MW01146692

WOOD'S BETRAYAL

STEVEN BECKER

Copyright © 2018 by Steven Becker

All rights reserved.

No part of this book may be reproduced in any form or by any electronic or mechanical means, including information storage and retrieval systems, without written permission from the author, except for the use of brief quotations in a book review.

Join my mailing list
and get a free copy of my starter library:
First Bite

Click the image or download here: http://eepurl.com/-obDj

WOOD'S BETRAYAL

1

STEVEN BECKER

A MAC TRAVIS ADVENTURE

WOOD'S
BETRAYAL

Mac was suspicious when Trufante said the dolphin were running, but not wary enough to stop him from loading the boat with bait and ice to give it a shot. His mate had several talents; finding fish was one, getting in trouble the other. Mac knew it was early in the season and with the strong cold front that had come through last week, he suspected the fish were either far offshore or still southwest of the waters near Marathon, making it an expensive proposition to go after them. The better plan would be to wait patiently for the Gulf Stream to bring them to his door. But inactivity was not something Mac did well and Trufante's prediction swayed him. He also knew from his three decades roaming the waters of the Florida Keys that fish seldom did what they were supposed to.

Surviving on the small chain of islands was tough and though known as a laid back, mind your own business kind of guy, Mac stayed busy by diversifying. Weather was always a factor here, and without a plan B, too many folks had nothing better to do than head to the bar when the wind blew. Besides being sought after for the more difficult salvage work that no one else would touch, he ran traps for lobster and stone crab, as well as fished whatever was in season.

He'd seen the look on Mel's face when he left the island retreat they shared, but there was something about Trufante that was like honey to a bear with him. Of course, she was right. He had pointed out that it was just a fishing trip, but her cynical view of the Cajun was unwavering. Ignoring each other, he walked down the stairs of the stilt house that Mel's father, Wood, had originally built and Mac had recently rebuilt. He left the small clearing just large enough for the house and a storage shed and walked down the brush lined path to the water. Wading into the gin-clear water, he released the line from the lone pile guarding the unmarked cut to the island. Using the dive ladder, he climbed aboard the forty-two foot custom trawler and glanced across the port rail hoping Mel had come to say goodbye, but the small beach was empty. Resolving to check in later, he moved his focus to the water in front of him.

The back side of the Florida Keys was like a puzzle. Navigating the shallow, shoal ridden waters dotted with mostly uninhabited mangrove islands was a challenge, even to the experienced boater. The shallow Gulf waters running adjacent to the northern side of the chain of islands were known by most as the backcountry. The reef, just a few miles off the southern shores, made famous for it's snorkeling, scuba diving, fishing, and treasure, usually occupied the spotlight, but it was the backcountry where other kinds of action took place. Smugglers and pirates had used these waters to hide since the Spanish explorers had started shipping gold back to Europe. There were no precious metals found here, just the Gulf Stream, which early navigators had used as a highway, known then as the Spanish Main to ship their riches home. Running just offshore of the island chain the strong northeasterly current aided the ships in their journey. But the deadly reef was also close enough that even a small storm could blow an entire convoy onto the treacherous reef. The 1733 fleet was the most famous, but many ships laden with treasure were lost in calm seas as well. Both wreckers and pirates flourished in these waters.

Mac reversed out of the channel that Wood had dredged years ago. It seemed counterintuitive, but the only way to Marathon from the island was to first head away from it. Spinning the wheel to port, he pushed down the throttle and the boat moved to the north. The markers for Harbor Key Bank were still in the distance when he made a hard turn to starboard and used an unmarked cut to gain the deeper waters of Spanish Channel. Now with the island on his starboard side, he looked across at the refuge, first built by Mel's father, Wood.

The old man had been Mac's mentor, and the two had worked together since Mel was in High School. There were some good times and some hard times, but they had remained close throughout. Wood had originally built his simple conch style house, using wooden piles to keep it above both the mosquitos and storm surges brought by the tropical storms and hurricanes that frequented this area more than most wanted. Mac had rebuilt it last year after a rouge CIA agent had burnt the original structure to the ground.

As he watched the island disappear behind them, he looked over at Trufante, napping in the chair to his left, hoping he was right and they would be back with a hold of fish. At least the weather was cooperating. It was that once a week kind of day, with barely enough wind to put a ripple on the surface of the turquoise water, and at least so far, there was no sign of the black cloud that followed the Cajun.

Mac followed the channel, staying straight where he would have veered to port if he were going to Marathon. Instead he headed toward the Bahia Honda Bridge. Lining up the bow with the missing section of the old railroad trestle bridge, he headed toward the deeper waters of the Atlantic Ocean. After navigating the churning water between the bridge piers, he accelerated on a heading of two-hundred-ten degrees. The fastest course to deeper water would have been due south, but he made the thirty degree correction to account for the distance he expected the Gulf Stream current to take them over the next few hours.

Five miles later, they crossed the reef line and he watched the depth finder plunge from twenty to two-hundred feet over the next half mile. The water changed with the depth, from a light turquoise, clear enough to see the coral heads that had taken so many unsuspecting ships over the years, to a dark indigo. Though it was dark, the water was deceptively clear, and the sunlight danced over particles suspended in the water column, making the ocean seem alive.

Once they passed four-hundred feet, Mac could see the outline of several freighters running southwest on the horizon. Their location told him where the inside edge of the Gulf Stream was running. The current ran like a river through the Atlantic, starting to the west of Cuba, and following the coast of Florida before veering east toward Bermuda. It was this current that was used to move millions of dollars of gold from the New World to Europe and still used today to save fuel for freighters and container ships moving up the coast. Nowhere did it run closer to land than it did as it passed the hundred-twenty mile chain of islands, and a slight navigation error or storm could easily lay a keel open on the shallow reef they had just passed.

"I got birds ahead," Trufante called out.

Mac hadn't even seen him wake up, but the Cajun's instincts were uncanny. Squinting into the glare, Mac turned toward a dark cloud hovering over the surface. "They're just tuna birds," Mac said. The gulls danced on the surface, darting here and there, and occasionally grabbing a small baitfish. He knew the birds were moving too quickly to be on dolphin.

Trufante was at the transom with two lines already out. "Black-fin'd be good eatin' and a skipjack or bonito'd make a nice bait." Just as he said it, the clicker on one of the rods went off. Trufante grabbed the rod and waited for several seconds, making sure the fish was hooked before he started to reel it in. Turning to Mac, he showed his famous thousand dollar Cadillac grill grin. "You gonna slow down and help me out here?"

Mac shook his head. He only slowed for a big fish. It was all good if you had the family out, but fishing was part of his livelihood and time wasted was money lost. "You're on your own," he called back.

Trufante tightened the drag and horsed the fish to the boat. A few minutes later, he swung the football shaped, dark black carcass, over the transom. Mac saw the stripes running vertically down its belly and knew he had made the right call. "Told you they was tuna birds.

Just a skip jack, all they're good for is bait. And don't bloody the deck with it. " He adjusted the course back to two-hundred-ten degrees and watched Trufante pull the hook and toss the fish in the box.

Another hour later, he checked the chart plotter and saw they were almost fifteen miles off the reef. The GPS told them they were making no headway and he knew they were in the Gulf Stream. Trolling against the current at six-knots left them standing still. "Where's the fish?" Mac asked.

"Maybe they's not this far yet. Try heading west some."

Mac spun the wheel to starboard, making a long easy turn so the lines didn't cross and tangle. "You know that or you guessing?" he asked. For better or worse, Trufante knew every captain up and down the chain of islands and for whatever reason, he had the type of personality, and primed by the ever present alcohol in those circles, they talked around him. Many including Mel, had a low opinion of him, but Mac knew the difference between a fool and acting foolish.

"Heard it was hot down off Key West a few days ago, thought they'd be up here by now."

That made sense except for the cold front that would have stalled them. Mac had a decision to make now. Either pull the plug and head back, wasting a hundred dollars in gas and bait, or pick up the baits and run. He chose the later and called back to Trufante to reel the lines in.

Subtle changes became visible as they cruised at twenty knots toward the waters offshore of Key West. The water temperature had increased two degrees and Mac was seeing more sargassum weeds in the water; both good signs. They would need a few days of south-east winds until they built into the huge weed-lines that blanketed the ocean, but looking down at the small patches he could see they held bait. As if on cue, he saw a pair of frigate birds circling ahead. "Put'em out," he called back. After setting the autopilot, he moved to the cockpit of the trawler he had customized to his needs and helped Trufante. After they had set five rods out, he went back to the wheel, hit the standby button on the autopilot and steered toward the birds.

The hit came quickly, and he could see Trufante's smile as two rods buzzed. A hundred yards behind the boat, he saw two splashes and knew they were onto some full-size fish, and hopefully a school. Dropping the RPMs to eleven-hundred, just enough to hold course, he set the autopilot again, and grabbed one of the rods. The fish had hit the outside, short rods and he decided to leave the longer lines out in case something bigger was lurking.

They fought the fish simultaneously, having to switch places several times before they were ready to be landed. Though nice size, neither required the gaff, and when the sixty-pound leader hit the swivel, they swung the fish over the gunwale. Mac immediately checked the other rods and the water, but these fish were loaners. There was no school.

Together, they reset the lines and Mac looked over at Trufante. "Seems like the action's to the west. What do you think about staying in Key West tonight, getting some provisions and chase them out of the Marquesas for a couple of days?"

"Shoot. I ain't gonna say no to that action."

"What about Pamela? She gonna get freaked out if you're gone a couple of nights?"

Trufante pulled back on one of the rods to shake the weeds off the skirted ballyhoo. "Ain't a thing. She'll be okay."

Mac knew better. Pamela had been around for over a year now, easily a record for the carefree Cajun, but there were questions surrounding her that no one could answer. Mel had even tried to run a background check on her, but it had come up empty. There was money, but to what extent or where it came from remained a mystery. "Your call."

"Could ask the same about Mel," Trufante said.

Mac knew he was right, but there was trust in their relationship and as long as he came back with a hold full of fish, she understood. It was the company he kept that bothered her. "She's got no use for me right now. Just got some satellite internet thing hooked up on the island. She's got her nose in some legal action about the Everglades trust she set up last year. We'll call them as soon as we cross the reef and get reception."

They picked up another half-dozen fish before the sun started to sink, but it was far from a full hold. To make the trip profitable, they would have to bring back a hundred good sized fish. The signs were all there, and that gave him some reassurance after the mediocre day. Plotting the hits in his head, he guessed the waters off the Marquesas, a small atoll of islands about twenty miles past Key West would make the trip profitable.

"Pull'em up. Let's head in and get some food. If what I'm seeing holds, a good day off the Marquesas will put some cash in our pockets.

Trufante hesitated. "We still stayin' in Key West tonight?"

Mac knew the draw the town had on his mate and had already thought it out. "I'll let you out of your cage for a few hours, but you're not going out of my sight, or staying. With the wind down, we can anchor up off Sand Key and get an early start tomorrow. He had thought about running at night, but they did need provisions, and allowing the Cajun a few drinks, would improve moral.

"Deal then."

With the lines in, Mac went back to the wheel, turned to starboard and set the GPS for the capital of weird.

2

STEVEN BECKER

A MAC TRAVIS ADVENTURE

WOOD'S
BETRAYAL

M ac eased the trawler against the fuel dock, cut the engine, and cringed at the price of diesel posted on the board. A fistful of bills later, his tanks were full and Trufante had shoveled the two gratis baskets of ice into the hold.

"Got any open slips?" he asked the attendant.

"Full up. Got some kind of freak show in town again," the man said. Mac eyed him as he replaced the nozzle. If his pink socks and toothless grin lent a definition to freak, then this was not a night he wanted to be around. Looking over at Trufante talking on his cellphone, he wondered if it might be better to leave the boat here for an hour, get some provisions and head out tonight. If nothing else, he'd get a better nights sleep and save a few bucks.

Trufante was still on the phone, which should have been his first clue that trouble was brewing. Rarely did he call Pamela, and with good reason. Her unusual habit of mixing song lyrics into her conversations was tedious, and he also knew his mate. Trufante would generally text women and call men. From his own experience, Mac couldn't fault that logic.

"Hey, what do you think about grabbing some provisions and hauling ass?"

"Shoot man, got my boy Billy comin' by for a beer."

"Billy Bones?" Mac cringed at the moniker the ex-Jersey pseudo gangster had claimed for himself.

"I'm going to the store. You do what you want, but this boat's pulling out at ten with or without you." Mac gave the ultimatum and climbed to the dock. After handing a twenty to the attendant, he helped Mac pull the trawler to the end of the dock with his promise he would watch it.

Mac looked at the boardwalk running the length of the marina. Tourists, mostly holding red solo cups or bottles of beer were gawking at each other and several groups were crowded around the charter boats where the mates were filleting their catch. Walking up to one of the boats he knew, Mac saw the dolphin on deck and smiled. He worked his way around the audience and stepped down to the cockpit, and climbed the stainless steel ladder to the flybridge. From ten feet above, he looked down at the crowd, now pointing to the hundred-pound tarpon schooling around the pier, fighting each other for the skin the mate had tossed.

"Hey, Rupert," Mac said, extending his hand.

The captain grasped it and laughed. "Mac freaken' Travis. In Key West. Wood's daughter get sick of you and toss your ass?"

"Naw," Mac said looking down to the deck. "Nice catch. I was hopin' to get into some tomorrow."

"If you want to spend the gas, you'll get past the schoolies off the Marquesas," Rupert said.

"Kind of what I figured. Started running into some twenty pounders off Sugarloaf. Thought there might be better numbers southwest."

Rupert nodded and took a sip of his beer. "Too far a run with the three-quarter day touristas, and they're happy catching schoolies anyway. If I didn't have a charter, that's where I'd be."

Mac nodded and looked down at the ten-pound plus fish fanned out on the deck like a billboard advertising the captain's prowess. If these were the size of the schoolies running here, he might just fill his holds after all. He left the bridge, said goodbye to the deckhand, and crossed the boardwalk to an alley that ran out to Elizabeth Street where he found a cab to take him to a grocery store on Roosevelt.

An hour later, he was loading food and beer onto the trawler. When he had finished stowing the provisions, he checked his watch and went for his phone. Realizing he hadn't checked in with Mel, he found her number on his favorites screen, where she had programed it, and pressed the call button. She was an exception to the call men, text women rule. He knew if he texted her, she'd know something was up.

"Getting a little late isn't it?" she asked.

"You know how it goes. Ran into them a little further to the southwest than I thought. We're in Key West gassing up and heading to the Marquesas. Should be back late tomorrow." There was no concern in his voice. After growing up in the Keys with her father, she knew how there were no schedules for fishing. If they were there you worked them, if they weren't you went home.

"Don't let that idiot run amok down there," she said. "Bring a load back. We could use some in the freezer."

He disconnected with the word *idiot* ringing in his ears. She made no secret of her distrust, bordering on dislike of the Cajun, but she also understood that as deckhands went, he wasn't, as her father said, *bad help*. The Keys were one of those places where people went to run away from either their past or themselves. Seeking employment was not high on their lists especially once the rent was paid and they had some beer money in their pockets.

But now, with Trufante's curfew coming up, he was worried. Trufante and Key West went together like crack and a pipe. There were several places he knew, the Cajun frequented and with his stomach rumbling, he headed over to the Half Shell Oyster Bar. After finding a seat at the crowded bar, he ordered a dozen oysters and a pound of shrimp. The long bar was lined with both tourists and locals. Only a few steps from their boats, many of the charter captains gathered here, talking story in exchange for drinks. More than one had learned how to attract charters with his tales, all the while drinking free liquor.

Sipping a draft, the only one he would allow himself tonight, Mac scanned the bar. Trufante, standing over six-feet was usually easy to spot, and hear, but there was no sign of him, or the sleazy Billy Bones. Not surprised, he finished the beer and food, paid the check, and started walking back to the fuel dock. It was an hour past sunset now, and the Mallory Square crowd had assimilated into the already boisterous mob. The bars were full, and the sidewalk crowded, but still there was no sign of Trufante.

The narrow boardwalk was moving at a snails pace so Mac decided to take the longer, but quieter route on the streets. From Margaret Street, he turned left on Caroline and after a few blocks, found himself back on Elizabeth. Where the street dead ended he wondered if he should continue on Greene Street, a move that would eventually lead him to Duval, the hub of the city's night life, but decided to wait out the Cajun on the boat. He left the street and found himself in a narrow alley.

By a dumpster, he heard men talking and suddenly one cried out in pain. Not one to get involved, he continued walking, risking a glance behind him, thinking he recognized the man on the ground. But if it was who he thought, he wouldn't stop. Something Wood had always told him about "not being able to save everyone" played through his head as he walked. Reaching the fuel dock, he saw no sign of Trufante. He'd seen this show before and had no intention of sitting here all night waiting. It would certainly be easier with his help, but Mac was entirely capable of loading the holds by himself.

He readied the boat and took one last look down the dock before starting the engines. After untying the lines from their cleats, he slipped one loop over them to hold the boat in place and offer a quick release. The easy thing to do would be to head back through the Northwest passage and run up the Gulf side to the island. He could be in bed by midnight, but his stubbornness wanted to both complete the trip and show Trufante he could do it without him. There was also the lecture that would inevitably come from Mel about Trufante and trouble.

Resigned to single handing the boat, he checked the wind and current, then released the bow line. The current swung him away from the dock, but just as he was about to release the stern, he heard the unmistakable sound of the Cajun. Looking down the dock, he saw the lanky figure darting back and forth as if avoiding something. He was less than a hundred yards from the boat when Mac saw the smaller man behind him.

Trufante landed hard on the deck and before Mac had a chance to cast off the lines, Billy Bones followed him. He landed badly and ducked behind the gunwale. Mac looked back and saw three men chasing them and though he wasn't positive it looked like at least one had a gun. He had no choice. Tossing the line, he ran to the helm and gunned the engine. Seconds later, the trawler, throwing a large wake, blew past the end of the pier and moved into the harbor.

"What the hell was that about?" he screamed at Trufante over the roar of the engine.

Trufante didn't answer and Mac knew better than to press him. His first priority was to get himself and his boat to safety. Then he would sort it out. He looked back, but the boats moored in the harbor blocked the view of the fuel dock. For now he was safe, but he knew his boat had been seen, and that made Key West dangerous. As if sensing he had safe refuge, Billy Bones stood and moved toward him.

"Damn Cubans," he said.

Mac didn't even look at him. The sooner he was off his boat the better. "I'm dropping your sorry ass at Sunset Key. You can make your way from there," he said, pointing the bow of the boat at the twinkling lights of the offshore resort. Less than a quarter mile off the mainland, the old fuel depot turned resort had several piers and a ferry service running from the back side of the island. He could get in and out of there before whoever was after them would know it. Another hour and he would be past the Marquesas.

A ferry pulled away from the dock causing him to wait offshore and just as he was about to pull into its place, he heard the roar of a boat speeding toward them. Looking back at his passenger, he saw the fear in his eyes and the bruise on his face.

"They coming for you?" Mac asked.

Billy Bones didn't answer, and Mac was glad for it. The last thing he wanted was to hear the fake gangster talk his way out of this. He racked his brain for any solution that would rid him of his passenger without implicating himself, but when the bullet slammed into the fiberglass beside him, he knew there were none.

At full throttle, he sped toward open water, but a quick glance told him he was underpowered. The boat was coming at them quickly and Mac could see the sleek shape and four outboards hanging on its transom. With no other options, he decided to raise the white flag and hope the men were reasonable when he turned over Billy. Flipping the switches for the spreader lights, he dropped to neutral and with the boat lit up like a beacon, he coasted to a stop.

The pursuers understood the gesture and came to an idle beside him. Mac called for Trufante to throw over the fenders and a line. With the boats tied together, Mac stared down Billy Bones.

"You can't give me up. They'll kill me," he pleaded.

"We just want our property," a voice called back. "He's not worth the bullets."

Mac couldn't agree more. "Give them what they want."

"Come on Travis. Show some mercy."

"I'll toss you over right now," Mac said, moving toward him.

"Okay." Billy removed something from his pocket and handed it across the gunwales.

Mac watched the man take what looked like a small rectangular metal case and wondered what this was all about. "You want him too?"

"No, just this." The man said, tossing the lines. The boats drifted apart and the outboards roared and buried themselves deep in the water, throwing a huge wake at the trawler before they pulled away. In seconds they were out of sight.

"You going to tell me what that was all about?" Mac asked, not really sure he wanted to know.

"You gotta help me," Billy Bones pleaded.

3

A MAC TRAVIS ADVENTURE
WOOD'S
BETRAYAL

Mac bit his lip and slammed the throttle to its stop. The engine noise created an invisible barrier between him and the two other men, allowing him to think. With the fuel topped off, he could afford to burn a few more gallons to both put some distance between the other boat and get a little quiet inside his head. He knew as soon as he dropped back into a more efficient speed, he would have to face Trufante and Billy Bones.

Trufante had done it again and as usual, he hadn't really done anything at all; just been in the wrong place at the wrong time. Mac killed the spreaders, leaving just the navigation lights and electronics on. With the bow slicing easily through the light chop, he cleared the shipping channel, cut the wheel to starboard, and checked his heading on the chart plotter. It wasn't a long run to the Marquesas; only twenty miles and there were still hours before dawn. Deciding it could all wait until he found an anchorage, he allowed the engine its head and like a racehorse it took it. The chop in the protected waterway turned into three foot seas when they hit open water. Spray crashed to the side as the deep V bow cut through the waves that barely slowed the speed of the four-hundred-twenty horse power diesel.

Half an hour later, Mac was in his happy place—alone on an empty ocean. His head started to clear and his anger diminished. The small horseshoe shaped chain of islands were getting closer and he slowed when he thought he saw the single white beacon of a masthead light. Zooming in, he used the chart plotter to guide the boat into a narrow channel. Instead of opting for the larger entrance leading to Mooney Harbor, he decided on the lesser know cut between several unnamed mangrove covered islands which led to a small lagoon.

Once they arrived, he ignored Trufante's questions and released the windlass. The anchor splashed and he waited the half-dozen seconds until it settled in the seven feet of water before pulling back on the throttle and releasing another twenty feet of chain. He locked the windlass and allowed the torque of the engine to dig the claw anchor into the muddy bottom. Mud wasn't the best bottom to anchor in, but with Billy Bones aboard, he doubted he'd be sleeping tonight. Anyway, he preferred the seclusion.

Trufante glanced over at him looking like a child that'd done something wrong and still wants a piece of candy. Finally, he gave in and nodded his head. The Cajun disappeared below and came back with six beers—three held in each of his large hands. Popping the top on his, he handed one to Mac and the other to Billy, then set the others on the deck. Mac thought about grabbing Billy's, but thought the conversation they were about to have would be a little better with some lubricant.

He waited until their beers were gone and Trufante went below for fresh ones before turning to Billy Bones. Mac knew the make believe gangster too well. He was just one of the constant stream of people running to the Keys every year, each for their own reason. They all thought they were unique snowflakes, but all had one thing in common—the real world wasn't working for them and somehow it was never their fault. Back in the early 90s Mac had made the trip to escape his past, hitchhiking from Galveston where he had been working as a commercial diver on the Gulf oil rigs. For him it had been the need to escape a crazy girlfriend that drew him here.

Mel's father Wood had been both his savior and mentor. A Navy man, originally stationed in Key West during the Cuban Missile Crisis, he had never left. After building or restoring half the bridges in the Keys, Wood had seen it all, and first pointed out the interesting migratory phenomenon years ago. Mac's observations had backed him up. According to Wood, there were degrees of running and it seemed like the hundred and twenty mile long string of islands acted as a filter allowing only the biggest nuts to reach the end of the line.

Billy Bones fell clearly into the bigger nut class. His story changed daily, but always had him as some kind of gangster sent from New Jersey to set up shop in the Keys. Why he would have sought employment from Wood on his way down was a question that was never answered. Wood always said, "you get what you get," and that perfectly summarized the employment situation in paradise. Billy had worked for less than a month, but it had been memorable. From creative excuses, to outright theft. He had left under the cover of night, much like he had tonight.

"So, you got a story?" Mac asked, finishing the beer, knowing he would need all the patience he had to listen to whatever fabrication Billy came up with.

"They got the wrong guy," he said.

So much for patience. "Let's start with the assumption that you're in trouble again. The bruise on your face, and those men after you would testify to that. I also saw the alley where you got the bruise, so no stories about some old drag queen that tripped you for your wallet. And they weren't Cuban either."

"Shoot Travis, cut a guy some slack."

Billy looked at Trufante for another beer, but Mac turned and shook his head. "I want the truth or it'll be a long swim back to Key West."

"Okay, but you gotta promise not to burn me."

Mac nodded, not knowing what he was talking about.

"There's these people, that smuggle hard drives into Cuba. Some kind of downloaded internet stuff on it."

"Doesn't sound like enough to get shot at over," Mac said.

"Maybe there's more to it. You see, since Obama's been all friendly like to old Raul, the immigration thing has gone sideways."

Mac had read about the increase in Cuban's attempting to flee the communist island before the United States normalized relations with Castro. He wasn't sure normal was a good word to describe it, but the two countries were talking for the first time in fifty years. Wet foot—dry foot, had been the policy for decades, allowing Cubans to turn themselves into a border patrol field office and receive asylum and an easy path to citizenship if they made it to land. If the Coast Guard picked them up at sea, they were returned to Cuba. With rumors the policy was about to change, tens of thousands of refugees tried to make the ninety-mile journey across the Gulf Stream, many dying in the process.

The influx had slowed now that the policy was on ice, but the Cuban peoples desire to leave the country hadn't. Now they were forced into using more sophisticated methods to reach the mainland. "Tru, get another round," he said, and waited for Billy to continue.

Billy Bones cracked the new beer, drank a long sip, and started. "There's someone told me that drives got more than YouTube and porn. Supposed to be some kind of encrypted file that gives them info on meets and times and stuff to get out."

Mac mulled that around for a while. He'd been to the island twice in the last few years, both times under less than ideal, or legal circumstances. What he had learned was that Internet service was almost non-existent. Unless you could afford a data plan for your phone, which most couldn't, the only access to the web was through government run Internet Cafes, which were still expensive and required the use of the governments computers. Neither was a good plan for someone looking for a way out. There were also parks and areas covered by Wifi, but the service was slow and there was the ever present government running the network. It made sense that the hard drives would be popular as a way to get some of the Internet experience offline.

"What were you doing with the drive?"

"We are in the business of helping people," he said.

'You're coyotes is what you are. What are you charging for bringing someone in?"

His expression changed. "Why you interested? This boat of yours, all hopped up and shit, could make you some coin."

Mac shook his head. "No. Wouldn't touch it. Just curious what your life's worth."

Billy spat over the side. Before he could come back with a smart ass comment, Mac heard the whine of a motor. It was an outboard for sure, probably an inboard, he guessed by the tone. The sound came closer and he could hear the engine slow. They soon felt a small wake lift the trawler as it pushed through the mangroves.

The movement caused Trufante to spill his beer. "What the hell? Damn fools ought to know this is a no wake zone."

Mac put his finger to his lips when he heard the motor drop to an idle. Sliding back to the helm he killed all the lights aboard and they waited in the silence. Another second later, he felt the direction of the wake shift parallel with the shore and he saw the beam of a searchlight filter through the mangroves. This was more than a cruiser looking for an anchorage. Anyone that knew the back channels between the mangroves here had a reason to. There could only be a few reasons a small boat was acting like this and he didn't want any part of any of them.

Trufante and Billy slid down to the deck and peered over the gunwale. Mac moved to his left, went down the three steps to the cabin and removed the shotgun from underneath the forward V berth. With a handful of shells in his pocket, he waited, not wanting to risk the tell tale sound when he chambered a round. The light from the other boat continued to play across the bushes and water. The channel was not marked, but neither was it hidden. If they were looking for it, they would have found it. The light settled on a particular spot and the engine died.

The only sound now was the buzzing of mosquitos and with the shotgun in hand, Mac moved to the starboard gunwale and using it for support, balanced the gun on it. There was no immediate threat, but after their escape earlier and the nearest police being twenty miles of open water away, he wanted to be ready for anything. For years the Marquesas had been a smugglers outpost, and with little surveillance and the mangroves for protection it was still a popular spot. The cruisers laying over in Mooney Harbor, though less than a quarter mile away were in a different world than back here in the mangroves.

Branches broke and the light moved, but showed him nothing. He could hear the low murmur of men talking, but they were too far away and it sounded like Spanish. He looked over to Trufante who could speak a little of everything, mostly enough to find a beer or bathroom, but it was more than he had. The Cajun shook his head in response.

Swatting mosquitos away from their heads and holding their bladders, they waited for what felt like an hour. Hearing only the muffled voices, they relaxed thinking there was no danger and an hour later, Mac was about to turn in when they heard another boat approaching. This one was bigger and by the sound of the engines, fast.

He was instantly on guard now. As the boat approached, he saw a searchlight flash, this time it was away from them and he knew they had stumbled on some kind of smuggling operation. The light flashed again. Mac could tell by the wake that the new boat had adjusted course and a minute later imagined it settling against the other boat. He looked over at Trufante and Billy, giving them a silent warning. As long as they remained quiet and out of sight, there would be no problem, but his grip tightened on the shotgun knowing with these two men aboard things just happened.

There were more men talking. It sounded like several were giving orders now and he felt the slight disturbance on the water echoing the shifting movement of the other boats. Finally, whatever business was being transacted was completed. He heard an engine start and felt the wake as the larger boat moved out. Slowly he could hear it accelerate, and he breathed deeply, waiting for the other boat to leave, except the only sound he heard was nature; mangrove branches rustling in the breeze and the mosquitos buzzing around his head. The other boat was still there.

4

STEVEN BECKER

WOOD'S
BETRAYAL

K urt Hunter idled the skiff up to the mangroves. He saw a ripple in the water ahead, killed the engine, and dropped the eight-foot power pole into the muddy bottom. Walking around the center console to the bow, he picked up the fly rod from the deck, pulled a hundred feet of fluorescent yellow line off the fly reel, and started to backcast. Slowly at first, then when twenty feet or so of line was out, he started to double-haul. The extra tension created by the second pull before he released the rod tip forward added momentum. The line snapped from the deck through the eyes of the twelve-weight rod and toward where he had seen the shadow.

The leader unwound, but a quick gust of wind came up ruining what could have been a perfect cast, and his first bonefish. Slowly he started to retrieve the line, but found the fly hooked to a branch. Frustrated, he pressed the up button on the remote and waited for the pole to extract itself from the mud. Using the line, he pulled the boat toward the snagged fly. Branches snapped as the tower and antenna encroached their territory and the before he could reach the branch, the boat would go no further.

His regulation footwear already cast aside, Kurt slid over the side, letting his bare feet sink into the mud, and waded toward the offending branch. Using the line to guide him, he entered the mangroves. Submerged roots caught his feet forcing him to shuffle forward and use his arms for support. Further in than he had expected, he saw the green and white shrimp pattern dangling from a leaf. Continuing to walk towards it, he pulled the branch toward him, and removed the hook. With the fly in hand, he turned back to the boat, only to find the line tangled. He bent down to retrieve it and saw something that didn't belong; faded white paint on a piece of wood planking only feet in front of him.

Leaving the line, he swept aside the branches and saw the transom of a boat. Something fresh and red dripped down into the water. He stood there for several long seconds trying to remember the protocol of the department. He'd been a Special Agent with the National Parks Service for half a dozen years, but back in the desolate foothills of Northern California, there was not much activity and no one to report to. That was until, under similar circumstances, he had been "patrolling" with his fly rod, searching for trout in the mountain streams of the park when he uncovered the largest pot grow to date on government land.

It would have been enough to just file a report, but his curiosity usually got the better of him and he slid his feet closer. Placed in the Park Service's version of the witness protection program, Kurt was sent cross-country to Biscayne National Park, where he now roamed flats and mangrove islands instead of mountain streams. Here, however, he did have a boss, and even though he was more interested in the condition of the grass on his favorite putting green than the sea grass below the pristine water in his charge, Kurt knew he needed to contact him before proceeding with the investigation. Reluctantly, he waded back to the boat.

He climbed back aboard the twenty-one foot center console and found his phone in the compartment below the steering wheel. After opening the contacts, he took a deep breath and called Ray Martinez, Special Agent in charge for the Investigative Services Branch of the Park Service—his boss. With the sense that he was being dealt with as an incompetent newcomer, Martinez told him to do nothing and wait.

Kurt sat on the gunwale putting his regulation socks and shoes on, then reeled in the fly line. He broke down the rod, setting the four-pieces in its sleeve and the reel in its compartment. The case was placed carefully behind a stack of PFDs in the center console. There was no reason for his boss to know how he had found the boat in the mangroves. He checked his boat for any other signs of his activity, drank from his water bottle, and waited for his boss. The bonefish would have to wait.

Mac left the cabin. It had been a warm night without air conditioning, but after seeing Billy Bones mosquito ridden body lying prone on the deck, he decided there was nothing to complain about. He would have liked to kick the man awake, but saw no point in it and climbed onto the gunwale to wake Trufante who was asleep on top of the cabin.

"We gotta go. Bite'll be hot in about an hour," Mac said, pushing the Cajun's shoulder. Mac had been up before dawn, trying to calculate the tides and currents of the offshore waters. There was an underwater seamount about twenty miles offshore he wanted to fish. The combination of structure and current were sure to attract bait and hopefully dolphin.

Trufante climbed down and both men ignored the inert body on the deck as they readied to depart. In their well-worn pattern, Trufante pulled a package from the chest freezer. He started to defrost and rig the ballyhoo while Mac started up the engine, checked the gauges and hit the windlass switch. With only twenty feet of rode out, seconds later, the anchor was swinging below the bow pulpit. Mac stopped the windlass motor and went forward to shake the mud off the claw before bringing in the rest of the rode and securing the safety cable.

Back at the wheel, he judged what the current and wind were

doing, then backed slightly, before pressing down the throttles and steering through the narrow channel. He had almost forgotten the smugglers from the night before when he saw what looked like an abandoned boat stuck deep in the mangroves. Not an unusual sight here, he was about to run past it when he saw the blood dripping down the gunwales.

"You see that?" Trufante said.

"Yeah. Something must have gone south with those smugglers last night." Mac pulled back on the throttle and coasted toward the abandoned boat.

"What are you doing?" Trufante asked.

"Having a look. What do you think? Might be someone alive," Mac said, leaning over the starboard gunwale. He noticed immediately the condition of the boat. The old wooden fishing boat was a sterndrive that looked like it was powered by a car engine from another era, and he knew right away that it was Cuban. The smuggling they had overheard last night must have been a refugee pickup. But that wouldn't explain the blood. The Cubans would be of no use unless they were delivered alive.

"Killed another batch of'em," Billy said.

Mac smelt the sour breath of the man standing behind him. "Another?"

"That's how it goes now. They pay up front and get one of those drives. Got no recourse."

Mac knew the golden era of political asylum, although it had cost hundreds if not thousands of lives, at least gave the refugees hope. If they could reach land and turn themselves in, they would be fast-tracked to becoming Americans. With the political asylum option off the table, and the Castro's still holding power over the island, the only way in was to hire a coyote.

Staring back at Billy, Mac thought he knew more than he was saying. "We ought to report it."

He heard the loathsome man clear his throat. "No need for that. These boats have been showing up here for years, abandoned with a story no one will ever know."

"That don't make it right," Mac said, coasting along the side of the boat and looking for any identifying marks. Were it not for the deck, glistening in the morning light from the blood splattered across it, he would have gone aboard and searched it. At least he could claim the salvage rights to the vessel. Though it was worth little, it could result in a lucrative towing contract from the government who paid generous contracts to remove the hazardous materials from the marine sanctuary.

"What about the bite," Trufante asked.

Mac looked at his crewmen. The boat was in a back channel of a backwater, and would not likely be found. Taking the chance it would be here when they returned, he snapped several pictures with his phone, reluctantly left the mangroves, and headed offshore. He would retrieve it and tow it back to Key West when he dropped off Billy Bones.

"AND HOW DID you find this again?" Martinez asked. The Special Agent in Charge, pulled on his waders and slid over the side. Kurt followed, catching a look from the older man. "You know it ain't good when this shit touches your skin," the man said, brushing the branches to the side with his long sleeved shirt.

"It's what I do. You said to patrol, so I've been patrolling. Learning the ins and outs of the park," Kurt said as he pulled aside the last branch revealing the transom of boat. Now that he looked again, he wasn't so sure it was blood on the transom and he regretted calling his boss without more evidence.

"From reading your file, that curiosity of yours almost got you killed out west."

"It thought that was the job?"

The man flashed him a look of warning. "You keep prowling around these mangroves, you'll find stuff for sure. Stuff you might now want to have seen. Shit flows in here twice a day with the tide and it don't usually come out."

Kurt didn't understand him, but they were at the boat now, and both men stared over the transom at the decks. Maybe the agent was right. This was something Kurt would not easily forget. Black flies and mosquitos greeted them and he backed away.

"Well, we got us a crime scene in the goddamn swamp," Martinez said.

"You want to tape it off?" Kurt said, eager for something to do that would get him away from his boss. "Call CSI?"

"No point letting anyone else know this is here. That yellow tape'll be honey to those curious tourists. We'll be spending more time pulling them off the sand bars than figuring out what happened here. As far as investigators, it's us until we can pull this thing ought of here and get it to land.

Kurt started to see the difficulty of working in the park. With the skyline of downtown Miami clearly visible to the north, and the chimney stacks of the Turkey Point power plant to the south, Biscayne National Park is ostensibly advertised as ninety-five percent water, which was true, but there were miles of mangrove lined shore stretching from Government cut at the bottom of South Beach to Card Sound road and the northern tip of Key Largo was filled with mystery and history. The cluster of barrier islands, some open to camping, and one that he lived on, separated the Bay waters from the Atlantic and the northern tip of the famous Florida Keys reef.

The tidal change only enlarged the territory, exposing many more acres at low tide. Standing by the abandoned boat, he realized the water had already risen almost a foot in the three hours he'd been here. Part of the crime scene was already gone. "How about I get the camera?"

"That's a good idea. We can document what we can and get the hell out of here before the bugs get worse," Martinez said, slapping a big black fly from his cheek.

Kurt felt them too and quickly waded back to the boat. The extra foot of water made it slow going, but he fought against the tide and returned with the camera. Martinez nodded at him and with a handkerchief over his face, waded back toward the boats, leaving Kurt alone with the crime scene.

Kurt started snapping pictures, walking clockwise around the hull as he went. Martinez yelled for him to hurry up. Trying to ignore him, he continued to document the scene when he tripped over a mangrove branch and fell against the hull. To his surprise the boat moved several feet. After regaining his balance, he stood staring at the mangroves realizing that this was probably not the scene of the crime.

5

A MAC TRAVIS ADVENTURE

WOOD'S
BETRAYAL

Mac started getting anxious about noon. Fishing had been good enough that even Billy Bones ineptness hadn't hurt, although he had, with Trufante's help, finished the beer supply. With his holds close to full, Mac's thoughts turned to the abandoned boat. Fishing was only one of Mac's income streams, and not the most lucrative. His unique skill set as both a commercial diver and his years working with Wood rebuilding bridges put him in an ever shrinking group of men. Working in the strong currents of the bridge cuts had given him the reputation of the guy to go to when the work was difficult. Since Wood's death, he had become more reclusive and stopped taking contracts and begun working freelance. Focusing more on private work had made for some interesting adventures and for Mac, it wasn't always about the money—it was the challenge.

There was nothing challenging about the abandoned boat in the mangroves. Aside from the twenty-mile tow to Key West, it was a routine salvage, and in this case had a nice paycheck attached. Word was out that the Marine Resource Board was paying good money to pull the thirty odd abandoned boats out of the Marquesas. Calling them environmental hazards and a danger to the migratory bird population, there was currently a bounty on their removal. For a several hours and a few dollars worth of fuel, Mac figured he could pocket about two grand.

The bite had died down with the tide, and Mac decided after watching Billy blow another gaff that it was time to go. "Pull'em up. We're out of here," he called, watching Trufante swing another fish over the transom and into the hold.

"A few more'll fill her," he said.

"Bites dying and I'm thinking of claiming rights on that boat back in the channel. We can tow it back with us."

"Shoot. May be a plan. Besides we're out of beer," Trufante said, looking at the location of the sun in the sky.

"You can thank your friend for that," Mac said. It was uncanny how Trufante could look at the sun and figure out that he had a good shot for a night in Key West. A glance at his dive watch told him it was almost one. An hour back to the Marquesas, another hour to rig the boat for the tow and a two hour run to Key West added up nicely to a Duval Street happy hour.

The two men reeled in the lines, and Mac turned the wheel toward the small cluster of islands on his GPS screen. Calculating the fuel, he eased back on the throttle. His three-hundred gallon tank would easily get him back to Marathon, but his fast run last night and the tow would cost him about a hundred gallons. The rods were stowed and Billy was quickly asleep on the deck.

Trufante sat in the adjacent chair. "We gotta ditch that dude," he said.

"If it were up to me, I'd have tossed him back in the Stream. I thought he was your friend."

"That boy is on the marginal acquaintance list. You know how it is, sometimes a man with his abilities is a necessary evil."

Mac looked at the Cajun thinking that description could also apply to him. "We're gonna have to put into Key West. Soon as we do, he's off."

Trufante nodded. "What're you thinking about that boat?"

Mac knew what he wanted. "Your cut should be about five hundred."

The famous Cadillac smile made an encore appearance. "That and the fish'll do me right till the first."

Somehow Pamela was always flush with cash at the beginning of every month. But as the days and weeks passed it dwindled, and Trufante became more motivated. He had always had a reputation as a flamboyant partier, and Pamela only added to that. But now, in the last days of May, Mac knew he was probably broke.

"Where's she get that money anyway?" Mac asked the question everyone in Marathon wanted the answer to.

"She don't say much about it, but it's got to be her daddy. Only one she talks about."

Mac noticed Billy Bones inch closer trying to listen in. "You know anything about her?"

"Meaning her past? Heck no. It's the Keys man: Don't ask—Don't tell."

"Ought to be a bumper sticker," Mac said, wanting to change the conversation before Billy Bones overheard anything. His thoughts drifted as he guided the boat toward the Marquesas. Preferring the touch of the wheel to using the autopilot, he gazed ahead. Trufante was as much of an enigma as his girlfriend. It had taken years and a whole lot of beers before he gave Mac a small glimpse of his past.

Before Katrina, and probably again, now that the storm had faded into memory, Louisiana was a part of the good 'ole boy belt of Southern States. The climate of corruption was rampant, and with his quick tongue, shifty mind, and malleable morals, Trufante, at least from his telling, had thrived. Through some combination of his attributes, working as a concrete contractor, he had somehow gotten a contract from the Army Corps of Engineers to reinforce the levies protecting the city. He wasn't the only contractor who's work failed when the storm surge flooded the city, but he was one of the handful without insurance. A fast escape in a "borrowed" sailboat ended with him landing in the Keys.

A small line soon appeared on the horizon, and Mac turned one eye to the chart plotter to avoid the shoals guarding the archipelago. As he approached, a plan formed in his mind to pull the boat out and he adjusted his course to the east. The islands grew as he approached and he easily found the channel.

"Going to head straight in and pull her lose, then we'll have to stake her out, and swing around for the tow," he said to Trufante. The wind had come up enough to make this a two person job. Entering the channel, he inched the boat forward until the bow rested against the blood-stained transom of the other boat. He nudged it to see how well grounded it was. The movement dislodged a cloud of flies and mosquitos that were feasting on the blood.

"Tide's left her dry. It's gonna take some torque to pull her."

"Right on. We could set the anchor and use the winch to pull'er" Trufante said, switching gears to work mode.

"Bottom's too muddy," Mac said, but liked the idea. He scanned the banks looking for a stout enough tree to hold the trawler, but there was nothing stronger than the mangroves. "Go on and take the cable over."

Trufante went to the winch, set it in free-spool, and started pulling the thick metal cable off the reel. With a cat-like move, he was over the rail of the trawler and aboard the refugees boat. "Ain't no bow eye," he called back from the bushes.

The eye, used for trailering was usually the strongest fitting. "Slip it around both transom cleats." Mac hoped using two stress points would help. He waited while Trufante rigged the cable and climbed back aboard. Billy Bones was by the winch, but the lanky Cajun pushed him aside. Mac put the transmission into reverse and slowly backed down until the cable was taut. Once he was happy with the rigging, he nodded to Trufante to start the winch. Rather than use the boats momentum to pull the abandoned boat off, he accelerated only enough to make a stable platform for the winch. In the close quarters of the mangrove lined channel, using the engine could send the trawler into the opposite bank when the smaller boat released.

Slowly the winch cable came in, and he adjusted the throttles to remain in place. Water churned under the trawler. The smaller boat creaked, sending a shiver down his spine, but the transom held, and the boat came free. He backed off the throttles. "We're good. Release her and I'll back in."

Trufante allowed the winch cable to bring the two boats together and when they touched he released the tension and went to the other boat. Once aboard, he went to the forward compartment. "Ain't no anchor," he called across.

Mac went below and came back with a small anchor which he dropped in the water, then tossed the Cajun the line. Once Trufante had secured the smaller boat, he backed the trawler out of the channel, spun the wheel around, and backed in. In this position, with the other boat free, it was a simple matter to set the tow rope and pull her out. The trawler pulled the small boat into open water, only stopping when Mac saw ten feet below him on the depth finder. After a few adjustments to the tow rope, he gunned the motor enough to get both boats moving, and settled back for the long tow to Key West.

MARTINEZ HAD BEEN GONE AN HOUR, leaving Kurt to stay for the tow. Aside from the bugs, he was happy to wait, and studied the tidal flat to pass the time. The wind was down and the water shimmered as if it was pushing the heat away. He thought about how far he had come from his home in the Sierra's. Making a decision for his new location based on fishing, might not have been the most logical thought process, but Biscayne Bay had lured him with its clear blue water. Tarpon, bonefish, permit, snook, and redfish were all seasonal predators on the flats, and with the thousands of acres of open water to explore, he had chosen this spot to relocate. It was also as far as he could get from the west coast cartel boss who had sworn to eliminate him.

He had found the pot grow in much the same manner as he had found the boat this morning. Patrolling the Plumas National Forest in Northern California, he was seldom without his fly rod. The four weight rod was smaller than the kit he had used here, but was in proportion to the fish. In his years there, he had found that walking the streams of the park, yielded him more than hiking the trails. Everything was centered around the water from illegal dredgers still looking for gold to the pot growers, needing the streams as a source of irrigation water. It hadn't come naturally, but over time, Kurt had learned to read water and could now see the main flow, currents, and eddies invisible to most. It was a small current that he had seen, and after investigation, he had found the end of the intake pipe covered with rocks. Had he not been in the water, pole in hand, he never would have discovered it. After chasing the pipe up the steep bank, he discovered the biggest pot grow ever found on public land and in the process made some serious enemies.

He missed the mountain streams and wilderness of the forest, but that was quickly forgotten when he hooked his first baby tarpon. He'd dreamed of his first hundred pounder that night but knew this was a learning process. The flats were a different kind of game than stream fishing. It had taken him a few years to master that, and he didn't expect overnight results here.

The other reason for exiling himself here were his estranged wife and daughter. There was little to no chance he could see them, at least for a few years until the danger from the cartel blew over, and he was not really sure where they were. Justine's sister was in Orlando, and only three hours away, he felt some comfort in their proximity. The US Marshall's had relocated them as well, with his wife insisting he not be given their location. Kurt guessed the bomb planted at their house in Quincy was the reason for that. Someday he hoped the chasm would disappear, until then he would fish and hope his daughter forgave him.

The sound of a boat coming toward him brought him back to reality and he stood in the bow waving his hands over his head until the Dade County Sheriffs boat approached and idled next to him. "Got the boat up in there," he called to the deputy.

The Parks service relied on the local Sheriff and the Florida Department of Law Enforcement for most of its backup. Martinez had told him the boat would be taken to the FDLE yard for forensics. The deputy tossed him a line. "Go hook her up."

Kurt knew the deputy was playing him, but went anyhow. If he were to survive here, he would need these peoples help. With his shoes on this time, to avoid adding to the cuts and scrapes from his earlier expedition, he slipped over the side, and waded into the mangroves trying to find a path wide enough to extricate the boat. He found what he thought had been the entry point and studied the branches. Several were snapped confirming his theory, and he catalogued the site in his head for future study.

Reaching the boat, now floating freely on the high tide, he swung it around and tied the line around the forward cleat. Using the line, he pulled himself back to the two boats and climbed aboard his. With water oozing out of his shoes, he made a mental note to get more appropriate footwear and released the lines from the deputy's boat. Once there were several feet of water between them, the deputy slowly accelerated until the line was tight and then with a quick bump to the throttle, pulled forward bringing the abandoned boat with him. He reached back and shortened the line before setting a course toward Government Cut and Miami.

Kurt sat on the transom and watched them until they were two specks on the horizon.

6

WOOD'S
BETRAYAL

Mac chose to wait until they were in site of Key West before calling the Coast Guard, and even then used the one-watt option on his VHF radio. The twenty-five watt setting had the range to make the call from the Marquesas, but would have alerted every boater within thirteen-hundred square miles. Most commercial captain's in the Keys were honest, but there were always a few on the lookout for an easy buck, no matter how it came. Salvage laws were antiquated and vague. After hearing his call on the radio there were several ways to either forsake or dispute his claim for the salvage rights before he arrived with the abandoned boat in tow. Even with Mel ever willing to go to battle, a legal battle over a two-thousand dollar payday was not going to be worth it.

After receiving an acknowledgment from the Coast Guard, he decided on taking the longer route around Sunset and Wisteria Islands rather than cruising up the channel for all Key West to see. Maybe the detour was paranoid, but he'd had more than one run-in in these waters including last nights, and both he and his boat were too well known for his taste. After passing the two islands, he turned to starboard and steered toward the far end of the harbor. Reaching the outside of the long pier where the Coast Guard vessels were docked, he found an empty space along the dock and pulled in.

"Go get some help," he told Trufante.

The Cajun hopped onto the concrete pier, taking a dock line with him. After tying the trawler off, he hurried to the office. Mac waited, realizing that with Billy Bones aboard, he still had a problem. The trawler had been confiscated once when Trufante had gotten sucked into a poaching endeavor by a woman, who had promised more than she could deliver. By the time he had proven his innocense the path of destruction included both his and Wood's houses.

"Why don't you hop off and disappear," he said to Billy, who was watching the dock.

"Might be a good idea," he said. "Be needin' my pay first."

Mac looked at his outstretched hand. "For what? Saving your sorry ass?"

"Days labor out there fishin' and then part of the salvage."

Mac clenched his fists and took a step toward him.

Billy backed away. "Okay, I can see you got your own thing goin' on. Let me get my stuff and I'm out'a here. You can catch up on my paycheck next time."

That was just another argument that would have to wait and Mac watched him go into the cabin. It took him a minute to question what he was doing down there and when he emerged with a bag under his arm, he was about to reach out for him when he saw the uniformed men approach. Before he could say anything, Billy Bones, avoiding the looks of the officers, scurried like a leprous rat down the dock. Mac watched him go, wondering what he had taken when he caught a glimpse of fluorescent green. He was about to check below, when the men hailed him.

"Captain," the officer said, extending his hand.

"Mac," he shook the man's hand and welcomed them aboard. A quick glance showed that Trufante was also missing. "Here she is," he said, nodding back at the old boat.

The officers moved toward the abandoned boat. One of them started taking pictures as he approached. "Good shape," he said.

"For what it is," Mac said.

"Curious thing though. Seen a few like this lately. The old days, we'd never see anything this seaworthy. Mostly they were rafts. The better ones had built up gunwales and old kickers or just sails. Now we're seeing legitimate boats."

Mac shrugged, wondering how you could call the boat either seaworthy or legitimate. But politics were not his thing. He only understood the machinations of the government enough to avoid it, and he was getting the feeling in his gut right now that he should be moving on. "Got some paperwork for me?"

"Gotta document it first. Could take a couple hours." The uniformed man continued to take pictures. When he was done, he and the other man donned latex gloves and climbed down to the boat.

Mac wondered why they needed to treat the boat like a crime scene. The blood was not indicative of a crime or an indication of a struggle, but he decided not to ask. "I'll go grab a bite while you do what you need." The man acknowledged him and Mac started walking down the pier. It was already late afternoon and his stomach reminded him that he hadn't eaten in hours. That was not his first concern though, he needed to find Trufante. And in a city like Key West, where there were two bars on every corner, that task wasn't as easy as it sounded.

Trufante, for all his larger than life persona, was a creature of habit, and Mac started to check his favorite haunts. Starting with the Half Shell Oyster Bar, he moved toward Duval street, finally catching a glimpse of him holding court at the bar at Willie T's. He entered the open air bar, and slid past the other partiers to the side of the lanky Cajun.

"Good timing, Mac. Could use an advance right about now."

Mac looked at the empty shot glasses on the bar and women on either side of him. With a nod to the women, he pulled Trufante off his barstool and walked him to the quietest corner of the bar. "What does Billy Bones want with my EPIRB?"

Trufante had a blank look on his face.

"I saw him take it."

"What that loser does, don't concern me. Now how about that advance?"

"Why don't you take it off the walls like you usually do?" Mac looked around at the money surrounding them. All kinds of currency was stapled to the walls, ceiling and columns. The predominant denomination was a dollar bill with the donors name and message written on it with a sharpie, but if you looked close enough, there were plenty of fives and a few tens unadorned of any signature. Poach a handful of those and you could drink all night.

"It ain't like that. But the options always open," he showed his grin and winked.

"Where can I find Bones?" Mac asked, pulling two twenties out of his pocket and handing them to Trufante.

"Heard he was holed up at a boat yard on Stock Island," Trufante said, grabbing the bills and looking at Mac like there should be more.

"That'll pay your tab. They should be ready with the paperwork by now and we need to head back."

"Shoot. Why don't you hang with old Tru for the night. I'll show you the town, Cajun style." Trufante said, flashing his thousand dollar Cadillac grin at the two women.

"Got no need for that. We gotta get back and sell the catch in the morning," Mac said. He looked over at the women. One looked back, catching his eye and it scared him. Middle aged women on the prowl were not his thing.

"They want to go to see the sights. You know how these old girls get when they get a few drinks in 'em."

Mac didn't need to say anything. He pointed Trufante in the direction of the bar with instructions to pay and meet him outside. A few minutes later the Cajun emerged with a sorrowful look on his face.

"They would'a been fun."

Mac ignored him. "Can you find that marina where Billy is staying from the water?"

"Sure enough, if your set on it."

They walked silently back to the Trawler and saw the abandoned boat tied to the pier in typical Coastie fashion. Four bright blue fenders separated the boat from the dock and besides the bow and stern line, they had added fore and aft spring lines. With no wind and little tide, that was overkill, but until he got paid, it was his investment they were protecting.

Trufante hopped aboard the trawler, and Mac continued to the office. The officer had the papers ready and Mac signed where he indicated. After waiting for his copies, he left the office and walked down the pier. It was almost sunset now, and he wondered if it was worth going after Billy in the dark. The numerous small channels in these islands were often hard to navigate by daylight. At night, one mistake by Trufante and he could run aground. He decided it wasn't worth the risk for what he had stolen and started the engine.

"We'll take the back way around to the island. You can stay on the boat tonight. Tomorrow, we'll head in and sell the catch."

"What about old Billy?" Trufante asked.

"I'm not done with him," Mac said. The conversation was over as soon as he started the engine.

BILLY BONES TOSSED the ticket stuck under his worn out windshield wiper onto the sidewalk and set the plastic bag with the EPIRB on the back seat of his beater Corolla. He said a quick prayer and turned the key. If he were back in Jersey, there was no way he would be caught dead in a beat up Corolla, but here in Key West, any car was a step up from a bicycle. This time the engine turned over, and before it could reconsider, he pulled into traffic, turned left on Roosevelt and headed off the island.

The car stuttered at the light before the Stock Island Bridge, but kept going long enough to turn into the driveway of the new condominiums. Stock Island had long been known as the cheaper alternative to Key West and many of the cities workers lived here. It was more commercial as well, but in recent years, developers had started

buying the old buildings and boatyards, and one parcel at a time were
converting them into luxury housing. He parked and looked at the
unique modern design of the building wondering what the architect
was on when he designed it. He guessed from the prices advertised
on the sign that claimed there were only a few units left, that the
smoked glass, exposed metal, and barn wood siding appealed to
someone, but he couldn't figure who. Either that, or the developer
was lying. That's what he would have done.

Waiting to be buzzed in by the intercom at the service entrance,
he looked down at himself, thinking he should at least button his
shirt. He set the bag down and did his best to look presentable, then
when the electronic lock, designed to keep his kind of people out
admitted him, he grabbed the bag and went to the service elevator.
Taking it to the top floor, he exited and turned right. Walking by the
polished steel doors, and smiling for the security cameras he
approached the last unit and pressed the doorbell. The door buzzed
and he walked in.

Billy Bones walked through the foyer and kitchen, glancing out
the smoked glass patio windows at the Atlantic Ocean. He turned
into a short hallway and knocked on the burnished mahogany door.
A man's voice called back. He turned the polished brass lever and
entered. Surrounding him was the lush office of Mateus Tabor, and
the man himself sat behind a large desk. The room was what you
would expect from a stateroom on a yacht, with polished brass and
gleaming mahogany everywhere. The standard nautical fittings were
present; all authentic and expensive. To the side of the desk were two
black leather chairs and a couch. Tabor motioned him over to one of
the chairs and came out from behind the deck.

Billy sat, feeling the expensive leather against his bare legs. There
was a slight smell of disinfectant in the the air, and he guessed it was
from the last time he had sat there. "I see you have something
for me?"

Billy Bones handed the EPIRB to the man, who took it and set it
on the table. The fluorescent green and clear plastic that housed the
strobe of the emergency beacon fit with nothing in the room, but the

man smiled. "That wasn't very smart taking that drive. My men told me they found you."

Billy rubbed the bruise on his forehead and shrugged. If Tabor wanted him dead, he wouldn't be sitting here.

"You just keep bringing me these," Tabor said, glancing over at the EPIRB.

"What do you do with them?"

Tabor looked over his reading glances, but didn't answer.

The pitch black pupils bore into him, and Billy Bones shrank in the chair. His hands clawed at the expensive leather, and though the room was cool, he felt several beads of sweat on his forehead. Back in Jersey, he had dealt with some low level mob bosses, but none put the fear in him like Tabor.

"Whatever you say. I can probably grab a few more tomorrow."

"You do that Billy," Tabor said, reaching into the pocket of his silk trousers. He pulled out a gold clip stacked with hundred dollar bills, peeled off half a dozen, and held them out. Before he could grab the bills, Tabor pulled them back. "There is something I need you to do for me." He fingered his billfold and took out five crisp hundreds and placed them next to the half dozen for the EPIRB on the desk.

Billy took money and thanked the man, wondering two things. Why would he he be paying a hundred dollars more for the EPIRBs than they were worth, and why give him more responsibility after the incident with the hard drive.

7

A MAC TRAVIS ADVENTURE
WOOD'S BETRAYAL

He knew Mel hadn't been happy about Trufante staying in such close proximity. Even having him on the boat was too close for her. It's not like she hated him, it was just the trouble that always followed. The guy's life was a rolling crap shoot.

She was already at work on her laptop when Mac got up. He walked over and kissed the top of her head, then went to the kitchen to make a fresh pot of coffee. While it brewed, he walked outside and stood on the covered deck that wrapped around the second floor of the house. By extending the eaves, the sun only penetrated the windows in the dead of winter. Weather was the number one topic on peoples minds here and Mac remembered a charter customer calling the climate here: seven months of summer and five months of hell.

Living on the island with no utilities was less of a struggle than one might think. If you were careful and kept an eye on things, the five kilowatt solar array provided plenty of power to the batteries that powered the lights and small appliances. The well was also solar powered, pumping water at a rate of three gallons a minute whenever the sun was out into the two five-hundred gallon tanks on the roof. The black plastic warmed the water enough that the small on-

demand water heater, powered by propane brought from the mainland, only had to boost it twenty degrees in winter and less in the
summer for a hot shower.

He brought the coffee pot over to the table and refilled Mel's cup,
catching what he thought was a thank you under her breath. When
she had her head into something, there was no conversation to be
had. "Gonna run into town and sell the catch. Need anything?"

She looked up. "No. Adding the Internet here has made all the
difference. Maybe see if anyone will take Tru off our hands."

The comment was said lightly, and he laughed as she went back
to work. He had resisted as long as he could. Maybe for her it was
better being hooked into the world, but he preferred the old days,
before cell phones, when VHF radios ruled the islands. Thinking of
the marine radio, he remembered the EPIRB. "Alright, I'll split whatever I can get for him with you."

Walking down the stairs, he did his usual weather check. The
palm fronds were moving slightly and there were some big puffy
cumulus clouds floating in the sky. No sign of a black cloud hanging
over the trawler where Trufante slept, or the anvil shaped thunder-
heads forming over the water that could ruin your day. It would only
take a few hours to sell the catch. If the weather held, maybe this
afternoon would be good opportunity to take Mel out in the center
console and do some scouting. He had just upgraded the electronics
in the unit and was curious how the side-scan sonar would work. A
friend of his who was the electronics guru at Marathon Boatyard had
told him it was supposed to expand the range of a standard depth
finder from the area underneath the boat to the width of a football
field on each side. Finding lobster required finding structure and the
waters near the island were sprinkled with coral heads and pot holes
only waiting to be found. He had a huge list of numbers, but with
each year the lobster and crab became less plentiful, requiring more
work to catch his limit.

At the beach he entered the water, wading to the lone pile that
both the trawler and center console were tied to. Releasing the line

for the trawler, he climbed aboard. Without disturbing Trufante, he untied the stern line holding the two boats together and gently pushed off the center console before taking in the two fenders he had placed between the boats. There was still no sign of the Cajun when he started the engine. With the transmission in reverse and his back to the wheel, he steered out of the unmarked cut. A small whirlpool appeared to starboard and he eased past the rock that was only visible on the lowest of tides. Turning to face forward, he accelerated into the channel. He had fifteen minutes of peace to enjoy the morning before he felt someone moving around below.

"Damn, we here already?" Trufante asked from the companionway.

"Be at the fish house in ten. Maybe you ought to call Pamela and get a ride. I'm heading out right after we offload."

Trufante disappeared for a few minutes. "She'll come get me. What do you think the paydays lookin' like?"

Mac tried to calculate the profit in his head. "It's still early in the season. The price ought to be high. Probably cover the extra fuel."

"What about the salvage vessel?" Trufante asked.

"You know it takes them a while to pay on those. You'll get your cut when I get mine." Mac said, turning away. He knew where this was going, and didn't feel like negotiating with Trufante for an advance. This was government work and they both knew they paid when they paid.

They had just passed the #22 marker and he changed course to run the channel between the Bethel Banks and the sandbar by the bridge. After clearing the shallows, he turned between two small islands and slowed to an idle. A rock jetty appeared and he steered a wide turn around it before entering a small harbor. To the right were slips rented out to sailboats and closer to the restaurant was a horseshoe shaped dock for charter boats. To the left was the more industrial area. He headed in that direction, passing several commercial fishing boats tied to the seawall before sliding into an open space near the end.

"You want to start unloading, and I'll get the boss," Mac said, climbing onto the rickety wooden dock with the bow line in hand. He tied it off to a piling and went toward the stern where Trufante tossed him another line. After securing the boat, he walked to the office to negotiate.

The women followed him to the scale and waited for Trufante who was navigating warped decking and trying not to dump the large wheelbarrow overflowing with dolphin. He reached the scale and together they piled the fish into large bins.

"Got some nice ones here," the woman said.

Mac knew she was prying for information. It was a big ocean and he didn't mind sharing, knowing it would come back his way sooner or later. "Been out by the Marquesas."

"I thought so. Haven't seen anything like this out here yet. They weighed the contents of a half dozen more wheelbarrows. "Come on in, and I'll take care of you," the woman said, writing the last weight on her pad.

Mac followed her back into the building and waited while she walked behind the counter to her desk. She added the numbers on her pad and wrote him a check.

"You know if you fillet it first, you get much more," the woman said.

"Yes ma'am, but then I gotta buy old Tru beer while he works, so it's about a breakeven."

"Good payday this early. Might be worth it to make another trip before the rest of the fleet find them."

Mac took the offered check. "Mind if I leave her tied up for an hour. Gotta cash this and pay off Tru."

She shook her head. "When are you gonna be done with that one?"

Mac shook his head not knowing the answer to the question everyone seemed to ask. He walked out of the office and looked for Trufante. One glance toward the trawler confirmed what he already knew, and he went over to the restaurant and tiki bar. Climbing the steps, he saw him sitting at the bar. A woman was next to him, and he almost turned around to leave, when she caught his eye.

"Mac Travis."

"Hey Celia," he said, frozen in place. She rose, her floral print dress undulating as she moved. Some of what it covered was in the right places and some wasn't. She extended her arms, covered with bright tattoos and gave him a hug.

"We're good my friend," she said. "You lost my babies, but that payday from the treasure and the insurance bought me another rig. Got five of those two-seventy-fives on the back of her now."

Mac laughed, relieved that she didn't harbor a grudge. The colorful woman had been of help to him in the past, and he would probably need her again. "How many boats are you running?"

She played at counting on her fingers. "Got half a dozen."

Mac was impressed. What had started with two broken down boats had turned into a pretty profitable enterprise for her. The small harbor was her domain, and she ran the captains and mates with an iron fist. There were charter docks all over the Keys, most doing little or no advertising. At most they'd hang their catch on a board or leave the spreaders on at night to illuminate the gleaming stainless steel superstructures. Celia had taken it a step further. Getting away from the old school, she went for bling. Colored LED lights lit her boats and multiple outboard engines hanging from their transoms powered them. It was a sexy look and it worked.

"Your boys catching?" he asked, following her to the bar.

"A little. Your boy told me you been to the Marquesas and scored pretty well. Towed in a refugee boat on top of it."

Mac knew the whole city would know by happy hour and just shook his head. There were no secrets when there was two feet of wood between Trufante and alcohol. He would offer whatever he had up for a free drink. "Going to cash the check. You coming?" he asked Trufante.

"No. I'm gonna hang here. Pamela should be by anytime."

Mac left the bar and walked out toward the street. After walking the mile round trip to the bank, he saw Pamela's car in the parking lot. Pulling the phone from his pocket, he texted Trufante to come down to the boat. It would be much better to pay him off away from the bar. Once the two of them got the scent of the money in his pocket, he would never get out of here.

Walking towards the trawler he felt the vibration of the phone in his pocket. He was going to ignore it, thinking it was Trufante acknowledging him, but it kept vibrating. He stopped and answered the call.

"This is the Coast Guard Station Key West," a woman's voice stated crisply.

Mac was surprised they had valued the abandoned boat already. "This is Mac Travis."

"Sir, this call is going to be recorded."

So much for a quick paycheck. "Go on."

"We have received a signal from an EPIRB registered to you."

He had forgotten to check for his. "Must be a mistake," he said.

"Can you confirm that?"

"Yes ma'am. I'm standing at the dock beside the boat now."

"No worries, sir. Happens all the time. Thank you."

"Any chance you can give me the coordinates where it went off?"

"If that will help you confirm the false alarm. 24 degrees 15.474' N, 82 degrees 35.807'W."

"Thank you ..." he started to say, but she had already disconnected.

Mac stuck the phone in his cargo shorts and strode to the trawler. Hopping on deck, he went immediately for the port bulkhead just inside the cabin. As he suspected the bracket was empty and he wondered what Billy Bones could want with the device. The units were registered with NOAA and were kept in a database accessed by a password account. He couldn't figure out why anyone would steal one.

He went back to the helm and started the chart plotter. Reciting the numbers in his head, he waited for the unit to start up and entered the numbers as a new waypoint. Pressing the *goto* button, he watched the screen zoom out and place a red flag on the coordinates.

Latitude and Longitude numbers to Mac were like zip codes or area codes to other people. He could guess the rough area the beacon was activated from the degrees. Knowing that Marathon was 24 degrees north and 81 degrees west, he calculated the beacon was just south and about a hundred miles west. The plotter confirmed his guess, placing the pin just below Key West.

8

M ac turned away from the empty bracket when he felt the boat move slightly and looked out at the deck to see Trufante climbing aboard.

"Payday?"

"Yeah," Mac said, pulling the stack of hundreds from his pocket. He counted out five bills and handed them over. "That's just the catch. You're gonna have to wait on the Feds to pay for the tow."

"Right on," Trufante said, folding the bills and putting them in his pocket. "What about making another trip? Bartender says the weathers gonna hold for another four or five days."

Mac shook his head at the source of the information. Even the weathermen couldn't predict the weather here, he wasn't going to listen to a bartender forecasting by watching a brick swing from a string. "We wait another week, they'll be offshore here. No reason to spend that kind of gas money chasing them."

Trufante nodded and turned to go. "Buy you a drink?"

Mac looked at the calm gulf waters, just past the breakwater. He wanted to be out there more than anything and he was as surprised as Trufante when he accepted. Following the Cajun to the bar, he knew the only way to find out what Billy Bones was up to was to pour a couple of drinks into his friend.

From the empty drink pushed toward the bartender and the one she was sipping, it wasn't hard for Mac to figure out that Pamela was already on her way. She nodded to Mac. Though there was a bond of trust between them, their relationship had always been a little uneasy. Neither really knew how to deal with the other, and when Mel was around, it was worse. Fortunately, Trufante had the innate ability to breach any social gap and got the conversation going. Mac ordered a beer and stared out at the water. Checking out the new sonar would have to wait; it would take a few drinks for Trufante to tell him what he wanted to know.

BILLY BONES OPENED the back door to the building fingering the money in his pocket. He looked around at the boats docked against the seawall, knowing most had the devices that Tabor was looking for, but decided they were too close to home, and exposed. He would have better luck in Key West.

With tourists coming down from the upper Keys for the nightly party, traffic had built since he left the island earlier. Normally, he would have been out roaming the streets, looking for whatever action he could find, but this afternoon was different. He needed a boat and quickly to fulfill Tabor's request. Instead of following his usual course to Duval, he turned on Palm, crossed over the causeway and parked in the city lot by the marina. If it were a few hours later, he suspected most of the captains would be in the bars, but now, they were still out or cleaning up if they only had a half-day charter.

He walked past Turtle Kraals and the Half Shell to the marina, avoiding the spray from the hoses washing the saltwater from the superstructures of the boats he passed. It looked like it had been a good morning, with dolphin, tuna, and snapper laid out on the decks. Beers were in most hands, and on any other day, he would have had one, but now he clutched the six-pack under his arm and kept walking. Nodding to some and ducking away from others, he passed the line of charter boats. Toward the end of the pier, in the cheaper rent district was the boat he was looking for. Unlike the fancy signs and carefully arranged catches displayed to entice future charters, the only advertisement was a pair of shark jaws hung from a crossbar in front of the *Shark Gunner*. This boat needed little more in the way of advertising. If you wanted to go shark fishing, this was the place.

"Billy Bones. What'ya got there?" The man called from the deck.

Billy pulled two beers from the pack and handed the man one. He took it, popped the lid, and drank half before looking back. If there was a reincarnation of Bartholomew Quint, the famous shark hunter from Jaws, he was looking at him. Unlike the rest of the captains in their new high-tech fishing outfits, he still clung to his old school khakis and long sleeve shirt. His face was unshaven and his hair groomed by the wind and spray. "How'd it go Wesley?" Billy asked.

"Shit for a morning. Damn environmentalists are killing my business. Lost a mako and took a thresher. The rest of 'em are all protected now."

Wesley Chalmers finished the beer and extended his hand for another. Billy handed it to him and moved close enough to have a discreet conversation, but not close enough to get the bloody chum still clinging to the boat on his clothes. "If you're needing some extra cash, I've got a job for you."

"Don't know about your jobs. Shark fishings tough, but at least I ain't doin' time."

Billy brushed off his concerns. "Just a boat ride. No contraband."

Wesley nodded and leaned closer. Billy held his breath to avoid the stench coming off the man. "Need to run out by Boca Grande Key. Meet a man."

Wesley screwed up his face and ran a hand through his hair. "Be about a hundred in fuel. Throw in an even five bills for me and you got a deal."

"Drop the gas and I'll pay you the five," Billy said, knowing Wesley wouldn't run past eight knots to save fuel. If he burned twenty gallons, Billy would be surprised. He pulled the crisp bills from his pocket. Other days when the timeline was not so critical, he would have worked him down another hundred, but he needed to make the drop in a few hours.

Wesley took the money and eyed the dwindling six-pack under Billy's arm. "We'll be needin' more beer."

"I'll get your beer if you take a hose to that thing," Billy said, walking away from the boat. "We gotta go when I get back."

A stream of water caught him in the back of the leg, but he kept walking. Reaching his car, he pulled a duffel bag from his trunk and went to the store for another six pack. Changing his mind to a twelve pack at the last minute, he paid for that, a bag a of chips, and some jerky before heading back to the *Shark Gunner*. Thankfully, the boat was clean when he got there and he handed over the beer and food to Wesley who was dripping wet after taking a shower with the hose. Billy climbed down with the duffel bag in hand and placed it inside the cabin.

"Whatcha' got in there Billy boy? I told you no contraband," Wesley said, making a move toward the bag.

"Ain't none of your business. If it helps any, it's a job for Tabor," Billy said, using the name like it should explain everything, which in fact it did. Mateus Tabor had a reputation in the lower Keys. His disdain for smuggling drugs and guns was well known. What Tabor smuggled was more delicate and more profitable.

"Tabor huh?" Wesley said, backing away. "Ain't bringin' nothing back are we?"

"Straight drop off. Like I told you."

Billy caught the look of uncertainty and knew he had made the right decision in buying the twelve pack. He quickly handed Wesley another beer before he reneged on the charter. It was pretty well known to most who knew the shark fisherman that it was lack of beer in his blood that caused more problems than too much. Wesley took another beer and after tapping the head of the hula dancer bobbing on the helm for luck, he turned the key. A puff of black smoke rose above the boat and the throaty roar of the old engine eliminated any possible conversation. That suited Billy fine, he handed Wesley a slip of paper with the coordinates and went forward to release the lines.

They idled out of the marina, and with another cloud of smoke, accelerated into the channel. Wesley tipped his beer to the crowded decks of the schooners and catamarans taking their passengers past Mallory Pier for a sunset cruise. A few minutes later, they were clear of the local boat traffic and Wesley adjusted the course to run parallel to the string of mangrove covered islands in the distance. Their destination, Boca Grande Key, was the last in the line.

MAC WAS GETTING edgy and the bar, with its clear view of the Gulf waters was not making it any better. Trufante was into his third or fourth drink while he was still carefully nursing his first beer. He stayed apart from the couple, watching the first hundred dwindle on the bar top. Mac tried to relax, but the lure of the water was too great. Even after twenty-five years here, when a day like this came, it was torture to be anywhere but on the water.

"I gotta get going," he said, finishing his beer and giving up on waiting for Trufante.

"Shoot, thanks for the work. How about we give it another go?" Trufante asked.

Mac could see Pamela looking over his shoulder. There were still five days left until the first, and the speed at which the first hundred was going, the money in the Cajun's pocket wouldn't last. "We'll see. Got something I gotta do first." Mac started to walk away, but turned, deciding there was nothing to be lost in asking. "By the way, what's Billy Bones up to?"

"What'ya mean? We just spent a day with him."

"No, I mean that story about the hard drive and the guys following him. Is he working for someone?"

"Rumors go around about that guy. Heard he was into something different though. Some high roller on Stock Island."

Mac scratched the stubble on his head. High roller on Stock

Island was an oxymoron. The island just east of Key West had long been the support and cheaper housing for the island. In recent years, expensive condos and marinas had been popping up, but it was still Stock Island. "What's his game?" Mac caught a look from Pamela to the Cajun, like he was going too far.

"Not drugs. I heard Billy was clear of that. Doesn't leave much else, if you get my drift."

Mac nodded and walked away. The what else, was not good. Drugs had never really hurt this community, in fact it had helped a lot of fishermen through some bad seasons. The Keys were a transport zone. There were not enough people or profit here to make it worth the dealers time to protect this turf for resale. The cartels and gangs stayed to the mainland.

The loss of the EPIRB still troubled Mac and as he climbed down the stairs, he decided to forego the afternoon on the water. His brain was working on a puzzle now and as much as the water lured him, the riddle would follow. Better to solve it now. He walked back to the office and talked the woman behind the desk into lending him her truck for an hour, and with the keys in hand and a vague promise to buy her a beer later, he found the old pickup and headed toward the Rusty Anchor.

Several miles up the road, he turned right after K-Mart onto the gravel road. A few hundred yards later, he pulled into a parking space and walked into the bar.

"Hey Rusty," he called to the bartender and owner.

"Mac Travis, been a long time," he said, reaching his hand across the bar. "Get you a beer?"

"Sure thing," he said, taking a seat at the end of the bar. The room smelled of good food and he realized he hadn't eaten all day. "If Rufus is around, I'll take one of those Hog Fish sandwiches too."

Rusty served a few customers and leaned across the counter so no one could overhear. "I know you're not one to stop by and say hi, though it's good to see ya. What's up?"

"Looking for Jesse," Mac said.

9

WOOD'S BETRAYAL

Kurt's calls to Miami-Dade and FDLE had gone unanswered, so reluctantly he called Martinez. The tone from the Special Agent in Charge was neutral and he offered no help. In fact, Kurt got the impression his boss wanted him to drop the investigation. Feeling like a red-headed stepchild, he was back at the site where he had found the boat. The mystery of the blood on the transom gnawed at him and he'd had little sleep the night before thinking about the fate of the refugees. Maybe the locals like Martinez were hardened after fifty odd years of the exodus, but this was new to him.

After realizing that the tide had moved the boat, he wanted to find the location it had been originally abandoned. There was no better way he knew to learn the water than to fish the spot, so he anchored close to where he had yesterday, and slid over the side of the boat. Black flies and mosquitos still patrolled the area, making crime scene tape unnecessary and Kurt found the site untouched.

Stepping away from the mangroves, he pulled line off the fly reel, letting it drift in the water by his side. After a dozen pulls, which he estimated at three feet each, he cocked the rod and with a flick of the wrist, started the casting motion. With each cast, the forward momentum of the line, pulled the excess by his side into the loop, and he was soon casting thirty plus feet. Now, with each cast he added a double haul, and pulled more line off. When he had about fifty feet in the air, he focussed on an imaginary target in the water and stopped the cast allowing the line to unwind. He frowned when instead of gracefully unwinding and setting the fly gently on the surface, the leader dropped in a pile with the fly on top.

Beside the heavier rod, line, and leader, saltwater fly fishing required a different technique than stream fishing. It was similar to the big rivers, but Kurt's experience was with mountain streams where every movement was subtle. The scale was smaller, usually only allowing him to cast ten or fifteen feet with a roll cast. Flats fishing required the same precision, but with longer casts and heavier gear. But reading water was how you found fish, and even though there were no visible eddies or flows like those seen in rivers, the flats were far from a static body of water.

It was only practice, and he respected the process, repeating it over and over until he had the fly dropping silently on the surface of the water. Now, he focussed on the water itself. It was about the same time of day as when he had discovered the boat, and he wanted to see how the water flowed to confirm his theory that where he had found the boat, was not its initial resting place. With each cast, he let the fly drift, carefully watching the nuances of the current. Once he was convinced he understood how the water moved, he stripped off more line and allowed the fly to float where the current took it.

He released line until the fly was a few inches from the mangroves. Looking back at the Bay, he judged the trajectory of the tide and put the rod back in the boat. Looking more official, with a waterproof camera around his neck, he slid his feet toward the mangroves and moved aside the broken branches the boat had left when it was towed out. Finding himself in the clearing where the boat had been discovered, he glanced over his shoulder and watched the water. Determining that it was flowing from about two-o'clock, he moved deeper into the mangroves. Several broken branches confirmed his theory and he carefully moved them aside as he went.

Last night, he had checked the tides and learned that the swing was only two feet from bottom to top. This gave him an idea how far to look and within a few minutes he was standing in a larger clearing. Inspecting the perimeter he knew whatever had happened had been here. With his camera he slowly documented the scene starting with the two openings cut through the mangroves. After photographing the scene, he started to carefully inspect the area closest to the open bay. What he found, was inconsistent with what he thought he knew. It looked like two boats had come into the clearing and after inspecting the torn branches, and seeing the fresh sap, he knew they had been here together.

He moved to the middle of the clearing, trying to envision what had occurred. It was clear that one boat was larger than the other and remembering the narrow beam of the abandoned boat, he guessed which was its point of entry. The other boat was much wider and taller. Broken branches hung from the overhanging mangroves close to ten feet off the water, indicating the boat had at least a T-top. Next he moved to the path he had entered from and found less damage. Only the smaller boat had gone this way.

The bigger boat must have backed out and he shuffled over to the opening. After inspecting the branches, he saw a scar in the bottom. If he figured the boats had met up about this stage of the tide, and the water, now above his knees, was about thirty inches deep, he could identify the boat by the draft, width and height of the entry. Retreating back to his boat, he took a tape measure and pad, which he stuck in his breast pocket and waded back to the site. He knew it was a long shot with so many boats that would fit the criteria, but he took the measurements and recorded them. Placing the pad back in his pocket he continued his survey.

Paint scrapings from the smaller boat were visible on some of the larger stumps and he imagined how the boat had sat. Beam to beam the boats could easily have fit here. The obvious answer was a smugglers rendezvous, but the other boat was a broken down wreck. Martinez in all his wisdom had said it was probably Cuban from the look, age, and design. That clarified things and he searched the adjacent mangroves for any sign of human activity. If the larger boat had offloaded refugees, there had to be something.

He found what he was looking for in the crooked roots of a large mangrove. The contents of the bottle glistened in the sun, attracting him like a magnet. Moving toward the plastic bottle, half full of a clear liquid, he almost dismissed it when he saw a blood smear on it.

First he photographed it in place, and then, reaching into his other breast pocket, he withdrew a pair of latex gloves which he slid on his hands before picking up the bottle by its top. With the bottle in his cargo pants, he returned to the clearing, but the rising tide had the water thigh deep and he retreated.

He cleaned up and pulled his cell phone from the water tight glove compartment. After finding Martinez's number he pressed the call button and waited for the agent to answer. The call went to voice-mail and after checking the time on the screen, he realized it was after two and his boss was probably on the golf course. He sat down on the bench seat and drank a bottle of water from the cooler, wondering what to do with the evidence he had found.

His job allowed him freedom, one of the reasons he had taken it. Martinez was technically his boss, but he had his area to cover which left him free to patrol when and where he wanted with surprisingly little paperwork. With Martinez not answering, and several hours left in the workday, he decided to take a run into Miami and visit the crime lab.

JESSE MCDERMITT WAS ON A LADDER, the upper half of his body buried behind the big radial engine of his old deHavilland Beaver. Mac waited nearby until the instincts of the former Marine told him someone was watching and he pulled his head out of the engine. "Hey Mac, what are you up to?"

"A little fishing, a little salvage," Mac said. He was usually close lipped, but of everyone he knew, Jesse was one to be trusted. They were actually neighbors. But unlike, the standard fences or bushes that marked property lines, theirs was water. About a mile as the crow flew from Wood's place, Jesse had his own island. More developed than Wood's, it had several structures, an aquaculture setup, and a boathouse. The plane, tied down beside the boat ramp at the Anchor, was just one of his toys.

"We ought to go out sometime. Maybe hit the mahi," Jesse said, cleaning his hands with a rag.

"They'll be here next week. We was down in the Marquesas and did pretty well with them yesterday."

"How's that old boy of yours?"

Mac knew he was referring to Trufante. "Same old." The conversation turning to the Cajun gave him the lead in he needed. "Listen, if you feel like taking a ride in that thing, I got something strange going on."

"Any excuse to fly is a good one."

"My EPIRB was stolen and the Coast Guard just called with a location it was set off."

"Where abouts?"

"Down past Key West. Near Boca Grande Key," Mac said.

"Tell you what. Give me a hand wrapping up this maintenance and we can take her up."

Mac helped where he could, and they finished the work. After cleaning up, Jesse boarded the plane, and a few minutes later, the engine roared to life. Mac waited on the pontoon for the thumbs up signal and released the tie downs. As Jesse worked the plane into position, Mac climbed into the right hand seat and buckled in. He started to yell over the engine noise, but Jesse pointed to a set of headphones.

While the engine warmed up, Jesse gave Mac a quick briefing of the radio and GPS, and when he had completed the pre-flight checklist, nodded to Mac and taxied down the ramp, and into the water. He shifted the landing gear to the retracted position and waited for the green lights. The pontoons cut easily through the light chop as Jesse positioned the plane in the center of the channel. Cut on a southeastern bearing, the original dredger's only aim was the shortest path to deep water, but with the predominant wind in their faces, it worked for a runway. Jesse revved the engine and the plane picked up speed, fishtailing as it broke the surface friction of the water and took to the air.

Before Mac knew it, they were over the Sombrero lighthouse and making a turn toward the Seven Mile Bridge. As the plane ascended, Mac could see more and more of the chain of islands. He searched to the east for Wood's island, picking it out as a spec on the almost clear water. Ahead was the large mass of Big Pine Key and then the channels of the lower Keys opened up in front of them. It was easy to see from this height why this area was a smugglers haven with its narrow, winding, mangrove shored channels.

"Key West up there," Jesse pointed out, then called Key West ATC. "Just letting them know who we are. Don't need any company from the boys at Truman AFB."

Mac nodded, and searched the horizon ahead for the small string of uninhabited islands that extended the Keys below Key West.

"If you've got numbers, enter them in the GPS and we'll do a flyover," Jesse said,

Mac pulled the paper from his pocket and entered the coordinates into the unit, then hit the *goto* button, noticing immediately that Jesse had corrected course.

"You want them to see us or not?"

"Better do the first pass up high. I'm not sure what this is all about," Mac said, holding onto the information about Billy Bones. He watched as the plane icon on the screen moved toward the waypoint and saw a pair of binoculars in the center console. "Right down there in the mangroves behind Boca Grande Key." He put the glasses to his eyes and focused on the two boats below.

10

WOOD'S
BETRAYAL

J esse dropped altitude and banked to the right to allow Mac a better view. The picture he had in his mind of the two boats in the Marquesas was playing out again in front of him—this time off Boca Grande. A fast thirty footer with four engines hanging from the transom was loading the passengers from the other boat that looked suspiciously like the abandoned boat he had just towed to the Coast Guard Station in Key West. They were too far above to see the faces of the people below, but Jesse must have seen the flash of the sun on metal and knew it for what it was.

He pulled hard on the yoke and it felt like Mac's stomach dropped to his knees as the plane gained altitude. It wasn't fast enough. The first bullet pierced the fuselage causing Jesse to bank hard to the right to avoid further damage. Before they were out of range, two more shots hit the plane. The two men exchanged looks. Neither was scared of gunfire, but both respected it. "Nothing vital, but what's going on down there?"

"I'm not sure," Mac said, focusing the binoculars on the boats below.

"There's a fly rod case behind your seat. Just in case. Let's get a better look. "

Mac released the seat belt and turned to retrieve the case. Opening the zipper he found the barrel of a gun in the rod holder. Assembling the weapon, he laid it across his lap and refastened the belt. Jesse banked to the right again and dropped toward the boats below. The fast boat, its bow now crowded with the refugees spun and accelerated. Mac saw the sun hit the rifle again and Jesse banked away to avoid the shot. He raised Jesses' rifle, but unable to get a clear shot of the driver without risking one of the refugees, set it down.

The shot went wide, and the man fired again. They were out of range now and Jesse carefully circled, closing on the abandoned boat with each pass. After confirming there was no threat, Jesse dropped altitude and changed course.

"Same as the one I just towed. Cuban for sure. Looks like the same old car engine for power. Someone's making these."

"Let's take one more pass and go after the other boat," Jesse said, easing the yoke in.

The plane dropped to a few hundred feet above the water and Mac stared out the window. "You want to drop me and I'll run it back to the Coast Guard? They're paying salvage on them."

"Got a tool box behind you. Seas are calm enough. I can land and get you close," Jesse said. "Then I'll do a high altitude recon on the other boat and see where they're going. I'll swing back before I head up island and make sure you're okay."

Mac gripped the edges of the seat as Jesse set up his approach. His stomach dropped as the flaps extended and the plane decelerated. The tops of the small waves were visible now, and Mac held tighter, wondering what would happen if the tip of one of the pontoons hit a wave badly. His worry was unfounded as Jesse executed a perfect landing into the wind. He spun the plane and let the waves bring them close to the boat. Mac unbuckled and reached into the tool box for a pair of wire cutters and two screwdrivers" Thanks man, I'll return these."

"Bring some beer with you. Sounds like it's gonna be a good story. You'll have to swim from here," he said, extending his hand.

Mac grasped the offered hand and the opened the door. He turned back and tossed his phone to Jesse. "Not much use out there."

"Not much use anywhere," Jesse said.

Using the strut for a step, he crawled onto the pontoon and eased himself into the water, stroking quickly to avoid the pontoon as the wind swung it back toward him. Once he was clear, Jesse taxied away and swung the plane into the wind.

Fortunately, he was downwind of the drifting boat and he waited while the light breeze caught the larger profile of the hull and moved it toward him. Just as Mac reached the abandoned boat, the planes engine revved and with one hand on the gunwale, he watched Jesse take off. Mac hauled himself over the side of the boat and looked back at the sky. The plane was just a dot on the horizon now and he turned his attention to the boat.

Attached to the transom were two fifty-five gallon drums. After giving them a quick shake, he realized they were both near empty. From the weight of the drums, he estimated they each held five to ten gallons of fuel. Enough to get him back to Key West. The larger problem was the sun moving toward the horizon. The last thing he wanted to do was navigate the busy channel leading to the harbor in Key West with no navigation lights, in this boat.

At an idle, which he suspected was all he was going to get out of the boat, he estimated he would need two hours to cover the fourteen miles to the Coast Guard Station. If not powerful, the car engines were efficient and he figured he could make it on the remaining gas. The barrels were attached with old line tied with half-hitches, which he easily undid. Once they were free, he tipped them on their sides to make it easier for the fuel pump to draw the remaining gas and hopefully spare the filter the residue surely residing at the bottom of the tank.

The hulls were similar; old fishing pangas probably salvaged and patched for the trip. The similarities between this boat and the one he had just recovered indicated they had been set up by the same person. Mac noticed the wiring and engine were virtually identical. He went to the helm and found, like the other boat that the key was missing. The ignition, like the engine, was fifties era Detroit, and he smiled when he slammed the end of the flathead screwdriver into the key slot. With both hands on the handle of the screwdriver, he turned it clockwise. The ignition started and the engine cranked.

The first three attempts yielded a single puff of black smoke and he leaned against the gunwale afraid if he didn't give it some time, he would flood the engine. With every effort he made to start the boat, the sun sunk lower and now he held his hand to the horizon. The orb was just over four fingers width from the water; and hour and a half tops to get the boat back.

A quick check of the rusty engine revealed no visible problems and he went back to the ignition and tried again. This time, to his surprise, it started and he quickly pushed the throttle down and swung the bow toward Key West. It would be a fine balance now between speed and fuel efficiency and he spent the next few minutes playing with the throttle, finally settling on a speed above a fast idle, but well below what he would need to get the boat on plane—if that was even possible.

Without gauges, he had to rely on the sound and feel of the engine. Half an hour into the trip, everything seemed okay, and he started to relax. Aside from losing daylight, he was satisfied. He was so tuned into the boat and engine that he barely noticed Jesse's plane fly over. He dipped his wings and was soon gone. Mac checked his watch again. After forty-five minutes he was still running on the first barrel, and straining his eyes, he could just make out the landmass of Key West on the horizon.

The outline of Fort Zachary Taylor built on the bluff guarding the harbor was just in site when the engine sputtered. With no way to lash the wheel, Mac was forced to reduce speed and idle toward Crawfish Key where he dropped the engine into neutral, leaving it running. If he could swap out the tanks before it died, he wouldn't have to worry about restarting it. The tide was coming in, pushing the boat to shallow water, and he hurried to the stern to make the change.

For once, something happened the way it was supposed to and he was able to change tanks without the engine stalling. Back at the wheel, he could only hope his luck would hold and he gently pushed the throttle down. The engine sputtered, but before it could die, he goosed the control. The added fuel flow revived it and he was back underway. He already knew he would be coming in after sunset and when the last of the suns rays faded into the short tropical twilight, he accelerated, trying to make it through the main boat channel before dark.

It wasn't the darkness, but the wake from a cruise ship that got him. The ship passed to starboard on its way out to sea after a day stop at Key West. The six foot wake rocked the small boat, and Mac lost steerage. He found himself beam to the large waves. The motion of the boat, now rocking side to side, allowed air into the fuel line and the boat stalled. Sunset Key was less than a hundred yards away, and he could hear the crowds at Mallory Square across the quarter mile of water to Front Street, cheering as the sun set. Mac didn't watch the orb disappear. He knew this entire exercise was in vain unless he could reach the Coast Guard Station.

Waiting until the wake passed, he tried to start the engine again, but after the third try, the battery started to die. Faced with this reality, he drifted, trying to think of a way to get to land. He decided to wait a few minutes to allow the battery to cool and the fuel to evaporate from the carburetor before trying again. Another few tries yielded the same result and with the battery dead now, he slumped back against the gunnel trying to figure out what to do.

Looking around the boat for anything that might help, he noticed a plastic water bottle sliding across the deck. He guessed it had been stuck somewhere and set free by the cruise ship's wake. Picking it up, he noticed that it was an American brand, and wondered for a second if they were available in Cuba. His throat was parched from the hot sun and before he could think it through, he opened the cap and took a long drink.

11

K urt pulled into the slip reserved for the Park Services' Vessels and tied off the center console. He stepped up to the floating metal dock and started toward the headquarters building just ahead. The building was a government effort to build in the Bahamas style, but they didn't quite pull it off. Located across the canal from Bayfront Park near Homestead, the Park service had several buildings: the offices, visitor center, and a maintenance building. Designed with the standard gingerbread and covered decks common to island architecture, the overall feeling Kurt got as he walked up the metal gangplank was that the entire complex looked too industrial—and had cost too much money without capturing the desired effect.

With the water bottle he had found now inside a gallon plastic baggie in hand, he entered the air conditioned lobby, nodded to Mariposa. The dreadlocked woman called a greeting from behind the reception desk in her Jamaican accent. After Northern California, Miami had been a culture shock. The people here were more guarded and less friendly. Mariposa was different. The receptionist had gone out of her way to welcome him and feed him little snippets of Park Service gossip that told him more about the park and its politics than anything he had been briefed on. He smiled back at her and went upstairs to Martinez's office.

The Special Agent in Charge was no where to be found, so he wandered down the hall to Agent McLeash's office. Susan McLeach was his equal, but you would never know it from her attitude. Based in the headquarters building, she obviously felt superior to the other two agents living on the islands. Kurt had a Park Service residence on Adam's Key, a small island near Cesar Creek, one of the navigable passes to the Atlantic. Steve Wells, the other agent lived on Elliot Key and was primarily a policeman, watching over the nearby lighthouse and the two campgrounds in the park. He and Steve had little interaction. Susan was often the person he had to go through to get to Martinez.

"Hey," Kurt said, sticking his head in the door,

"Island boy, what brings you to civilization?" she asked, barely looking up from her paperwork.

"Looking for the boat that was towed in." He decided against telling her about the water bottle.

"They don't bring them here. There's a yard up the Miami River they take the wrecks before they demolish them."

"But it's a crime scene," he said.

"Once we sign it over to FDLE, it's not our concern. Just concentrate on keeping the Park safe." The look on her face was enough to make him regret saying anything.

"Right. I'll catch you later," he said, and left the office without waiting for a goodbye. Kurt walked downstairs and went to the reception desk. "Hi Mariposa," he started.

"Mr. Kurt. How is the island?" she asked in her melodic Caribbean accent, as if she were genuinely interested.

"Could use a few less mosquitos, but it's all good." In fact the mosquitos were as big as B52s and aggressive enough to keep you indoors between sunset and sunrise.

She laughed. "That's what they say."

"Would you know where they would tow an abandoned boat we found yesterday?" he asked.

"They take them up the Miami River. By the airport is a yard."

"Thanks," he said, and added, "just curious."

He caught a look from her and at first thought he was in trouble. "You need to come to dinner. Look at you, skin and bones. Mariposa will fatten you up and my husband has some Jamaican rum that I only let him break out for special guests."

"That's something I'll take you up on. I need to sign out a car."

She handed a clipboard over the counter with a set of keys. He signed and handed it back to her "Thanks, I'll drop the keys in the box."

"Don't be a stranger," she said warmly.

He smiled. Taking the offered keys he went outside and around back where he found the car, and with the aid of the navigation app on his phone he headed out of the park. Turning out of the parking lot, he followed several of the straightest roads he had ever seen with canals running beside them. The last one ran by the monstrous Homestead Miami Speedway where he turned right and headed for the Florida Turnpike. The roads were quiet now, and he couldn't help but wonder what it would be like when the Speedway emptied out. Heading north on the Turnpike, he was lucky that most of the afternoon traffic was heading south, but as soon as he merged onto the Dolphin Expressway, all bets were off and he glanced at his phone wondering if he would make it in time.

When he reached the Palmetto Expressway, traffic was at a standstill. Kurt alternated watching the heat waves coming off the stopped vehicles and the clock that kept ticking as he inched his way toward the 836. Finally, at 4:45, he found the marina. He parked in front of a portable office, that looked like it was permanent, and got out. Just when he reached the office door, it flew open, almost hitting him in the head and a middle aged woman emerged, squinting into the sun. The daylight wasn't kind to her made up face or died hair and the small dog clutched under her arm appeared to have the same disdain for the weather here.

"Afternoon ma'am," Kurt started.

"Sorry, we're closing up. Just on my way out. Whatever it is, it'll keep 'till morning," she said, checking the lock. Without a word, she moved past him in the direction of a sun baked sedan.

He caught her before she opened the door. "Just looking for the boat that Miami-Dade towed in yesterday."

She ignored the interruption. Pushing him aside, she opened the door, released the dog, and dropped herself into the seat. The engine started and Kurt was about to jump out of the way for fear of being run over when the window cracked opened. He could feel the air conditioning escape.

"That old Cuban beater is tied up to the dock. Better get what you want, it's scheduled to be hauled out tomorrow. Lock the gate when you're done."

The window closed and she quickly reversed before he could respond. He watched her pull through the gate and realized it was only due to pure laziness on her part that he had gotten access. But lucky breaks made cases and he turned his attention back to the facility. From the modular office, the seawall was just visible across the pavement. Several lifts lay idle near concrete ramps, and boats were scattered through the yard. The place looked deserted.

Kurt walked across the hot concrete, checking out the boats either dry-docked or under repair. From the look of the yard and its surroundings, this was the more industrial area of the river. They were several miles inland and he guessed that closer to the Atlantic the more upscale the facilities would be. He reached the seawall and saw the derelict boat tied up between two old tugs. Made to service larger boats with higher gunwales, he had to drop to his knees and sit on the hot concrete before his legs would reach the boat.

He was not certain what he was doing here, except things were nagging at him. The fact that refugees had come across the Gulf Stream aboard the rundown craft, gave it life. There was a story here, and even if there were no laws broken, the human drama fascinated him. Maybe he would become immune, as many of the locals appeared to be, as he saw more of it, but fresh from the West coast, he couldn't deny his interest. He worked his way from the bow to the stern. The boat was empty, as if whoever picked up the Cubans had taken everything off. That alone, made it suspicious. The ninety-mile journey could take anywhere from one to three days. There should be evidence of food, water, or tarps used to protect the occupants from the elements, or at least trash from the journey.

His first pass revealed nothing, and he went back to the bow, this time running his hands in the concealed areas. Surprisingly there was nothing hidden in the forward section. He would have though that refugees would either hold personal items on their persons or if they were too large, hide them.

Kurt was on his back, using his phone to see underneath the helm. Compared to modern boats with all their electronics, the wiring was simple. Even with his lack of boating experience, the ignition controls, and the steering and throttle cables were easy to identify. Something else was there; a rectangular metal box that had no wires or cables run to it. Curious, he reached to his belt and removed the multi-tool from its case. Squeezing his body further into the tight space, he cut the ties holding the box in place. After extracting himself, he sat against the gunwale and stared at the unit. It was wrapped in plastic, but looked like a piece of computer equipment.

He place the unit in an evidence bag and sealed it. Moving to his knees, he checked the rest of the boat, but found nothing. He climbed off and took one last look at the boat. The blood he had seen on the transom was dry now.

He had no expectations before he started and had to admit a certain victory in finding the metal box. With the evidence bag in hand, he walked back to his car and set it on the passenger seat next to the bag holding the water bottle. Before leaving, he checked his phone, entering the address for the FDLE crime lab. Making sure to lock the gate, he left the yard and followed the directions from his phone.

It was almost six o'clock when he reached the station, but that was good. He felt more comfortable coming in after hours as he really had no authority here, and if anyone questioned him, he doubted they would know his day shift boss. Thinking Martinez was at the bar after a quick late afternoon golf game, he decided to try his luck. Entering the station, he approached the desk and after showing his ID, asked for the forensics lab. The officer buzzed the door open and directed him down the hall and to the basement.

He shivered when he reached the lower level, both from the cooler air, and the sterile environment. Everything in sight was tile, glass, or stainless steel. The plastic sign on wall told him he was here, and he opened the door to the forensics lab. Facing him were several rows of stainless steel tables with test equipment. Off to the side were several cubicles, most looking as sterile as the rest of the lab, but he heard the faint tones of Bob Marley coming from one in the back.

"Hey," he called out. The music continued, but no one answered. He assumed whoever was working, was away from their desk. Walking past the cubicles, he saw in each the standard formica desk and standard calendar, family photos, and cut out comic strips pinned to the cushioned walls. Reaching the last cubicle, he stuck his head around the corner. "Hey!," he called out again, knocking against the fabric covered partition.

A woman looked up, startled. She pulled the headphones from her ears and he could clearly hear the reggae. It took her a second to find her phone and pause the song. "Hey back," she said.

"Kurt Hunter, from the Park Service," he introduced himself.

"Janet Doe," she nodded.

"Really?" he asked, looking around the cubicle for a name plate. Immediately, he saw a difference between this and the other work areas. The pictures were more of friends, beaches, and sailboats. And there were a lot of them.

"Doechynski," she said.

"Got it," Kurt said, slightly embarrassed. He thought he blushed when she looked at him. The pale green eyes and braided blonde hair, set off a face that could have been on a magazine cover.

"And you're here because ..."

He awkwardly handed her the evidence bags, realizing how stupid he looked with the latex gloves still on.

"You shouldn't have," she said.

"No," he stuttered. "They're from a crime scene, or at least I think it's a crime scene."

She sat back in the chair and he saw the contours hidden behind the lab coat. "You think it's a crime scene? Like and imaginary one?"

He started to explain about finding the boat, but saw her eyes drift past him toward the door. His first thought was that he had lost her, but the door opened and a man in a cheap suit walked in. The first thing Kurt thought was that it could be Martinez's brother.

"Hey Doey, you got my results yet?" he asked,

"Hi Dwayne," she said, drawing the name out to emphasize the redneck connection. I'll have them in an hour or so."

Kurt could tell by his body language that he was not happy.

"What, you got a new boyfriend jumping in line in front of me? Thought you'd be hangin' with some hippie guy. Didn't think you liked the uniform types."

She leaned behind the cubicle and stuck her tongue out at him. "No baby, tests just takes some time. I'll call you as soon as we have the results."

"Just don't be putting that Park Service crap in front of real police work," he said, coming toward them.

"Right. That's what you're doing. Real police work."

He turned and walked out without a word. Kurt watched her eyes as she followed him through the glass wall and he noticed his pants were torn.

Janet must have noticed too. "Gator gotcha?"

The door slammed behind him and when he was out of sight, she started laughing. He sat there confused.

"Don't mind him. Just another dick. You were saying about the refugee boat?"

There was something about the way she said refugees. As if there were some empathy there that she clearly didn't have for whatever the detective wanted. It took Kurt a second to regroup. Figuring out the politics of the FDLE would have to wait. At least he had her attention. Continuing with his story, she pulled a pair of gloves from her drawer, put them on, and took the bag. "Let's go run some tests," she said.

"What about the detective?"

"I got his done an hour ago. You've got to be careful with these boys or they'll be sitting here watching you work. You coming?"

12

A MAC TRAVIS ADVENTURE

WOOD'S
BETRAYAL

M ac fell to his knees, tried to rise, and found himself flat on the deck. He dropped the water bottle and watched as the last few drops poured out. Slowly he crawled onto his knees and looked over the gunwale at Sunset Island looming large on his port side. The lights from the cabanas and restaurant were blurred together and halos encompassed the ones further away. His throat was dry and his mouth had a bitter taste. He knew something was wrong, and he looked at the empty bottle for answers.

Unable to rise, he crawled to the helm and grabbed the wheel, using it to pull himself up. Without the engine, there was not much he could do, but try and hold the boat steady as the incoming tide carried him toward the beach. An outgoing tide would have been disastrous, carrying him into the Gulf Stream, and he thanked the sea gods for their grace when the bow brushed against solid land. Picturing himself adrift in the small boat in the Gulf Stream made him feel something for the refugees.

The island he found himself on was formerly called Tank Island, aptly named as it had been originally built as a fuel depot with the spoils from the dredged channel during the cold war. Never used for its intended purpose, the island was sold off in the 1980s and had been renamed Sunset Island and converted to a Westin Resort in the nineties. It was a high scale neighborhood now. Trying to focus he squinted and scanned the beach to see if any security guards had seen him land. With few choices, he decided that the best outcome from this situation would be to abandon the boat and walk over to the ferry dock where he could at least catch a ride to Key West. He would give up the salvage value, but at least stay out of jail.

Slowly he climbed over the gunwale and set foot on the beach. He was a little shaky at first and it took a major effort to reach the palm trees and find the path to the resort. Once on the footpath, he wobbled slightly, but probably no more than a tourist leaving the bar. He walked around the registration desk, past the bar and saw the long pier jutting into the water. Two ferries were tied up and he could see the wake from the third as it made its way back to Key West. At the end of the pier, he found a bench and waited.

The rumble of the motor must have woken him. Not sure how long he had been out, he shook his head, got up, and walked to the gate. The twenty-six foot *Sierra* was just backing into the dock. The handful of passengers disembarked and Mac boarded with a few late diners and staff. The ferry was a free service, and though they checked passengers boarding in Key West to see if they had reservations at the restaurant or were staying on the island, on the return trip, no one questioned him. The ferry crossed the channel and deposited the passengers at the dock, this time there were no passengers to pick up, and it backed quickly out of the slip to make its return trip. Mac walked out to Front Street and found an alcove where he could take stock,

Turning out his pockets he found some soggy bills and whatever you called wet lint. He remembered he had left his phone with Jesse so it would not get ruined on the swim. With his boat at the dock in Marathon, he was wondering if there were still pay phones where you could make a collect call, when he saw Billy Bones coming toward him. He tried to duck back in the doorway, but it was too late.

"Mac Travis, on Front Street of all places," Billy said, coming toward him.

"This can't be a coincidence," Mac said.

"Just running my rounds."

Those words might have been as close to the truth as Mac had ever heard from the man.

"Happy hour at the Half Shell, Mallory Square for sunset, now I'm heading for Duval."

Mac had no doubt he followed the same route and schedule every day. Prowling was what he did; on the lookout for anything he could make a few bucks on.

"You got Tru's number?" Mac asked.

Billy pulled his phone from his pocket. "Right here," he said, holding it just out of reach.

"Can I just make a call?" Mac asked.

"Now, that would be a favor you're asking, and old Billy don't recall you treating him kindly enough to return a favor."

"I saved your ass from those thugs," Mac said, reaching out for the phone. His patience was running short. Billy handed it to him and he scrolled through the contacts until he found Trufante's number listed as it probably was on half the phones in the Keys as "The Cajun". He pressed the icon and waited for the unlikely situation where Trufante would save him.

"Billy the Bones," Mac could hear the slur.

"It's me," Mac said, holding the phone away from his head as if he might catch something by touching it.

"Mac?"

"Yeah. You sober enough to get down to Key West and pick me up?"

"Ready and able," Trufante said. "Go over to the 2 Cents. I'll be there in an hour."

Mac disconnected and looked at the phone, thinking he should call Mel, but the last thing he wanted was a record of her number on Billy Bone's phone. He handed the phone back and started to walk away.

"You ain't gonna buy ole Billy a beer for the call?"

Mac was about to blow him off when he remembered the stolen

EPIRB. Drinking wasn't really on his mind after the drugs which still had a lingering effect on him, but the pieces of the puzzle were slowly falling into place and he wanted to see if he was right.

"Sure. Tru said to meet him at the 2 Cents. You know where it is?"

"That I do. Bacon happy hour."

Mac followed Billy, careful to stay an extra step behind in case he was recognized. They cut through several side streets and entered an open courtyard with tables. Grabbing an empty table in the corner, Mac sat and waited for Billy to say hello to whoever he knew. The waiter came over with a basket of bacon and Mac took two pieces and stuffed them in his mouth. He ordered a beer and pointed to Billy Bones with the instructions for the waiter to get him what he wanted. The waiter handed him a die. Mac looked at him and he nodded for him to roll. It came up a six and the man scooped it up and informed him his beer was going to be full price. In return, Mac scooped the rest of the bacon from the container and asked for a refill.

He was nursing the beer and eating bacon, when Billy finally came back to the table. He set his backpack down by his feet and finished the beer. Looking at Mac, who nodded, he caught the waiter's eye and ordered another. Mac moved closer. It was time for some quality time with Billy Bones.

"So, what's the word on the Cuban deal? I know the wet foot - dry foot thing is over." Mac offered trying to lead him into a conversation, although he didn't expect him to be forthcoming.

"Just a different Castro's in charge now. The brother, Raul, is just as bad as Fidel. The people still want out. But Obama's changed the playing field; they gotta have a coyote now." He saw Mac's look. "You know, someone to run them over the border, so to speak. Like they do to get across the Rio Grande. Except here they do it with boats and call them Remoras."

Mac sipped his beer. A remora was as good a description of Billy Bones as Mac had ever heard. The suckerfish, as it was known, attached itself to sharks—a parasite on a predator. It perfectly described the caricature of a man sitting across from him. He let the silence hang for a minute, not wanting to appear too anxious. "How do they set it up?"

"You thinkin' about getting in the people business?"

"Just askin'. Those guys were ready to shoot you for that hard drive." Mac reminded him.

"Well that's the thing. The whole operation is all technical and shit. They use them hard drives to kind of smuggle the internet in, but for an extra fee, they give you a password for one of the sites. That's where it gets really illegal."

Mac nodded and took another sip.

"There's instructions to find this guy over near Mariel. It's close enough most anyone can get there from Havana without attracting attention and industrial enough that the government just takes its cut and leaves them alone."

"What happens there?"

"They hook up with this guy that runs a boat yard. He'll set them up with a boat like we found the other day, and send them off."

Mac already knew how they signaled to be picked up, but asked anyway. "How do they get picked up?"

Billy started to get nervous and inched the backpack closer. Mac let him off the hook, knowing what he suspected was correct. "Trade secrets, right?"

"Yeah man. Got to go pretty high up the food chain to get anymore info."

Mac heard the roar of pipes come up the street and stop behind the wooden fence at his back. A minute later, hair tied back in a pony tail, and the Cadillac grin on his face, Trufante walked into the bar. He saw Mac and Billy.

"Ain't you two best buddies?" he laughed.

Mac was stuck between a rock and a hard place, or an idiot and a crook. "We got some work to do," he said. "Good seeing you Billy," Mac got up quickly and made a move to the door. Trufante moved to the side, but he was too slow and Mac's foot snagged one of the straps of Billy's backpack. He dragged it several feet across the floor before there was an open space where he bent down to remove it. Knowing he might not get another chance, he turned his back to the table, and opened the zipper. The bag was full of bright green EPIRBs.

Billy grabbed the bag and quickly closed the zipper.

"Got mine in there?" Mac moved toward him. "Maybe there's a little more to this refugee business than you told me."

Billy looked around for a way out, but Mac and Trufante were standing in the only aisle. "Got to make a living you know. These do save lives." Before Mac could respond, Billy pulled two of the devices from the bag, released the safety and pressed the button to initiate the distress signal.

"We got to go Mac," Trufante said, already moving for the door.

Mac had no idea how many outstanding warrants were out on the Cajun, but he did know that half the police in Key West were now on their way here. "Right," he said and turned to Billy. "I'm not done with you." He followed Trufante to the street, waited for him to start the bike and got on the back. There was of course no helmet, but that was the least of his concerns as the first police car stopped only feet behind them. He tapped Trufante on the back and he quickly wove his way between a car and a delivery van. They had the advantage on these streets with the bike and were able to work around the vehicles, bicycles, and pedestrians crowding the sidewalks and overflowing onto the streets.

"Slow down around that corner," he yelled in Trufante's ear.

They turned left on Whitehead and Trufante slowed after a quick right on Angela. At the curb, he left the bike idling and turned to Mac. "What's that boy into?"

BILLY BONES WATCHED Mac and Trufante go. He quickly reached down and secured the safeties on the devices, stuffed them in his bag, and took off through the restaurant's kitchen. Ignoring the cooks, he slid out the back door. He ran through an alley and looked both ways before stepping onto Southard Street. He sensed the police behind him, but with the EPIRBs no longer transmitting he knew he was just another dude with a backpack and the best place to blend in was Duval Street. Turning left, he walked a half block and before he even reached the main street, he was invisible.

Now he had to think. It had been a profitable day. After dropping the first load, as Tabor had instructed, with Wesley, he had cruised the marina and restocked. This EPIRB business was one of the sweetest deals he'd ever fallen into. Tourists were all over the docks here and boats were seldom locked making it easy to gain access and steal the devices. Tabor was paying top dollar for whatever he brought, and an hours work could bring in four or five units. For little effort, he would walk away with a couple thousand dollars cash. When people started getting suspicious here, he would just move up the chain of islands. In the Keys there were no shortage of boats.

As cocky as he was, he had the paranoid gene of most successful scammers and felt the heat of the units in his bag. The sooner he could get rid of them the better. Reversing course, he crossed the street and headed back down Duval. He slid into an alley and glanced back at the street. On seeing the law enforcement activity, he turned and picked up his pace. Dripping sweat, he arrived at his car, tossed the ticket off the windshield and opened the door. After starting it, he wasted no time in pulling into traffic and heading for Stock Island.

13

K urt leaned over the counter watching Janet as she added drops from several small vials to the row of test tubes she had partially filled with water from the plastic bottle. He wasn't sure what to expect when one of them changed color. Looking at her now, he waited for the results.

"Got a positive for rohypnol."

He looked back at the tubes. The second to last had turned blue. "The date rape drug?"

"The one and only. Everything else is negative."

"But why?"

"You want your people docile and to have short memories, that would be the drug of choice," she said.

Kurt thought about this. It had been odd that the water bottle was an American brand. "They could offload them and get them where they want to go a whole lot easier if they're zombies. What about the blood?"

"It's not blood until I say it is. She took the bottle and sprayed something on the red stain. It immediately reacted. "Okay, now it is."

"Can you get a print off anything?" he asked.

"More than likely, but if they were handled by the refugees, it's a long shot we'll get a hit."

He nodded and watched as she pulled a jar of powder and a brush from a shelf. "Old school?"

"Still the best," she said. Shaking the jar, she opened the lid and lightly touched the brush to the contents. When the powder was applied to the bottle, a blurry print emerged. Janet pulled the backing off a piece of clear tape and captured the image, then placed it on a card.

"How long till we know?"

"Probably be a while if there are no matches as I suspect."

"Then why bother?"

She smiled. "You never know and because I'm intrigued. Most of what I do here is ballistics. Simply match the bullet to the barrel stuff. No stories. This has real people involved."

Kurt thought about that for second. "Same here. My boss told me to wash my hands of it as soon as the boat was towed."

"You still have the boat?" she asked.

"Yeah. I had a look earlier and pulled that box from it. Couldn't see anything else."

I'd like to have a look."

"Like CSI?"

She smiled again. "I don't get out much."

Kurt realized she was throwing softballs. "We have to go before tomorrow morning. The woman there said it was being hauled out." He hesitated. It had been a long time since he asked someone out. "If you get a dinner break, I'd be happy to buy."

"We have a winner." She went back to her desk and pulled a file from a stack of paperwork. Leaving it on the counter by the door, she removed her lab coat, and hung it up on a hook.

'You gonna call that guy?"

"He'll be back every hour, mostly trying to flirt me up," she said, opening the door. "Coming?"

They left the building and decided on Kurt's company car. "You want to eat first?" he asked.

"Let's check out the boat."

He wished he hadn't locked the gate. "We have a fence to climb," he said, starting the car.

"All good, as long as they don't have guard dogs or cameras."

He suspected neither. There was nothing there worth any money, and being the last one out, he hadn't seen any dogs. "Not as far as I saw." He pulled out of the lot and followed the same route back to the boatyard.

"You're not kidding there's nothing here," she said when he pulled up to the locked gate.

After maneuvering the car so its back bumper was against the chain link fence, he shut off the engine and went to the back of the car. Using the bumper, he stepped onto the trunk and with two steps was over the fence. He looked back to help Janet, but she nimbly dropped by his side. Using the security lights, to guide them, they walked through the dark boatyard to the seawall. It was high tide, and the boat rode higher now, making it easier to board. He was just about to step down when she stopped him.

"Let me have a go at it."

He moved back and watched her walk the seawall, studying the boat from bow to stern. After watching her lean down and take a few pictures, she pointed out several scars and marks he hadn't bothered to look at. "There's some blood on the transom—I think," he said, feeling amateurish in what he thought had been a thorough investigation. Satisfied with her inspection of the hull, she hopped down to the deck.

"Can you hand me my bag?" she asked.

"What do you see?" Holding it by the strap, he suspended the messenger bag to her. After removing gloves she continued her investigation shining the flashlight methodically across the interior and taking pictures as she went.

"I've got some blood," she said. With a knife, she chipped off several pieces from the boat and placed them in plastic evidence bags. "We'll see if they match what you found."

Again, Kurt was impressed with how thorough she was and was

surprised when after taking several more pictures she moved the two drums away from the transom. She leaned over and he saw the flash go off. A minute later, she reached back and removed a long set of tweezers and took another bag from her kit. Bending down again, Kurt waited impatiently to see what she had found. A minute later, she handed him an evidence bag with a piece of cloth.

"Well I guess we have a choice. Dinner or this?" he asked.

"How about both. We can get some takeout and bring it back to the lab."

"Cool," he said, anxious to both spend more time with her and see what they had found.

"Sounds good. I'm still buying," he said, wondering if it would be bad form to submit the receipt for a quasi date as a reimbursable expense. "Chinese?"

"Thai, would be my choice," she said. "There's a place I go to around the corner from the office. "You like spicy?" she asked with a grin.

As they walked to the car, Kurt thought about the spicy comment, wondering if it was some kind of invitation. He was becoming as fascinated with Janet as he was with the case. "Your call." He caught a glimpse of her smile again when he opened the door for her and studied her profile for a long second before closing it and going around to the drivers side. She had strong features, almost like a model, but with a little bit of a groovy kind of look that he really liked.

They passed the twenty minute ride with small talk about their families and where they grew up. Kurt suspected that they both wanted to talk about the case, but neither wanted to sound like they were all work and no play.

At this time of night, the restaurant was quiet and they were seated quickly. He let her order, relieved that she didn't ask for *Thai hot*. The food was good, and they relaxed in each others company. He did have to admit he felt relieved when the date portion of the evening was over and they were back in the lab.

KURT STACKED the evidence bags on a stainless steel counter, while Janet set up another table with lights and a camera. She took the plastic bag with the box and placed it on the table. He went over and stood behind her as she first photographed the entire package, then cut away the plastic and set it aside. Kurt tried to hide his impatience at the process as she began to photograph the case. He could see it was a hard drive now that the plastic was removed and was anxious to see what was on it.

Ignoring him, she set the drive down and dusted it for prints. After processing these, she used a miniature screwdriver to remove the cover. His hands were sweating just watching her as she set aside the last screw and pulled back the lid. With the cover open, she photographed the inside and then examined it carefully with a magnifying glass before reassembling it.

"Sure it's not a bomb?" he asked to break the tension and stepped back, as Janet moved past him.

"Got to trust the process," she said, setting the device on a counter next to a dual screen computer. She fished through the drawer, finding a cable that she inserted in the drive and then the computer. Kurt moved next to her.

"Ready," she asked.

He inched closer, looking over her shoulder as the right hand screen showed the files and directories. Just before she clicked on the first file, her phone rang. After speaking for several minutes, she closed the screen. "Crap, I gotta crime scene."

Kurt looked at his watch. It was almost eleven and he was faced with a dark ride across the bay to get home.

BILLY BONES PARKED in a space by the dumpster. He hadn't called Tabor, mostly out of fear. But he had a half-dozen EPIRBs in his bag and wanted to unload them before word got out that two had been activated. He grabbed the backpack from the passenger seat and left the car. There was no point in locking it here. If a thief wanted something, his would be the last car in the lot he would chose. Walking past the late model Lexus, BMWs and Jaguars, he stayed to the shadows, knowing there had to be security cameras. He made it to the service entrance, slung the backpack over his shoulder and called Tabor.

It wasn't the warmest greeting, but seconds later the electronic lock buzzed and he pulled the door open. Moving quickly to the elevator, he pressed the up button and tried to get his breath under control while he waited. The beep when the cab arrived made him jump, and he stood back when the doors opened. Fortunately the elevator was empty, and he slid inside and hit the button for the top floor and then impatiently pressed the close door button.

After buttoning and smoothing down the front of his shirt, he stepped out of the elevator and walked towards Tabor's unit. He was about to ring the bell when the door opened.

"Come in Billy," Tabor said.

Billy slipped inside and followed the diminutive man to his study. Tabor sat behind his desk and waited, using the silence as a weapon

"I got some units for you," Billy said nervously.

"Why don't you tell me why the police in Key West had a call to check out simultaneous alerts from a bar there."

Billy had expected him to know something—he knew the man was wired in, but was surprised he had the details this quickly. "It was an accident."

"And I suppose the reason for your visit at this time of night is to unload what you have in case I hadn't heard what happened?"

"I meant to tell you in person. You said to be careful on the phones."

"Yes. So, let's assume that your intentions are good and you were going to tell me the truth."

Billy breathed out, thinking he was off the hook.

"And, let's also assume that it wasn't an accident."

Billy gasped. He had thought for a second that he was off the hook. Now he needed to come up with a story that was good enough to stem Tabor's worries enough to sell him the EPIRBs. From his experience the best way to push the fault away from him was to put in on someone else. "Trufante. Crazy Cajun from up in Marathon. He grabbed the bag and set them off."

Tabor looked at him over his glasses. It was creepy the way the man could remain so still while he exerted so much pressure. "The lone Cajun theory?"

Billy looked at him not understanding.

"Never mind. But, I'm guessing it's a little more complicated than that," Tabor said.

"There are two of them. This guy Mac Travis. One of the units I brought in the other day was his. Trufante's his sidekick. I think he was on to me. He grabbed the bag, and the only way I could get away was to create a diversion.

"And then you run here."

Billy's stomach dropped. His half-baked plan to sell the units had just backfired. "I came to ... "

Tabor cut him off with a look. "You'll leave the units here for safe-keeping. I will make them disappear." He touched his fingers together and was silent for a minute. "How much do these men know?"

Billy spilt his guts. He told Tabor everything he knew. From the hard drive to the abandoned boat, carefully removing his name whenever possible. When he was finished he watched Tabor.

After what seemed like an eternity, like a judge handing down a guilty verdict, the man spoke. "I'll be needing to meet these two men."

"I can maybe get one of them, not both together by myself."

"You don't have to take them, just lure them here. Find something they'll come after and take that."

Billy sat in the sterile leather chair, afraid to move or the friction of his skin against the material would make noise. He had met Mel, Mac's girlfriend once, and there was no way he was going to tangle with her. Pamela would be an easier option.

'Yes sir," he said, and almost crumpled on the ornamental carpet when Tabor dismissed him.

14

STEVEN BECKER

A MAC TRAVIS ADVENTURE
WOOD'S
BETRAYAL

M ac gritted his teeth as the bike roared up US 1, sure that Trufante in front of him had his mile-wide grin as they cruised down US 1. He could take all the horsepower a boat could put out, but transfer that to two wheels and he was not happy. On top of his own discomfort, there was Trufante's innate nose for trouble and Mac suffered the gut clenching, white knuckle ride, hoping it would end soon. For the first time he could remember he was grateful for the endangered Key Deer and the thirty-five mile an hour, readily enforced, night time speed limit on Big Pine Key. But the torture resumed and by the time they reached the Seven Mile Bridge, his arms were numb from clinging to the handle behind the seat—there was no way he was holding on to the Cajun.

They arrived at the Rusty Anchor just before closing. Rusty must have seen the look on Mac's face when he walked in because there was a beer sitting on the scarred wooden top waiting for him. Mac took a long draw from the bottle. "Thanks Rusty. I could sure use that Hogfish sandwich I never got this morning if Rufus is still around," Mac said. The spices from the crafty Rastafarian cooks meals clung to the air.

"I'll see what I can do," Rusty said. "Him too?"

"Yeah, gotta feed him," Mac said. With good reason Rusty was wary of Trufante. He hadn't reached persona non grata status here, but he wouldn't come in without Mac.

They finished their beers and Rusty put two more on the counter when he returned. "Should just be a few minutes on the food." He walked down the bar and came back with a slip of paper and a cell phone. "Jesse left this for you."

Mac took the paper and opened it up. *They headed to Stock Island* was all it said, but that was enough. Next, he powered up the phone and immediately saw the missed calls from Mel. He procrastinated calling back and sipped the beer, taking a few minutes to allow his brain to unravel after the bike ride.

His thoughts soon turned to the missed payday. It was too bad about leaving the boat on the beach at Sunset Island, but there might still be a chance to recover it. He'd come in after dark, and there was a strong possibility the boat had not been discovered. If he got down there early enough, maybe he could still salvage it before the maintenance crew found it. "What do you think about heading back down in the morning and bringing that boat in?" Mac asked.

Trufante finished his beer. "Two things you don't have to ask me twice about: going to Key West and making easy money."

"Okay. I'm going to call Mel and stay on the boat tonight. Be aboard at 4:30 tomorrow morning and we'll run down there." Mac figured with the early start, they'd arrive just at sunrise giving enough light to tow the boat across the channel. For a couple hundred dollars in fuel, it was worth the risk.

He picked up his phone, went outside to the deck and pressed the icon to call Mel's cell phone. She picked up on the second ring.

"Hey," he said. "Just got back in town." She was quiet while he explained what happened. Knowing she'd get the truth eventually, he offered as many details as he could remember up front, carefully leaving Trufante's name out of it.

"Two abandoned boats, stolen EPIRBs, and drugged water?" she summarized. "This is intriguing. I wonder what happened to the refugees?"

Mac's face changed. The worried look was gone, replaced by something that was hard to describe. He hadn't intentionally tried to lure her in, but her sense of justice and years of protecting the downtrodden had fine-tuned her radar. "Listen, I'm going to stay on the boat tonight and head back to Sunset Key early to finish the salvage on the boat." He held his breath, hoping for an easy approval. The connection fell silent, and he was just about to ask if she was still there. He'd expected some resistance and started to pace.

"I want to see the boat," she said.

He released his breath. "What's up?"

"I've seen some stuff posted on message boards lately about the changes in Cuban immigration since the Wet foot - Dry foot policy was abandoned. It's got me curious."

Mac knew from experience that at this point, things could go either way. Mel had a nose for the truth, and more often than not, got justice, but there was often a cost. "I already told Trufante to come," he said, wanting to get that out of the way. "I'll need him for the tow. It's dicey across that channel."

"He's your business," she said. "Are you at the Anchor?"

"Here now, but the boat is at Keys Fisheries, on the commercial side. We were going to meet at 4:30."

"Better. See you then."

Mac ended the call and stared at the phone. Her response was not at all what he expected, not that he had ever been able to read her, and he wondered what was running through her mind. It was not having her take the boat ride to Marathon in the dark that worried him. She was good with boats, and knew these waters blindfolded. Having the trawler over at Keys Fisheries on the Gulf side made it easier for her as well. She could make the trip without having to cross over to the Atlantic. What really bothered him was that Mel, and her sense of justice was as dangerous as hanging out with Trufante, and with both of them together, there was no way this was going to be a standard salvage trip.

He went back inside, paid the tab and said goodnight to Rusty. Rather than walk, he took a ride back to the boat from Trufante.

Music and conversation filtered down from the Tiki bar across the way, and he thought after the busy day, that he'd be able to ignore it and sleep, but that was not the case. He found himself sitting out on the deck of the trawler, staring at the stacks of lobster and crab traps piled in the parking lot, and thinking.

THE WHINE of an engine cutting through the night woke him. Boats had unique sound profiles and he recognized this one immediately. It was still a ways off, but coming closer. He rose and stretched, then went to the wheelhouse and turned his spreaders. Going forward he watched the green and red bow light of the center console approach. The boat slowed at the entrance to the breakwater. It dropped in the water as Mel hesitated for a minute, then she got her bearings and idled over to the trawler.

This time of night, all the boats were in, leaving no room against the dock. Needing to raft the boats together, Mel eased the smaller center console beside the larger boat and tossed the lines up to Mac. He dropped fenders and tied her off. They would have to swap positions when they left. He helped her aboard and went below to make coffee. Just as the pot finished brewing, he heard the roar of pipes and the single headlight of Trufante's bike turn into the parking area.

The Cajun hopped aboard and they quickly swapped boats. Several minutes later, they were underway. Despite the underlying tension between Mel and Trufante, Mac was relaxed. Mel knew that if nothing else, Trufante was a competent deck hand. With Mel sitting in the seat beside him and Trufante sprawled out on the V-berth in the cabin, probably already asleep, Mac steered out of the small harbor and turned to port. He had already decided on taking the ocean side down and turned toward Moser channel. There were faster ways through the Seven Mile Bridge, but in the dark, he preferred the safety of the main pass. Once they cleared the bridge, he followed the channel markers until passing the red #2. Steering straight, he waited until he entered the deeper water of Hawks

Channel before cutting the wheel to starboard. From here it was a straight shot. He set the autopilot to two-hundred-forty degrees and motioned Mel over.

"What is it you want to see?" Mac asked.

"I won't know until I see it."

Mac understood. "But why the interest?"

"An old colleague of mine is from an big Cuban family. I saw a post from her on Facebook about her cousins. She knows they paid a coyote and she has confirmed that they left Cuba, but they never arrived. I reached out to her to see if I could help from here, and she referred me to several message boards. They're loaded with missing persons reports."

'That's not all that unusual. I don't want to be the pessimist, but I saw the numbers from last year," Mac said.

"I know. Those idiots in D.C. Can't see past their own noses. They have no idea about the unintended consequences of their policies. By broadcasting the end of Wet foot - Dry foot, they started an exodus almost as large as the Mariel boatlift. Thousands died."

Mac glanced at the water. The southeast wind had them in a generally following sea, making the ride smooth despite the four foot swells. "How is it different now?"

"You said it yourself. They were in real boats, not rafts, and the stolen EPIRBs lend this an air of organization. If you're right about the water being drugged ... I fear the worst for these people."

"What about your official contacts?"

He knew from her look, that angle wasn't worth pursuing, and he agreed. Even before Wood's death, they had been skeptical of what the government could accomplish. Mac had found the old missile in thirty feet of water out in the Gulf, abandoned after the Cuban Missile Crisis and offered irrefutable proof to the authorities of a plot to blow it up. It had been the alphabet agencies lack of action and corruption that had almost killed a President. It had been Wood who had saved him and it had cost him his life. "I hear you. But can we agree to take this one step at a time?"

"Agreed," she said.

But he knew it would likely turn out otherwise. Mel moved back to her seat, and he checked their position. After adjusting course slightly, he saw there was still an hour to run. Leaving the autopilot on, he went below to refill his coffee mug. Back at the helm, he slid into the seat and set his feet on the dashboard. Sipping the coffee, he watched the water flow by, occasionally glancing at the passing islands on the starboard side, wondering what he had stumbled onto.

The following sea and current had them ahead of schedule and off Sunset Key just before sunrise. He wasn't sure if he should be relieved or not after seeing the determined look on Mel's face when she saw the boat on the beach, There was little chance to turn back now and pretend this never happened.

He had decided on towing the abandoned boat rather than waste time trying to refuel and restart it. After explaining to Trufante and Mel what he needed them to do, he went back to the helm and nosed the trawler to the beach. When the depth finder read eight feet, he stopped and called for Trufante. The lanky Cajun, stripped down to his shorts and with the end of a hundred foot line in his hand, he jumped into the water. He swam a few feet, then found his footing and waded to the beach.

Rigging the bridle took only a few minutes and after Trufante signaled that he was ready, Mac reversed the boat, using the torque of the engine to slide the bow of the refugee's boat toward the water. With the two boats aligned bow to bow, Trufante hopped into the abandoned boat and Mac, still in reverse, pulled it off the beach. Once they had enough water between them and the island, he dropped to neutral and swung the stern to the beach. Grabbing the line as it swept past the gunwale, he took the end and looped it around one of the stern cleats before tying it off. Back at the helm, he spun the wheel and waited for the stern to take the weight of the tow before releasing the line from the bow cleat.

"I want to have a look before we turn it into the Coast Guard," Mel said.

Mac frowned. "I can take it out behind Wisteria Key. We'll have to get Trufante off sooner or later."

The thought of Trufante riding the tow put a smile on both their faces. For the moment they were both happy. He had the abandoned boat to broker and she had a mystery. Mac changed course, bringing the boats behind the mangrove covered island just off the end of Sunset Key. He wanted to be out of sight of land before bringing the boat alongside. They weren't doing anything wrong, but it might look that way to the wrong set of eyes and they were dangerously close to the Coast Guard Station.

Mel retrieved the slack line when Mac stopped, reversed, and backed down on the boat. A few minutes later, the old boat was tied alongside them and Trufante jumped onto the trawler. Mel gave Mac the come with me look and crossed over to the refugee boat. Looking back, he saw she was right behind him.

15

It took Kurt a few minutes to realize where he was. Daylight streamed through the sliding glass door, penetrating the thin curtains and illuminating a room that wasn't his. He cast off the light blanket, set his feet on the carpet and stood. From the couch, he could see the indicator light on the coffee machine and a half full pot. Moving toward the kitchen, he took his shirt off the chair and put it on. The clock on the microwave read 9:30, and he looked around for Janet.

Just as he lifted the coffee decanter, the door opened, causing him to jump. With her hair tied back in a pony tail, and beads of sweat glistening on her mostly exposed, deeply tanned skin, Janet entered the apartment and grabbed a towel from a hook by the door.

"About time you got up," she said, wiping her skin dry and moving behind him. She reached into the refrigerator and grabbed a water bottle. With the towel wrapped around her shoulders, she sat at the dining room table.

He followed with his coffee and sat across from her. After getting called to the crime scene she had logged the evidence into a file on her computer, and then placed everything in a bin which was placed on a shelf with the other active cases. On their way out of the forensics lab, he had made a vague comment about having to make the drive to Homestead and then the boat trip home, and she had offered her couch. It wasn't the offer he really wanted but he took it.

"Nice tan," he said, feeling awkward, but she looked very different, in a good way, in the light of day.

"There's a few perks to working nights," she said.

"Good run?" he asked.

"Paddle actually. Took the paddleboard out for a five-miler."

"I'd love to try that sometime," he said.

"And I'd like to take a boat ride and see where the boat came from."

"Deal. Can we get a look at what's on that hard drive?" he asked, knowing bringing up work with a partially dressed woman across from him was not his best opener, but he felt awkward sitting here with her. It wasn't tense, just that neither knew what to do.

"I'll give it a shot when I go in tonight, but it's going to have to be on my time." She must have seen his confused look. "It's not really a crime yet. I have to log my hours and submit them. Last night I can slide by, but any more time and I need authorization."

He sat quietly for a minute wondering how Martinez would react to his pursuing this case—if it really was a case. She was right, a hard drive, a bottle of drugged water, and some blood from an old boat didn't constitute a crime.

"I'd be up for a boat ride, and if we just happened to cruise by the spot where you found the boat, well, that would just be a coincidence," she winked.

"What about work?"

"I don't go in until five. Got my paddle in, and I'd like to see this through. Besides, you're kind of fun to hang out with."

He felt the blood rise to his face and noticed her eyes boring into him. It had been a long time—a really long time, since he had had to deal with these kind of feelings and he had no idea what to do. Justine, had been his high-school sweetheart and they had married after his two-year stint in college. They were both small town raised and always assumed they would stay together. It was a good life until the difference in the definition of a small town started their struggles. Her's had five figures on the population sign when you entered the town; his had three. In retrospect, it was boredom that had started their problems. Allie's birth had solved that for a while. Thinking about his daughter, he felt a muscle flutter under his heart. Now fourteen-years old she was never far from his thoughts. Sitting here now, in Janet's apartment it felt like he was doing something wrong. His phone vibrating on the coffee table, broke the spell.

"It's my boss Martinez texting. Wants to know what I'm doing."

"You're not getting in trouble over this are you?" she asked.

"No, probably saw that I signed a car out late yesterday and haven't returned it." Kurt texted him that he was following a lead and would be back by early afternoon. "That should get him off my back for a while." It had only been a month since starting his job here, and there had been nothing to indicate in his boss's behavior that he cared what his underlings were up to. The return text surprised him. "Drop it and get back on the water."

"Bad news?" Janet asked.

"That's weird. I've gone days without touching base with him and now he wants me to drop something he doesn't even know about." That made Kurt think. Someone had told Martinez.

Janet read his mind. "How did he find out?"

Kurt shrugged and got up. "I gotta do what he says, but I can be a little late. Are you okay if we take two cars? I'd still like to have a look at the refugee boat."

"Sure. This keeps getting more interesting."

Kurt followed Janet back to the boatyard. They parked by the office. "I'll check in with them if you want to get started," Kurt said, walking toward the office, while Janet, with her crime scene case in hand, went to the seawall. The woman in the office was on the phone when he walked in, and aside from a scowl from her for him to close the door, she just nodded and dismissed him. Back outside, he walked to the seawall where he saw Janet with her hands on her hips.

He joined her and together they stared at the water. The boat was gone. They both turned in opposite directions, scanning the yard for any sightof it. A forklift was moving in the distance. "Let's go see what he knows."

The driver stopped, removed his hardhat, and wiped his brow. "What can I do for you?"

Kurt saw him looking at Janet and let her answer.

"The refugee boat that was docked over there last night?" she asked, pointing at the seawall.

"Y'all are a little late to the party. That one went out early this morning. We've got a contract with some guy that takes them. Probably just a bunch of splinters by now."

They thanked him and walked away. Kurt didn't have to turn around to know the man was staring at Janet's butt. "I guess all we have are the samples and the drive."

"That could still be a lot."

"I gotta get back to Homestead ..." he said, letting the sentence trail off to a pregnant pause.

"And I'd love a boat ride," she said. "Think you're boss will be okay showing a FDLE officer the scene of the crime?"

"We can try." Kurt said.

Kurt tried to think, but every time his brain started to gain traction, it slipped into neutral when he looked in the rearview mirror and saw Janet looking back at him. It wasn't Justine, but Allie, who was spinning him out. Their breakup had been brewing since he took the job in Quincy. The small one road town in Northern California was just too small for her. She didn't want to be there, and she had made it clear that she didn't want to raise their child to be a hillbilly. But Kurt was happy wandering the forest, fishing the streams, and playing with his daughter. There wasn't anything a city had to offer him. What was already cold, turned to ice when he discovered the pot grow and his family incurred the wrath of the cartel.

Taking sole custody of his daughter, with no visitation, was done under the premise of safety, and after a ten-minute court hearing, they were gone. His lawyer had tried to explain that when a drug cartel blows up your house, the safety of the family might be at risk, and he understood, hoping time and a change of scenery would heal the wounds. He assumed they were in Orlando, where her sister was, but he didn't know for sure. Maybe in a few years when things had faded into the past, he would look for them. Deep in his heart, he knew Justine had no ill will toward him; she was just looking out for herself and Allie.

He looked back and saw Janet brush the bangs away from her eyes wondering what he was going to do if this went any further. The witness protection program and his exile to an island had sat well with him—until now. Unable to clear the clutter from his mind he almost missed the exit, and whispered an apology to Janet in the car behind him as he hit the gravel shoulder a little too fast and skidded off the Turnpike. Checking his mirror again to make sure she was still there, he headed east, and then turned left just in front of the speedway. They reached the Park Office and he pulled into the back lot, leaving the car in the same space as he had taken it from yesterday, and met Janet in front.

"Better let me see him alone," Kurt said. "The boat's over there. I'll just be a minute."

He watched her go, then took a deep breath, wondering what Martinez wanted. Mariposa greeted him and after signing the clipboard, he handed her the keys.

She smiled. "Mr. Kurt got a friend?"

He returned the smile, but didn't offer any information, but she knew and winked at him. Turning away, he climbed the stairs to the second floor, turned down the corridor and went to Martinez's office. He knocked on the jamb and entered. Martinez sat behind his desk talking on the phone. With his free hand, he motioned Kurt to sit and finished the call that sounded suspiciously like he was making a tee time.

He set the phone down and leaned forward. "You tryin' to stir some shit?" Martinez asked.

He was more menacing than large, but Kurt instinctively sat back, knowing too late it was the reaction the man was seeking.

"Just got curious about some stuff. I found at the scene ... "

Martinez clenched his fists. "Curious? There is no scene, because there was no crime."

Kurt sat back deflated. "But, I thought ... "

"Okay, you're new. I get it. Once a hero, finding that pot grow, always looking for another taste. Things are different here. We're pretty much begging for everything. We have no tow boats, no lab, not even a maintenance department. Welcome to the National Parks Service."

Kurt breathed deeply. If he could just lay out what they had discovered, he was sure he could calm Martinez. "We found blood, drugs, and a hard drive."

"Jeez, Hunter. You're not getting it. All kinds of shit floats up in the mangroves. From bodies to square grouper and everything in between. If there's no body, we clean it out and let it go. There's other agencies that have actual budgets to chase this shit down." He breathed out and leaned back.

"Sorry, boss. I got it." Kurt said, looking at the door. This was not a fight he was going to win. Martinez nodded and he quickly rose and left the office before the Special Agent in Charge went into another rant. None of this sat well with Kurt as he descended and walked to the exit.

"Don't mind him," Mariposa said, running her hand against the tip of her cornrows. "And maybe Friday night, you come over for dinner and bring your new friend."

He smiled back, and left, wondering how every one here knew what was going on except him. The humidity weighed on him when he left the building, and his head was down when he reached the dock.

"What's wrong?" Janet asked.

He stood with his hands on his hips. "They shut me down."

"What?" Even FDLE wouldn't ignore this. They call it and FBI sized clue."

"Maybe that's who should handle it." Kurt said, looking up at the Martinez's office window which had a clear view of the docks. "I think we better take that boat ride another time."

"Yeah. Bosses huh," she said.

He looked back and watched her walk away. He had promised himself when he took this job that he wasn't going to let the work get in the way of his life and as she turned the corner and disappeared, he knew he had done just that. Before he could go after her, he saw the car turn out of the parking lot and onto the road.

16

"That's dried blood," Mel whispered to Mac. Trufante was watching over the gunwale of the trawler, but they used their backs to block his view. The less he knew the better.

"Not unusual. It could be fish blood for all we know," Mac said.

"This boat is different. You've towed these before. Ever see one left like this?"

Mac knew she was right. The wave of Cuban immigration flowed like the tides with highs and lows over the years, but some things were consistent. He had found all manner of craft; from inner tubes with plywood mounted on top to homemade floating houses and everything in between. It was rare to see one with a working engine and even more unusual to see a boat this clean. In all cases, with the exception of these two, they had been filthy and littered with refuse. In its own way, each told the tale of the crossing. Blood was not that unusual, fish blood that is. Many dragged fishing lines trying to pull a meal from the fertile Gulf Stream waters on the way over. As far as he knew, there was no way to tell the difference between fish and human blood without a lab.

"I know its clean, but what about it?" He asked, instantly regretting it.

"The only reason someone would go to this kind of trouble would be to cover something up. My guess is they're drugging and offloading the refugees. What happens after that we have to figure out."

"Isn't that ICE's job?"

"Not if they're dead or never set foot on American soil."

The wake from a large ship rocked the two boats. The fenders did what they could, but the difference in freeboard and design of the hulls knocked them together. "Whatever you decide, we can't sit here," Mac said, looking at the old blue paint that had rubbed onto his hull.

"We'll have to trust the Coast Guard, but let me do the talking," she said, climbing back aboard the trawler.

Mac followed her, and released the lines holding the boats together. With Trufante's help, they adjusted the tow line and twenty minutes later they pulled up to the Coast Guard dock. Mac eased the trawler against one of the cutters allowing the refugee boat to drift into a space against the seawall. After sending Trufante over to tie the wooden boat off, he backed against it and secured the trawler on the outside of the smaller boat.

Mel moved quickly across the smaller boat and Mac had to jump onto the seawall to catch her before she reached the office without him. He knew he had little choice but to let her do the talking, and that was fine, as long as he didn't lose the salvage rights. They reached the office together and he grabbed her arm just as she was about to open the door.

"Listen. Let me get the rights before you go off on them."

She nodded. "You're lead until they sign, then I'm taking it."

Together they walked to the desk where a petty officer sat. Mac recognized her from the day before.

Before he could say anything she greeted them. "Got another one?"

Mac wondered how she knew and then saw the small monitors off to the side showing the dock and yard from several angles. A group of uniformed men were already aboard. "Yeah. What'd you do with the other?"

"I think they pulled it yesterday. We have a contract with someone to pick them up. I think they salvage what they can and then scrap them," she said.

Mac wondered about the similarities between the two craft and thought there might be more to it. If they were sophisticated to use EPIRBs to locate the boats, why not recycle them.

"Any way to check," Mel asked.

Mac looked at her, noticing immediately that her body language had adopted her lawyer pose. "I'd be curious about that too, but can we do the paperwork on this one first?"

The woman nodded and opened a drawer. She removed the same two-page form he had filled out yesterday, put it on a clipboard, handed him a pen, and motioned him to one of the plastic seats to the side. He knew the drill and sat down to complete the paperwork, but Mel stayed in place.

"How about the other boat?"

"What's your interest ma'am?"

"My interest will be your superior officer if you don't help me."

Mac felt bad for the woman; he knew it was a bluff, but the petty officer didn't. Mel had no standing, but the intimidation seemed to work and after a few seconds of silence, the woman told her to wait a minute and picked up the phone. Mac put his head back down, hoping they had survived a potential showdown when the security door buzzed open and four armed men came through with their weapons extended.

"Drop everything and spread eagle on the ground," one of the men yelled.

Mac looked at Mel, who was about to launch into a tirade. His look tried to caution her against it. There was nothing to be gained until they could speak to an officer. She, of course ignored the warning.

"What is the meaning of this?" she asked.

"You want my superior officer, you'll meet him on his terms. And don't think you can treat a Petty Officer of the US Coast Guard like a receptionist," the woman said.

"On the floor ma'am," the man repeated, this time moving toward her with the tip of the barrel almost touching her arm.

Mac breathed in relief as she complied and lay down next to him. They were frisked and led into the back of the building. After being led down several halls they were deposited into an interrogation room with security glass in the window and told to wait. The door slammed behind them and Mac's stomach tightened when he heard the magnetic lock.

"What the hell?" Mel asked.

"I have no idea. How do we get out of here?" Mac asked, checking his back pocket for his phone. He hadn't felt it, but in the confusion they must have taken it. A look over at Mel showed hers was gone as well.

"They're not going to leave us long before sending an officer in to talk to us. Nothing to do except chill until then," she said.

Mac wasn't so easy going. He walked the perimeter of the room, looking at every nook and cranny for a way out. Mel sat in one of the chairs, bolted to the floor by a table. It was classic interrogation room, from the bright fluorescent lights to the soundproof walls.

"Relax Mac, they'll be here soon. They know who you are already from the paperwork. There's probably still red flags on both our names from some of the other adventures that Trufante has embroiled us in."

He felt the burn when she said *adventures*. She was right, of course. There had been several interactions over the years with law enforcement, and none in a cooperative or collaborative manner. In most cases, Mac found the government a bunch of worthless bureaucrats and avoided them whenever possible. He knew Mel shared the sentiment, but had too much respect for the legal process to disregard it.

Mac paced the floor and silence enveloped the room until the door buzzed and a single man walked in. From the four stripes on his epaulets he was a captain, and Mac sat next to Mel after he motioned him to the chair.

"Mac Travis and I'm guessing this is Melanie Woodson," he said, looking at both when he said their names. Opening a file and setting a legal pad in front of him, he sat, clicked his ball point pen and started writing.

"Yes, that's me," Mel said. "Why are you holding us?"

He turned to Mac. "You brought in another boat yesterday?"

"Yes. That's kind of what I do," he said.

"It was your EPIRB that went off yesterday. That's a felony by itself. And, we found blood on both vessels," the man said. "I am holding you and the boats until we can complete our investigation."

"Holding me for what?"

"It's really very clever, getting rid of the refugees, cleaning up the boats, and getting the salvage for them. Sounds like you're pulling down a profit from all sides."

Mac started to rise and felt Mel's hand on his thigh. "Are you making a formal charge here?" she asked.

"We've got forty-eight hours to hold him before charging. That should give us enough time to complete the forensics on the boats. We'll also need DNA samples from both of you."

"Got a warrant?" Mel asked.

He hesitated. "We'll get to that."

"I'll be Mr. Travis's legal representation. Please leave me alone with my client for minute," she said.

The man rose and left the room. Once he was gone Mac turned to Mel, who put a finger over her mouth. He understood and they leaned in close, speaking in whispers. "Can you get me out of here?" Mac asked.

"They've got their forty-eight hours, but I can try and find a judge that'll listen."

"Fat chance of that. Guess I'll be catching up on my sleep," Mac said.

"Don't worry Mac, I'll figure this out," Mel said, kissing him on the forehead. They embraced and she went to the door, knocked, and waited for the lock to disengage.

He gave her a reassuring look, and set his head in his hands.

AFTER STARING down the Petty Officer at the front desk until she returned her phone, Mel walked outside without looking back. She had taken the officer's card and said she would be in touch, but didn't want to give them any reason to detain her as well. At a fast walk, she strode down the pier, hopped across the refugee boat, and released the lines for the trawler before stepping onto the gunwales and boarding.

"Hey!" she called for Trufante. There was no immediate answer, and she went to the helm. Guessing, he was probably in a bar already, she started the engine and set the transmission to forward. It had been a long time since she had piloted a boat this large, and she bumped the Coast Guard Cutter docked in front of them before turning and exiting the channel.

Ten minutes later, after entering the Northwest Channel, Trufante came onto the deck rubbing his eyes. "Where's Mac?" he asked, looking around to get his bearings.

"They're holding him."

"Damn Coasties is always trouble," Trufante said.

Mel ignored the comment, but motioned him to the wheel. Anyone with a uniform was trouble for him. But he knew how to run a boat, and she needed time to think. "Take us the back way to the island," she said and went to the transom where she stared back at the pier and Coast Guard building receding into the horizon.

"What are we going to do about Mac?" Trufante asked when she came back to the helm.

"We?"

"You just tell me what you need. I'll be there for you."

Mel knew he was sincere, she just couldn't take the chance of having the black cloud that followed him shoot a stray lightning bolt her way. It was better to work alone. "We need to get back to Marathon. I'll be in touch when I figure it out." She let him down easy. Despite her feelings for him, she might still need him.

She tried to think through the problem, but the ride was uncomfortable heading into the seas and she couldn't concentrate. The chorus of *You got me babe* broke the silence and Trufante pulled his phone out.

"Pajamabama," Trufante answered. "Just heading back, babe."

Mel had already figured out who it was from the ringtone. She started to back away to give him privacy, but the tone of his voice suddenly changed.

"What the hell? What're you doin' with my girl?"

Trufante looked distressed and she studied him, moving closer so she could hear the conversation. He held the phone so they could both hear the voice on the other end. She recognized the accent immediately and mouthed "Billy Bones?" Trufante nodded his head.

"Shit boy. You and you're buddy Mac stepped in it this time. You guys back off the whole Cuban thing and I'll do my best to get her back to you. For now, she's security."

Mel reached for the phone, but Trufante used his long arms to put it out of reach. "Listen here, Billy, anything happens to that girl and it's on you. Put her on."

Mel had never seen Trufante like this. Pamela was back on the line, and he turned away so she couldn't hear the conversation. Mel moved away to let him have his privacy. As whacky as the woman was, she understood what she was going through. She left Trufante at the helm and went forward where she sat with her back against the wheelhouse thinking about the layer of complexity that had just been added. It didn't take her long to figure out that from what she knew of the operation, it was way over Billy Bone's pay grade. She had to find out who he was working for, and her best source was Alicia and TJ.

17

K urt had a lonely ride back to Adam's Key. He knew he should have let it go, but he wasn't one to let himself off the hook. It was just a job, and she was the first woman that he'd had any interest in since moving here—and a long time before. He slammed the wheel of the boat, wishing he had handled things differently and Janet was beside him. The last look, etched in his mind, before she turned away, made it worse. He knew she wanted to be here too.

His mind was elsewhere and the cracking of wood and tearing of fiberglass brought him back to reality when he came in too hot and slammed against the concrete dock. The hull bounced against the seawall again and he scrambled to toss over the fenders and stem the damage.

Just as he had gotten the boat under control, the door of his neighbor's house opened and a woman, clutching a toddler came toward the dock. Almost knocking them over as it ran past, a mostly black dog with a white patch on his right eye bounded toward him. Wagging its stubby tail and barking as he came, the dog acted more like a lab than a pit bull mix. "Put a lid on it Zero,"the woman yelled at the dog, and turned to Kurt. "Y'all call ahead on the VHF next time the wind's up like this," she said, taking the dock lines and expertly tying the boat off while still holding her charge on her hip. She stooped over and looked at the damage. "That's a nasty bit there, clear through the gelcoat. I can get Ray to have a look and keep it off your record." Her accent was from the deep south, forcing him to concentrate on her every word.

"Thanks Becky. I still need some practice. How's junior?" he asked.

"I tell ya what, this boy's a handful. Ray's off working, but we's here." She stepped back allowing him some space to hop onto the dock. "Seen you wasn't home last night."

It wasn't a question. If this were a neighborhood, she would be the woman who knew everything. In fact there were only two houses on the island and she did know everything. "A little late business with the forensics lab. Stayed over." He could see from the look on her face that she only partially believed him. Reaching down, he patted the dog on the head and changed the subject. "Zero's a good alarm."

"'Bout all he's good for is barking. I swear, as soon as the baby goes down for a nap, he's off barking, barking, barking. Got no peace 'round here."

Kurt started along the walk and turned to the right when it split by his house. "I'd appreciate it if Ray could have a look at the boat," he said.

"Sure. You got a beer, he'll be over to look. Just make sure that pantywaist Martinez doesn't see it. He'll write you up for sure."

Kurt thanked her and walked toward the single story, plantation style house. The two homes on the island were miniatures of the headquarters building in Homestead, and looked so similar it was like the Park Service had gotten a discount on the plans. Though cookie cutter, the design was effective, with the Bahamian shutters and large eaves blocking the sun. On most days he relied on the sea-breeze to cool the house and had only run the air conditioning several times.

The house was his, but it wasn't home. The sparse furnishings were either left by the last occupant or from Ikea, shuttled across the

Bay and assembled here. Just as he was about to go for a shower, he heard a light knock on the door.

"Kurt, I'm leaving Zero with you. This babies gotta get a nap, and mama needs some downtime. You good with that?"

The door opened and the dog bounded through, skidding across the tile floor. All of a sudden it felt a little more like home. The dog nuzzled against him. Like there was a choice, he called back that it was okay. After a shower, he sat at the small bar in the kitchen with his laptop in front of him, a bottle of beer on the counter, and Zero snoring by his feet. He pulled up a blank incident report and started filling in the details. It was straightforward until the question of whether a crime had been committed or not.

This was the first time he had to think about whether to check the box or not. Each park had their own *top incident lists*. Biscayne was no different. Out west, he had most of the reports were for mining related accidents, and dredging without a permit, or disputed claims. Personally, he left the fishermen alone, only checking for licenses if something looked wrong. Here, by far the largest source of paper-work were groundings. Cesar Creeks's winding channel, visible outside his window, caught its fair share. Even though it was well marked, people often got lazy and went outside the lines, only to find out that the markers were there for a reason.

Finishing the beer, he got up and grabbed another, then walked outside onto the deck with Zero following behind. He sat in a fake wood Adirondack style chair provided with the house, whose plastic boards were supposed to outlive him. The splinter-less wood was no more comfortable than the real thing, and he soon got up and went to the rail. The house had a deck around three sides, all with water views. To the east, was Cesar Creek, named after the famous pirate, Black Cesar, and to the south and west were views of the bay.

His thoughts alternated between the checkbox and Janet. Knowing the two were tied together, he decided the best way to put Martinez in his place and get Janet back was to find a crime.

～

MAC PACED AROUND the ten by ten room like a caged animal. It had been several hours since Mel had left and besides a bag of takeout breakfast burritos, he'd had no contact with anyone. Though he was tired, he couldn't relax knowing the door was locked and he was suspected of doing something he had no part in. This wasn't the first run-in with authority that had gone badly for him, in fact there was quite a long list.

He knew that this kind of thinking was not getting him anywhere and he sat staring at the blank yellow pages of the legal pad one of the men had left. Maybe they thought he would have momentary lapse in sanity and write a confession. He took up the pencil, but instead of writing the words, sentences, and paragraphs, his captors wanted, he drew a diagram.

He put Billy Bone's name in the center. There was no way he was the boss, but his fingerprints were on everything. From there, he drew arrows leading out to the items: EPIRBs, refugee boats, hard drives, and drugged water. Staring at the page, he struggled to connect the dots when he heard activity outside the door. Crumbling up the paper, he jammed it in his pocket and felt something hard. Realizing it was a trolling weight and a bunched up piece of monofilament he had cut for a leader when they were fishing, he rolled the oblong lead shape in his fingers. They had taken his cell phone, but never really searched him. A wad of bills and a few barrel swivels were all he had otherwise.

Escape was always an option, and if he were going to be held and charged, as he expected, he needed to do it quickly. This would be the least secure setting he might see. Glancing around the room, his eyes fell on the return air grill for the air conditioning system. Unlike the movies, where escapes were made through the ductwork, he knew it was too small. The only other point of egress was the door, and just as he turned to it, the lock buzzed and it opened.

The officer that had talked to him earlier walked in and glanced at the pad. "I guess you haven't come to grips with what you're dealing with here," he said, moving toward the table. A uniformed man with a sidearm entered and stood by the door.

"I told you. We just found the boats. It's what I do," Mac said. He stuck his hands into the pockets of his cargo shorts, again finding the comfort of the weight.

"We are prepared to move forward on the felony charge of unlawfully deploying a radio beacon. We'll figure out how you're tied into the refugee thing from there," the man said.

Mac sat down, hoping to buy some time. If they charged him, he would be moved either to a more secure cell here, the navy facility nearby, or the county lockup. None would afford the ease or opportunity for escape as this room. He saw the frame job coming, and knew he had to act now. Slouching in the chair so his pants were hidden by the table, he pulled the weight and line from his pocket. It was awkward, trying to hold the man's attention and tie a knot at the same time, but Mac had spent almost three decades on the water. "It's Billy Bones you want," he offered.

"Yeah, we know about him. Your girlfriend threw his name around on her way out. Problem is, there is no one with that name in any database."

The hole was getting deeper and Mac looked the man in the eye while his right hand worked frantically to tie the Palomar knot. With the weight resting on his thigh, he doubled the leader and worked it through the hole in its end. "It's an alias. Every cop in this town knows him."

"We called over to the city guys too. They got no record of him. You're going to have to go higher on the food chain if you want out of this."

Mac had the overhand knot tied now and was working the weight through the loop. It slipped and he was barely able to catch it against his thigh. Coughing to disguise his movements, he spun the weight through and cinched the knot.

"If you're not going to cooperate, I guess we don't have a choice," the officer said, and turned to the guard. "Why don't you take Mr. Travis in for processing."

There was no way of knowing if the leader was tangled, but if he was going to try something, he needed to do it now.

The officer moved toward the door and the uniformed guard moved toward him. Just as the automatic closer on the door started its work and hoping for the best, Mac dropped the weight, flinching when it bounced on the hard floor. The leader fell in a loop at his side. The moment the officer was out of the room, Mac swung the weighted line up and spun it toward the table. He slammed it against the metal top. The guard jumped, not knowing what had happened, but instinctively stepped back giving Mac enough room to swing the makeshift bola at the overhead light. There was a loud pop as the fluorescent light exploded. The shattered glass fell on both men, but Mac had been expecting it and the guard hadn't. With no other source of light, the room was dark, lit only by the small crack of the door which was closing quickly.

Mac lunged for the handle, needing to reach the door before the electronic lock caught it. He pulled the door open, and before the guard could react, closed it and threw the bolt. He looked both ways and after seeing no one in the corridor, he took off toward an exit sign. Not knowing where he was inside the building, he would only have seconds before the guard called for help. Running, he hit the exit door hard, not stopping when the alarm went off. The door opened onto the seaward side of the building and he glanced at the dock. The trawler was gone, but the refugee boat was still tied off and he ran toward it.

He reached the boat, and untied the lines. Staying low, he peered over the gunwale and watched as a half dozen men frantically searching around the building. They split up and moved toward the parking area, thinking there was no means of escape on the dock. So far, he was in the clear, and now, he just needed a bit of luck. Staying low, he crept toward the fuel tank, and pushed the primer ball. Reassured when it filled, he moved to the helm and with a quick glance toward shore hit the ignition. Surprisingly, the engine coughed and started. Mac had no idea whether the Coast Guard had charged the battery, or the rest allowed enough juice to flow to the starter, but he didn't question his luck. Now he had to get clear of the pier before they saw the boat moving.

Two miles offshore lay a cluster of mangrove islands, if he could reach their protection, he might have a chance. Pirates and smugglers had been using these waters to escape capture for centuries. He needed a little of their luck and all the subterfuge he could muster now.

18

Kurt scanned the mangroves, thinking he should have placed some kind of marker to find the crime scene. The wind wasn't helping either as it whipped the branches making the shoreline even more indistinct. He cruised at idle speed into the twenty knot breeze, barely making progress against the small white-capped waves. Several times he thought he had found the opening only to find it was a dead end. Finally, he decided he would have better luck wading through the brush and anchored at what he thought was the far northern end of the area. Under normal circumstances, he would have used the power pole attached to the transom to anchor, but when he tried it, he felt the tug of the wind driven current against the boat. The tide was high and the pole had only a foot of bite into the mud. One large wave would easily lift the boat. Moving to the bow, he dropped the Danforth anchor and fed out the rode. After he was sure the anchor had set, he let out a seven to one scope, just like the book said, and after counting out sixty feet of line, tied the nylon line off on the forward cleat.

He checked the anchor twice more and finally satisfied, he donned his waders and slipped over the side. With a flashlight in hand he moved toward the mangroves, glancing back at the boat several times to make sure it was still there.

Fighting against the small waves he reached the shoreline and started pulling the larger branches aside. The high water and wind waves made it hard to move, but he would gladly trade that for the relief from the smell cast by the rotting vegetation at low tide. Once inside the bushes, he was sheltered from the wind, and at high tide, found himself in a new ecosystem. Thinking he was a predator, small baitfish broke the surface in front of him, and he jumped back when he came face to face with a hunting egret. There was a momentary standoff until the bird determined there was better fishing elsewhere and using its long legs, waded out of sight.

After a hundred yards he saw broken branches and started to slow down and examine every bush. The combination of the elements was disastrous for a crime scene. The wind, sun, saltwater, and tides destroyed everything in their path, but he was confident something had happened here. Thinking of how he had found the suction line in the river out west that had alerted him of the pot grow, he breathed deeply and observed. The wind turned from a nuisance into a blessing, showing him the hidden channels he hadn't seen before. Standing completely still he watched the flow of the water as it moved through the roots. Reading water was the same whether in a river, a stream, or the ocean, and he soon started to see the main current and eddies off to the side.

Following the faster water, he moved deeper into the brush, pushing aside branches that had probably never known the touch of a human hand and soon found himself by a mudbank. Leaning against a large limb, he took the water bottle from his pocket and drank deeply. Just as he was about to move around the bank, he thought he heard branches moving. His first thought was a crocodile. Florida is famous for its alligators, but it is the saltwater crocodile that is the real danger and a known resident of the Park. Kneeling into the mud of the bank, he crawled onto the porous surface. Branches moved again and he froze. Now that he was out of the water, he felt safer, until he heard the sound of a man's voice.

His hand went to his side, but he had left his sidearm aboard the boat. There were only two reasons he could think of that men would be in here: poaching or doing what he was doing, except with the intention of removing evidence, not finding it.

Without a weapon, he was helpless and slid around the back of the bank, staying low as the men approached.

"We were out there," a voice said.

"The tide might have brought it in here," another man said.

The little bit of reassurance that he was on the right track was on the back burner now. Leaving only his head above the water, Kurt slid down into the muck. Cool water poured into his chest high waders and the first thing he thought of were leeches, but the voices distracted him. He dropped another few inches leaving his nose an inch above the water. With his waders full of water, he stayed perfectly still—there would be no escape if they found him.

"It could be miles from here," the first voice said.

"With all this crap. No way. It's here. Keep looking."

Kurt felt the small wake from the men as they moved around the area. Hidden by the back of the bank, he could just see the open water of the bay through the branches and felt the men moving on his left. Without thinking, he slid to the right, away from them, but something stopped him. The men were loud, almost on purpose to scare away any predators and he was able to move without being heard. Slowly he reached his hand forward to move what he expected was a downed branch. Grasping the object, there was no doubt he was touching human flesh.

The men were closing in on the bank when the crocodile grunted. What he had originally been worried about was now his savior. The men must have heard it too, because they froze and whispered not realizing the crocodile would feel their vibrations with every move they made through the shallow water. Kurt froze, still grasping what he thought was a human arm.

"Where is the bugger," one of the men whispered.

Another grunt came from Luke's left. The crocodile was behind the men. Suddenly a shot rang out, followed by a half dozen more as one of the men emptied the magazine into what he hoped was the crocodile.

'Got the son of a bitch!" the first man exclaimed loudly.

"Be a damn nice trophy."

"No way. We need to get out of here. We'll come back and look for the body later," the other man said. "Let's get out of here before the sharks smell the blood in the water."

Kurt waited as the men moved through the brush and finally, when they were out of sight rose to his knees. He felt like the Michelin Man with his waders full of water and sat on the bank taking them off. He dumped the water out, relieved when he didn't see any critters and put them back on. They were wet and clammy, but he could move freely now and listening closely in case the men returned, he returned to the body.

His first thought was to drag it onto the mud bank, but he knew the protocol was to leave it as he found it. It had already been moved by the current and tides, maybe several times, and he decided that preserving the remains was more important than the exact position he had found it. Grabbing the corpse of what appeared to be a middle aged, dark skinned man by the arms he hauled the bloated body onto the mud, nearly gagging when it released some of the putrid gas stored inside.

With the body on semi-solid ground, he wanted to get eyes on the men. Listening carefully, he made his way back to the Bay. Not realizing how dark it was in the bush, he was temporarily blinded by the sunlight. Holding his hand to his forehead to shield his eyes, he scanned the water looking for the men's boat. It was nowhere in sight and he waded to the Park Service boat. The men must have come up from the south and not seen it, or they would never have entered the brush.

Once aboard he pulled off the waders, thankful for the breeze that quickly dried his skin. At the helm he started the boat, and pushed the throttle forward to a slow idle, ran to the bow, and started hauling in the anchor line. The chain rattled on the deck as he secured the anchor. Moving quickly back to the helm, he pushed the throttle down hard before spinning the wheel toward the east and open water. He wanted to get a look at the boat and maybe a visual on the men. By appearing from the east he could make it look like he was coming from the barrier islands. Steering a south-easterly course, he moved away from the mangrove lined shore until he could see the boat and spun the wheel ninety degrees to the west.

They were about to get underway and he thought about making a routine stop to check fishing licenses. If they had only taken the carcass, he would be sitting on a legitimate poaching arrest. Without proof, they had broken no laws. They were armed though and he eased back on the throttle, pulled his gun belt from the console, checked the pistol, and secured the webbed belt around his waist. He was about a quarter mile away and studied the other boat, noticing the three engines hanging from the transom and the narrow beam and lines of the thirty foot hull. He didn't need to consult a naval architect to know that even with the wind driven chop, the boat could easily outrun him. All he could do was to try and follow, and he eased his course to the south.

A swath of white foam came from the transom. The men's boat came up on plane and turned in a wide circle heading toward Miami. Kurt was far enough behind that he could turn without causing alarm and he pushed the throttle down. Staying closer to shore to obscure the men's line of sight if they happened to look back, he followed them north.

IT HAD TAKEN all Mel had to get Trufante home without doing damage to himself. The way the dice had landed, Pamela and Mac's fates were now intertwined. She knew she was probably going to need his help and the last thing she needed was the Cajun out on a binge. With a promise of getting ahold of Alicia and tossing around all kinds of legalese, she all but guaranteed action in the morning. After a quick stop at Keys Fisheries, Trufante had left on his bike and wanting a friendlier anchorage, Mel had taken the trawler around to the canal behind the Rusty Anchor

With Trufante gone, she had time to think. The Coast Guard had only threats and the clock was ticking on them to release Mac if they didn't charge him, and even if they did, the EPIRB charge would never hold up. Fingering the officer's card, she placed it beside her legal pad to call first thing tomorrow. Unfortunately, there was not much she could do for Mac tonight.

The cabin was stuffy, and she moved outside to get some fresh air. Rusty had offered to hook the trawler up to shore power and water, but she declined, wanting to be able to drop lines and take off quickly. She looked at the handful of sailboats tied up to see if anyone was around that might overhear her conversation. Music and laughter drifted down along with the smell of Rufus's specialties and she figured the boats occupants were up at the bar. With her phone in hand, she thought for a minute if she should really involve Alicia, but knew there was little choice. The ex CIA analyst, now part-time dive boat operator and contract agent, had a soft spot for Mac and Trufante. They had helped guide her from her desk to the field and introduced her to TJ, who she now lived with in Key Largo. Between her and TJ, the couple had the unique skill-set and discretion that she needed.

She pressed the button on her screen and waited for the call to go through. It rang four times, and she was already composing a voice-mail message in her head when she heard the mildly shrill voice answer.

"Alicia, how are you? It's Mel." They exchanged pleasantries for a minute, but neither woman could be described as chatty. Mel briefly outlined what had happened.

"Let me get TJ. He's down in the shop. Call you back in a few," she said and disconnected.

Mel stared at the blank screen, unsure what to do when the smell of fried hogfish caught her attention. All the wheels were in motion now and she left the boat, walked up the dock toward Rufus's shack, and ordered one of his famous sandwiches. She made small talk with the ancient Rastafarian cook until her sandwich was done. Thanking him, she took it back to the boat.

Back on deck, she stared at her phone. Waiting was not something she did well, and fortunately, the phone rang and Alicia's name appeared on the screen. Pushing the plate to the side, she answered the call.

"There's nothing in the Coast Guard network about Mac. We expanded the search and checked the NCIS station up on Boca Chica Key and the county lockup on Key West. He's not showing up anywhere, which leads me to believe the Coast Guard is still holding him." Alicia said.

"I did some checking too. It is a felony to set off an EPIRB, but ninety-six percent of all reports are false alarms. Mac said they called him and he told them it was stolen and he had no idea where it was. That should have settled it."

"You'd think that would have cleared him. The tie in with the refugee boats is interesting, but I'll need some time to figure it out. Give me a few hours."

Mel thanked her and disconnected. She'd been around long enough to know that Alicia Phon was one of the few people she could trust to do what she said. That very reason was part of her reluctance to involve her in the first place. Once she had her teeth into something, it was like a dog with a bone. She wouldn't let go until it was over, an attribute she knew she resembled all to well.

Taking the sandwich on deck she sat in the captains chair and ate.

19

M ac nudged the throttle, trying to find the sweet spot. Heavy and underpowered, the refugee boat was running rough. It sputtered and would not come up on plane, but he knew he was lucky it had started. He was stuck plowing through the water, needing to find the right combination of speed and fuel efficiency. It was a painfully slow trip through the main channel running adjacent to Fleming Key. When you were on open water, it was often hard to tell the difference in speed. Surrounded by landmarks he was constantly reminded how slow he was moving. Forcing himself from looking back, he focussed on the water ahead. As soon as he reached the last marker, he cut the wheel to the left and went cross-country heading toward the cluster of mangrove islands that made up the Calda Bank.

Instead of having to navigate protruding obstacles as in an off-road course, in the back waters of the Keys, cross-country meant avoiding the hidden dangers. Dangerous coral heads, lurking only inches below the surface were all but invisible in the fading light and could easily tear the bottom from the boat. Mud flats and sandbars were scattered through these waters as well and could ground him.

Maybe in full daylight, from the deck of a larger boat, or poling platform of a flats boat he could see where he was headed, but he had neither and was relying on gut instincts.

Dropping speed to allow the hull to sit level in the water didn't help him either. At six knots, a good kayaker could catch him. Now exposed in open water, there was nothing to do except hope he could reach the first island before the Coast Guard could organize a search. To make things worse, he knew this water would be no problem for their inflatable zodiacs that could run at full speed in only inches of water.

The first island was approaching and he chanced a look behind him. There was boat traffic in the channel, but none looked to be official. Unless someone had noticed the missing boat, they would be focussing their search on land. That theory faded when he heard the roar of two outboard engines. He could just make out the low profile of the zodiacs, but the bright orange life vests of the crew stood out like a neon sign saying the Coast Guard is on the way. He could only hope the reverse were true and that he would be invisible to them.

In order to avoid the zodiacs he needed the cover of the mangroves. Still looking back, the first branch slapped him in the face and he focussed ahead. He had made it to the first island and cut the engine. Using the protruding branches, he pulled the boat around the back of the island. Without the engine noise, he could hear the outboards coming, and when he thought he had escaped and was out of sight, the boat grounded. Jumping over the low gunwales he landed in calf deep water and walked to the transom. With his back against the wooden hull, he pushed as hard as he could. The effort did little but sink him deeper into the muck, but like every other boater in the Keys, he had been here before. There was an old adage that if you hadn't grounded yet, you either would or you were lying.

Finally his feet found purchase and the boat moved forward. After several attempts it crested the shallow spot and floated freely. The water still had not reached his knees, and he knew adding his weight to the boat would only ground it again, so he continued to push it back into the bushes. The mangroves were too dense and resisted his efforts, and all he could do was hope the other islands would cut down the angles from the channels.

Whether his ruse had paid off or the crews weren't looking his way, he would never know, but he saw the two inflatables move past the cluster of islands. They disappeared leaving him wondering when they would return. With the onset of twilight the mosquitos descended on him, and he had to decide what to do. With no phone or radio, he couldn't risk going further into the backcountry, especially with his limited fuel. The only way out was heading back to Key West. Looking toward land, he noticed the closest lights were from the Army Special Forces Underwater operations school at the tip of Fleming Key. Thinking the Coast Guard and Army probably communicated as well as every other government agency, he decided to take a chance.

Mac pulled the boat out of the mangroves and pushed it ahead of him until the water was thigh deep. Hopping over the gunwale, he started the engine hoping he had enough gas to reach the back side of the base. The Coast Guard would never think to look for him on an Army base. Looking both ways for boat traffic, he turned to starboard and accelerated toward the lights of the base. It was a much shorter run than he had made from the Coast Guard pier and he was soon passing around the northern tip of the island. Ahead was a dock, which he gave a wide enough berth that without running lights he would be invisible to any guards. Once he was a few hundred yards past, he turned toward the island and ran the boat hard aground against the shore.

Fleming Key was two miles long and only a quarter mile wide. With only one road running from the bridge to the Army base, he found it easily. Staying off to the side, he followed the road, ducking out of sight whenever he saw headlights approaching. Half an hour later, it was full dark when he reached the short bridge leading to Key West. He waited for a break in the traffic and dashed across the bridge. To his right was the Coast Guard headquarters he had escaped earlier, which he avoided by cutting through the Navy base. Rows of drab two story stucco buildings were ahead and he fought his desire to run, and walked through the parking lot next to the helipad. This section of the base was not restricted and he knew that running would only attract attention. Even then he stayed in the shadows whenever he saw headlights approach.

Several minutes later the base was behind him and he entered a residential area. There was enough foot and bicycle traffic now to relax and he walked on the sidewalk, wondering what he needed to do to get the Coast Guard off his back. Remembering the diagram in his pocket and that every road led to Billy Bones—the person he least wanted to see in the place he least wanted to be. With no other choice, he walked toward the center of Key West's nightlife glancing at every corner store to see if they had a payphone he could use to call Mel. Several blocks later he found what might be the last one on the island.

Entering the store, he grabbed a bottle of water and bag of chips. Realizing how thirsty and hungry he was, he doubled his order and approached the counter where he dug out the wet wad of bills, paid, and got change for the phone. With no idea what a call to Marathon cost, he dropped all the quarters he had into the slot, waited for a dial tone, and punched in the numbers for Mel's cell phone.

He knew she wouldn't answer, especially this late and without caller ID telling her who was calling. Leaning over, he peered at the space where the number should have been and saw nothing there. His watch said it was nine o'clock and he left a message asking her to pick him up at the West Martello tower by the beach at midnight. However this went down he had three hours to find Billy Bones, extract the information he wanted and meet Mel.

KURT FOLLOWED the boat as it cruised toward the skyline of downtown Miami. It had already passed the closer Bayfront Park and it was clear now that their destination was probably Government Cut.

The inlet was the main boat channel in Miami. Behind the breakwater, he could already see the towers from the cruise ships tied up on Dodge Island. The speed boat had to slow to avoid the heavy traffic in the inlet and Kurt closed on them, using the bulk of several freighters, escorted by tugs, to screen himself.

The towering condos of South Beach passed by to starboard and the cruise ships were directly ahead as Kurt throttled down to obey the idle speed sign. He matched the speed of the other boat and followed as they went toward the backside of Dodge Island. The skyscrapers of downtown Miami dominated the skyline now as he entered the Miami River a few hundred yards behind the men. As he passed through downtown, the buildings decreased in size, turning to palatial residential homes with yachts moored at their docks. As he passed I 95, the housing standards were lowered and dropped even further after going under the bridge for the Palmetto Expressway.

He looked around, realizing the surroundings were familiar. They were close to where the refugee's boat had been towed. The speed boat swung towards a dock on the left and he recognized the boats tied up on the seawall. Kurt immediately dropped speed and coasted to the far side of the river. There was little traffic here and he decided the best course of action would be to pass the boatyard as if he had business upriver and come back on foot. Pushing the throttle to a fast idle, hoping his indecision hadn't been noticed, he cruised past the yard. Another facility appeared a few hundred feet ahead. Looking back, the other boat was out of sight and he crossed the river. Misjudging the current, he slammed the dock, but instead of hitting the concrete seawall, he hit one of several large tires hung from the wall. Several men came toward him and he fumbled for the dock lines and fenders he should have already had in place. Feeling the scrutiny of the men watching, he tossed his lines up to them and looked at the man he thought was in charge. The one looking nervous.

Using his authority implied by his uniform and the Park Service boat he called to the man, "Just need to tie up for a minute and check something at the next yard."

The man's anxiety dropped and he smiled, instructing his men to tie off the boat. "No problem, officer. We're happy to help."

Kurt knew it was a lie, and wondered if there wasn't something to look into here as well, but it was out of his jurisdiction. He knew he had already gone farther than his authority or boss allowed. Deciding he was on questionable ground, he nodded to the men and felt his phone vibrate in his pocket. He pulled out and cursed to himself when he saw Martinez's name on the screen.

"Where the hell are you? We leave our agents on long leashes around here, but what's so important in the Miami River?"

Kurt bit his lip, cursing himself for not thinking the Park Service boat and his phone would both have GPS trackers. "It happened fast. There's a body in the mangroves and I followed these men who were looking for it to a boatyard here." He almost said the same yard the refugee boat had been taken, but wasn't sure he should disclose last nights activities.

"And you took this long to call it in?"

"Can't talk over the engine and I didn't want to lose them," Kurt said, hoping to calm Martinez.

It didn't work and he listened to a barrage of regulations he had apparently broken. "Stand down, agent. That's and order."

"Yes sir," Kurt answered. "What about the body?" There was no way Martinez could dodge a dead body in the Park.

"I'll send the coroner to meet you there. You will go directly to the scene, do you understand?"

"Yes sir," Kurt said and disconnected. He looked back at the boat, and figured even if Martinez was watching the GPS tracker in real time, he could explain away fifteen minutes. He went back to the boat and dropped the cell phone on the seat.

The foreman was standing by the boat, an amused look now on his face. "Trouble?"

"Bosses," Kurt said.

"I hear that," the man responded and went back to his crew.

Kurt walked down the seawall, hoping the yards connected. The closer he got to the perimeter, the more of a junkyard feel the yard had and he was soon skirting discarded engines and parts only to find a chainlink fence with razor wire running between the properties. The clock in his head was ticking and he started running along the fence. His eyes shifted between the obstacle course in front of him and the yard next door. Suddenly he stopped when he saw the men.

20

M ac had to slow his pace a block before he reached Duval Street. Between the bicycles on the sidewalk and the groups of tourists in the street, navigating the mob was a free for all. Cars pushed forward slowly trying to find parking, fighting a losing battle against the revelers. He reached the famed strip and stood on the corner staring at the neon signs. Billy Bones would be here somewhere, he just didn't know where. There was always the chance he had missed him at the dozen bars lining the historic seaport, but that was too close to the Coast Guard base for comfort.

Sloppy Joe's was to the right and he walked toward the white stuccoed landmark. There was a line out the door and a bouncer collecting a cover charge for the band. Doubting Billy would pay a cover charge, he stood on the corner of Duval and Greene watching the crowds. To his right was Front Street and the cruise ship pier. The restaurants got more expensive and the stores more exclusive in that direction. To the left was where the action was.

He took a deep breath and mixed with the scantily clad tourists, most with drinks in hand. Channeling his inner Trufante, he went with the flow of humanity in search of their next drink, checking out the open fronts of the bars as he walked. He was past most of the action now, and losing hope that he would find the degenerate when he saw someone with a women on each arm heading into a turquoise building on his left. At first, he ignored him thinking it hard to believe he could attract even one woman, but he saw the trademark backwards visor and unbuttoned Hawaiian shirt.

Mac pushed toward him, through a crowd of giggling, half drunk girls with devil horns on their heads. Caught in their group he moved toward the entrance and waited while they dug out their ID's and credit cards. On full alert, he felt something unusual to his side and when he looked up, he found himself standing toe to toe with the largest woman he had ever seen. And then it dawned on him—it was no woman. He turned, thinking he should escape the line and wait outside for Billy to leave, when another group of middle aged women, wearing too few clothes and too much makeup pushed him forward. He was squeezed between the two groups front and back and with the drag queen on his right. His only option was to turn toward the bouncer.

"I got no cash," he muttered, hoping he would be escorted outside, but one of the women behind him must have heard and looped her arm around his and walked him in the door calling back to her friends to cover him.

The music was loud and lights flashed everywhere, making it hard for Mac to see anything but the stage. Slowly, as the women escorted him to an upholstered bench seat on the right, his eyes acclimated and he scanned the room. There in the front row with two women that were way over his pay grade was Billy Bones. Mac was about to confront him when he found himself sandwiched between two of the women on the bench. They were cheek to cheek and with the small cocktail table in front of him, there was no escape. The best he could do was hope they were enough insulation between him and the drag queen that had just taken the stage.

The lights were down now. He averted his attention from the stage, trying to keep an eye on Billy Bones, but not really needing to watch the man, for he was clearly having a good time with the two bimbos. Tossing singles at the performer and sucking on his beer, he wasn't going anywhere. But if there were a choice between watching Billy or the show, be chose the former.

"Come on! Live a little," one of the woman yelled in his ear. Handing him a shot glass she clinked glasses and before he knew it he was downing the fiery liquid. The women around him were moving to the music holding dollar bills over their heads and waving for the queen to come over. Mac winced when she moved away from Billy and started working toward his group. One of the women handed him a bill.

The drag queen was upon them now, leaning back into Mac as the women took selfies with her. A hand grasped his arm and guided his dollar bill toward the performer. With a wink, that he thought he feared he would never forget, the queen took the bill and stuffed it in her cleavage. Finally she moved to the next group and he took a deep breath. The women were hooting and calling after her, but she was gone. Now they turned their attention on Mac. He felt them brushing against him and another shot glass was in his hand. Vowing this was the last one, and that he would wait outside for Billy Bones, he drank with them and excused himself to use the restroom. Moving past the stage into a dimly lit corridor, he tried not to touch anything and stood in the stall breathing deeply. It was time to get out of here.

Turning left instead of right when he left the restroom, he went for the back door, disappointed to find it locked. There was no way out but the front. He started down the hallway, waving at the women who appeared to be screaming and pointing at him as made his move for the exit. Two steps later, he saw what they were focussed on when the large queen stuck something in his face and reached for his package.

He brushed the hand away and saw Billy Bones, front row center laughing at him. This was as far as Mac was willing to take this and he went for the man, grabbing him by the ear and leading him out of the club. The crowd was yelling after them, probably not sure if this was part of the show or not, but Mac was not stopping until he reached the street.

Once outside, he pushed Billy Bones against the building. He caught a look from the bouncer, which he returned and the man looked away. "Where is she?"

Even though his mouth said otherwise, Billy's eyes showed he knew what Mac was talking about. "I'm just having some fun."

"You don't have the kind of money or looks to have this much fun," Mac was in his face. "Where's Pamela and what the hell is going on?"

PAMELA FOUGHT against the restraints wondering why she had disobeyed her instincts and opened the door. Her first thought had been that something had happened to Tru when she saw Billy Bones standing on the porch picking at the ridiculous soul patch on his chin. Opening the door was one thing. Inviting him in another and she had leaned against the door jamb clearly blocking his entrance.

He had been acting unusual, even for him, and when he reached behind his back and she saw the glint of metal, she tried to pull back inside and slam the door, but he was able to grab her arm. With the pistol held gangster style against her head, he pulled her away from the house, pushed her across the porch, and downstairs to his car.

It had been a slight relief that the passenger seat was cleaner than his. She suspected not many people rode with him voluntarily. After pushing her into the seat, he quickly ran around to the driver side and got in, placing the gun under his left thigh, and out of her reach. With his twisted grin, he had pulled out of the driveway and a little over an hour later turned off US 1 on Stock Island.

Now she sat in the dark wet hold of a derelict ship dry docked in a boat yard. Tied to an eye bolt screwed into the bulkhead, she had just enough room to adjust positions, but not to stand. Usually there was some kind of music in her head, a choice lyric she had chosen for the moment, but rage engulfed her and her mind was blank. Her pockets were empty as well, her credit card left by the computer on the kitchen counter.

It was not in her DNA to give up. She'd been in challenging situations before and had come through. There had always been a rebellious streak running through her, and it was often out of her control. Even as a child, boredom had set in too easily and her solution was to find the edge. This of course hadn't gone well with her parents. Through high school she had gotten by with little work; able to hold a B average by just showing up once in a while. Growing up in Tuscaloosa, Alabama, her lineage and looks had her pegged to be a debutante. But that was not the path that called. A pretty girl who looked older than she was, from a wealthy family in a college town, there were just too many options, and most of them led her down streets going in the wrong direction.

It had come to a head after she graduated high school and sat in her fathers study. She had been excited, and expected as "daddy's little girl" there might be a cool and expensive graduation gift on the table, but what she had faced was tough love. After a stern lecture, she realized that for the first time in her life, she had to start making decision. Even with his threats, she knew her monthly allowance was a pretty big parachute, but this time he held the release. Unless she chose college, the party was over.

Community college was an easy gig and allowed her the luxury she was used too, but again boredom took its toll. She had met Chase on her twenty-first birthday, and for the first time in her life she felt a purpose. The only problem was Chase was just like her. With their combined math skills, they had figured their allowances could rent a place, put some food on the table, and leave enough for some partying. So they moved in together. That had lasted, as her father had predicted for just long enough to put a ding in her credit record before the couple split. But now Pamela had a taste of independence and liked it. Tuscaloosa had become too small a town.

Loading her tricked out Cabriolet, she took a tour of her friends colleges, finally settling at the infamous University of Miami. The combination of tropical air and the South Beach night life were intoxicating and she spent the better part of her twenties living large in Coral Gables. It turned out her father's threats were just a bluff and the allowance continued. With the next step on the partying ladder only three hours away, she had taken several trips to Key West, only the last one had ended badly. Her risk taking had gotten bolder over time, and she had gone with a guy she barely knew. It was Trufante who had found her wandering the streets of Key West rolling around her suitcase with no place to go.

Surprisingly to anyone that knew either of them, they grounded each other. It was not a yin and yang thing, but more of a party of equals, and one of them somehow had enough sense to watch the other. She liked the mix of the Keys; the tourist money and local eccentricities. Trufante, though older was thoroughly entertaining and had a sixth sense about when she was running low on her allowance. He had no problem throwing money into the party when he had it.

There was no question in her mind that Mac Travis and Tru would find her . She just had to be patient. Rubbing her wrists together, she wished she had some of Cheqea's medicinals to get her through this. Slumping to the floor, she stretched out her long legs and felt something with her foot. Pulling it back she slid off her flip flop and reached out again. This time with her bare foot she felt the skin of another person. Suddenly a moan came from somewhere near her head and she realized she might be in more trouble than she thought.

21

WOOD'S
BETRAYAL

K urt knew he should have returned to the scene. The decision to follow the men could easily ruin his career. But he knew this might be his only chance. The Medical Examiner was probably hours away and unless another predator found it, the body would still be there. The men in the adjacent yard were in no hurry, making it easy for him to navigate through the discarded boat parts lying against the fence. Although he wasn't able to get a good look, he followed them until they reached a white pickup with a boat trailer behind it. He stood stunned at the site of the expensive truck as it pulled out of the lot pulling the refugee boat on a trailer behind it.

Running for the street now, he paused long enough to pull his phone from his pocket and open the camera app. Leaning against the end of the fence, he waited until the truck approached, and snapped a picture realizing as it passed, that unlike California, Florida only required rear license plates. Turning quickly, he stepped into the street dodging a car with windows so heavily tinted he didn't think they could see him, and a delivery van that saw him but didn't care. Jumping out of its way, he shot a picture of the rear, this time getting the tag.

The truck and trailer moved off into traffic and he breathed deeply. Returning to the sidewalk, he looked at the two pictures. Surprisingly the first showed the outline of the two men, which was more than he expected. The second was a clear shot of the license plate and he stood there wondering what to do with it. Martinez would be no help. Once the body was removed from the Park, he would close the case file and either bury it or pass it along to the FDLE. It would be a major inconvenience for him to waste a golf game if it went to trial. With the phone still in his hand, he looked at the time. It was already four o'clock and he thought of Janet.

With an hour to kill before her shift started, he went back to his Park Service boat and retraced his route. Staying just above idle speed, he left the river and entered the Bay, where ignoring the chop on the water, he pushed the throttle forward and suffered the jarring his body took with each wave. The beating paid off and he reached the mangroves before the Medical Examiner. It was just after five and he searched the horizon. There were several other boats, all just dots, and none looking like they were approaching.

Sliding the boat up to the mangroves, he anchored and stared at his phone, wondering how this was going to go. With nothing to lose, he scrolled through his recent calls, found the number, and dialed. A bored voice answered and he asked for the crime lab. He felt that pulse in his heart, usually reserved for his daughter, when she answered on the third ring. There was a pregnant pause on the line and Kurt heard her say hello twice while he summoned his courage. He visualized her hand moving the receiver back to its cradle when he replied.

"Hey, it's Kurt."

"Hey Kurt."

He pause again, and he sensed her impatience. "Listen, about before."

"It's no big deal. I see it all the time; detectives getting wrapped up in their cases."

He'd heard that too—from Justine. "It's not right. I promised to take you out on the bay and I let my work get in the way. My boss is such a dick. Can we start over?"

She laughed. "Wow, a man that can see the error in his ways. Sure, I'll take another shot at it."

He was relieved, but now had a problem. Just as he was about to wreck it and ask her to run the plate, he heard a fast boat approaching and looked up to see a sheriff's boat come down off plane. "I gotta go. We found a body and the ME's here. Call you later?"

"You found a body? You better call me. I want details."

Hearing the enthusiasm in her voice, he smiled and pulled on his still wet waders. Cringing as the damp material clung to his legs, he slid over the side. Leaning against the boat, he waited until the Sheriff's boat tied off to his and the two men aboard were suited up. With the deputy dragging a backboard behind him, they entered the mangroves. Looking through the dark shadows cast by the branches, Kurt breathed a sigh of relief when he saw the outline of the body where he had left it.

"This where you found it?" The coroner asked, looking at Kurt over his reading glasses. He looked like he should be in an accountant's office staring at ledgers rather than wading through the mangroves.

Kurt pointed to the mud bank. "It was high tide then, and the body was mostly submerged. I dragged it onto the bank so it wouldn't get washed out. The man responded with a humph that Kurt wasn't sure was good or bad.

He scratched his head. "Probably the right call. Like to leave them where we find them in the future," the ME said, looking over his reading glasses, like a teacher scolding a student.

"Yes sir," Kurt said, hoping that would end the lesson.

The ME stuck a large thermometer in the mans side. "Eighty-two degrees," he called out to the deputy who was taking notes on a pad. "Been in the water a while. Couple of days from the looks of him."

Kurt wondered if he should be taking notes too, and tapped his pocket, only to find it empty. "Sounds about right with when we found the boat."

"Give me a hand here," the ME called to the deputy who placed the notepad in his pocket. Together the men rolled the corpse over. "First thing to go's always the lips and eyes. Damn crabs." Removing a flashlight from his pocket, he started to examine the body.

Kurt stared down at the dead man. His lips and eyes were indeed gone. Maybe an artist could reconstruct his likeness, because after two days in the eighty degree water, Kurt doubted the man's own mother would recognize him. Despite the damage from the water, he could tell he was definitely Hispanic and probably Cuban. His age was harder to determine. The wrinkled skin showed a man to be anywhere from twenty to sixty, though the hair was still jet black. The ME called for the backboard and the deputy looked at Kurt for help. "How old do you think?"

The ME looked over his glasses as if Kurt were an interruption. "You're new here?"

Kurt nodded. "Just over a month now."

"Oy." He swatted a mosquito from his forehead. "Gets ugly when the sun goes down," he said, motioning for the board to be slid in place.

Together Kurt and the deputy slid the body onto the board and strapped it in place. Between the bloating of the corpse and buoyancy of the board, they were able to easily push it between them. When they emerged from the mangroves, Kurt was surprised to see the sun setting. Getting the board over the gunwale took a little work, but it was soon loaded on the sheriff's boat and the men were back aboard stripping off their waders.

"I've got a light load and the night shift to work. Think I'll do the autopsy tonight before it decomposes any more," the Medical Examiner said across the boats.

"I'd like to watch," Kurt said. What he did on his own time was none of Martinez's business, and he was pushing overtime now.

"Hope you've got a strong stomach. Floaters are always the worst," he said matter of factly. His eyes looked over his glasses at Kurt when he offered no excuses. "Suit yourself. By the time we get back and get some dinner..." He looked at his watch. "Nine o'clock?"

Kurt wondered how the man could eat a meal and then do an autopsy. "That'd be good." He thought for a second, remembering there would be no way to get the keys to a Park Service vehicle. "Can I ride with you?" he asked, hoping Janet would be interested enough in the story to pick him up. Maybe he could make amends for earlier.

Kurt followed the Sheriff's boat back to Dodge Island and tied off the Park Service boat. He helped load the backboard into the Medical Examiners van and went to the passenger side. With a grunt, the ME climbed into the drivers side after thanking the deputy for his help, started the engine. The tires squealed as he cut the turn too fast pulling into traffic. He accelerated and switched lanes, cutting off a truck. Kurt looked over at him and if he were not scared for his life would have laughed. Clearly of Jewish descent, his bald spot cropped by the remains of his hair. He was hunched forward with the seat too close to the wheel, projecting his nose even further forward as he squinted over his reading glasses. The van swerved again and Kurt was almost ready to ask if he could drive when he screamed something in what must have been Yiddish at the driver who honked before changing lanes. He was clearly enjoying this and Kurt, with one hand on the door handle and the other on the dashboard held on.

They pulled into a strip mall and parked. Fortunately the Cuban restaurant the Medical Examiner, who finally introduced himself as Sid, chose was loud enough to preclude conversation. Once the food arrived, Sid's mood improved quickly, but they spoke little and all Kurt came out of the meal with was a full stomach that he expected he might lose, and the man's name.

They rode together to the morgue and waited while two men loaded the body onto a gurney and wheeled it into one of the sterile examining rooms. Sid motioned to a dressing room where Kurt put on the mandatory gown, mask, and eye protection and minutes later they stood in front of a stainless steel table with the body on it.

Sid went quickly through the description of the deceased;

measurements and distinguishing features were recited in a monotone drawl as he talked into a recorder that would later be transcribed. Kurt, bored by the monologue stared at the face of the dead man wondering what his story was to take his mind off the grimness of the event. Sid finished with the posterior of the corpse and with Luke's help, they rolled the man onto his back.

"Cause of death right here," Sid said, using a stainless steel instrument to tap a puncture wound at the base of the man's scalp. He swung a magnifying glass with a light over the wound and side by side, they looked at the blow that had killed the man. Sid measured and photographed the area and moved on with the autopsy. Kurt became less interested as it went on.

He helped turn the body again and just before Sid was ready to make the incisions to open the man's chest, he decided there was nothing else to be gained except an embarrassing moment when he lost the meal that had been pushing against the back of his throat.

"Thanks Sid, but I'm going to pass on the rest."

"Can't say I blame you. Report should be available sometime tomorrow," he said, making the first diagonal cut.

Kurt was surprised there was no blood and out of a grim fascination almost decided to stay when the first of the gasses hit him. "Are you going to do toxicology?"

Sid looked up over his glasses, now hidden behind the plexiglass face-mask. "Wouldn't ordinarily. We already have the cause of death. Why?"

Figuring there was nothing to lose by telling him, Kurt explained what Janet and he had found.

"If you give me the drug, I can get tests for that."

Kurt thanked him and left the room. In the hall, he ripped the mask off and with his hands on his knees inhaled a half dozen deep breaths of air conditioned sweetness. It took a full twenty minutes before he felt normal again, but the smell still lingered in his nostrils. He looked up at the clock and seeing it was almost midnight, reached into his pocket for his phone and called Janet.

WHEN MEL SAT BACK DOWN, she noticed the missed call and voicemail. Thinking it was too soon for Alicia to have any information, she picked up the phone and heard Mac's voice. She had to replay the message several times before it sank in that he was out of custody. It was already ten o'clock and she needed to get going.

The boat was not an option and she looked up at the Rusty Anchor, thinking she could borrow a car from Rusty. Then Trufante came to mind, something she never wanted, but this time with Pamela likely down there, she couldn't ignore him. Looking down at her phone, she found his number and hit the call button, wondering if this was the right thing to do, or if she was just inviting more trouble. Before she could decide, he answered.

"Mac's out somehow, and wants us to pick him up in Key West at midnight."

"Be there in ten."

She thought about the drive down and traffic in Key West, making a quick decision. "Bring me a helmet. We'll take your bike," she said and disconnected. That decision might haunt her, but she expected traffic to be heavy and navigating around the island in a car was difficult.

Mel heard the roar of the pipes long before she saw the headlight coming down the crushed shell drive. She walked out to meet him, took the offered helmet, and hopped on the back of the bike. Trufante spun around, his trademark grin replaced by a deep frown. Without a word, he sped out to US 1 where they turned left. Traffic in Marathon was fairly light, but Mel knew that once they got closer to Key West that would change. She wrapped her arms around the lanky Cajun and with gritted teeth and butterflies in her stomach, clung to him as he accelerated onto the Seven Mile Bridge.

22

The backwards visor fell to the ground when Mac slammed Billy Bones against the turquoise stucco. He held him there long enough that the texture of the cement surface would leave its mark on the back of his head for a week. Grabbing him by the shirt collar, he pulled him forward and looking him square in the eye, he was about to ask again where Pamela was but decided against making a scene in the middle of Duval street.

"Let's go," he said, pushing him against the wall before releasing him.

"Ease up, man," Billy said, straightening out his Hawaiian shirt.

Mac looked at him again, wondering if it was worth the time. But with no other place to turn, he pushed him ahead. Deciding they were better off away from the crowds, he turned right on Truman. "Walk in front, and no crap."

"I can get my car. We don't have to be hoofing it," Billy started. "Where are we going anyway?"

Aiming to stop the chatter, something Mac knew Billy Bones excelled at, he closed the gap and gave him a sidekick to the back of his knee. Billy fell forward onto the pavement and slowly picked himself up. He turned, and his mouth was about to open, but the scowl on Mac's face must have deterred him. The two men walked forward with Mac in the lead now. Too close to be strangers and too far away to be friends, to an onlooker it might appear like a man was walking his dog.

After a dozen blocks, Mac turned right onto White Street, and looked behind to make sure Billy Bones followed. A glance at his watch confirmed that the meet was a half-hour away. With a mile to the old fort, he increased their pace and soon saw the old brick building. What remained of the structure, originally built as one of two advance batteries to protect Fort Taylor, lay ahead. The red brick walls had never served their intended purpose, but now meticulously landscaped by the Key West Garden Club who had taken over the fort in the seventies, the old brick fort finally had a reason for being built.

They left the gardens and headed out to the long concrete extension of White Street. Mac had chosen the site for the water access. Built well out from the south facing shore which was mostly flats and beaches, the pier was in deep enough water for a boat. There were no other harbors on this side of the island and he hoped they could get in and out without running into the Coast Guard. Billy Bones hesitated when he realized where they were going, probably thinking he was only fifty yards from his death. Mac stopped suddenly, surprised when he heard the roar of a bike. Backing up a few steps, he looked down Atlantic Boulevard toward the source and saw two figures on the Harley. He was about to turn back toward the pier when the, helmet-less driver, smiled.

"Shit. Thought you was going to toss me off the pier. There's sharks out there you know."

Mac just stared at Billy, not acknowledging that he was even human. He walked toward the street and hugged Mel who had dismounted and run to him. Trufante parked the bike and strode toward them with more urgency than he was usually known for.

The lanky Cajun faced Billy and jabbed a finger in his chest. "What the hell have you got into now?"

Billy went to swat the finger away, but Mac cuffed him in the back of the head. "You see that look in his eye? That's the look of a desperate man. I imagine you've been desperate before, but not like this. It's a different feeling when it's about someone you love. Right now, I'm your best friend," Mac said, pulling Trufante back. "Start talking."

Billy looked down. "Guy I know. He's got this thing going on. You guys got too close."

Mac struggled to restrain Trufante. "You really want it to go like this?"

Billy dropped his head again. "Mateus Tabor. He's running Cubans."

Mac knew the name, but couldn't come up with a face or where he had heard it. "That's better. Now where is Pamela?"

"He's got a couple of old ships up at a marina."

"Take us there," Mac said.

Billy looked at the bike.

Mac caught his glimpse. "Where's your car?"

"Off Duval."

Releasing his grip on the Cajun, he spoke quietly to him, "Go with him and get the car, come back, and pick us up."

Trufante nodded and climbed onto the bike. Billy Bones followed, reaching out to Mel for the helmet. "Your greasy ass head ain't touching my shit," Trufante spat.

Mac and Mel stood side by side as the pair sped off.

"What do you plan to do?" Mel asked. I have Alicia working on what little information we have. She reached into her pocket and checked her phone. "Missed her call." She tapped the screen several times and pressed the speaker button.

Mac walked her onto the pier, away from anyone that could hear. The phone rang three times before Alicia's answered. "Hey, Mac said. Here with Mel, and we have you on speaker."

"Hey back." she said and started her report. "There's definitely an increase in EPIRBs reported stolen. The same serial numbers all correspond to false alarms reported by the Coast Guard. The phone vibrated and they stared at a map on the screen. "You can see on the map that all the activations have been from the Tortuga's up to Palm Beach."

"They follow the Gulf Stream and stop just before it heads offshore," Mel said.

"Exactly. Fill in the blanks and you have a line to Cuba. Running refugees is a different kind of business now. You can't just walk onto American soil and get a welcoming handshake," Alicia said.

"I found two boats in as many days. Both were the same. Old wooden hulls with adapted car engines. Not anything I'd cross the Gulf Stream in, but better than the home made rafts they were using," Mac said.

"They call these new runners Remoras. Kind of like the Coyotes on the Mexican border," Alicia said.

"Remoras that suck Cuban blood," Mel said.

Mac could see her temper rising. "You know the name Mateus Tabor?"

There was silence on the line for a moment and Mac could almost hear the keys clicking in the background and imagine the data flowing across the multiple flat screen monitors mounted on the wall of the war room. "Shipping. Based out of Stock Island. Don't see anything unusual. There are a half-dozen law suits—all settled. Nothing looks out of place for that kind of business."

The line went quiet again. Mac and Mel waited patiently, knowing Alicia was working frantically to provide whatever information was available. Mac had no idea how she did what she did, but she was the best.

"Robbie's marina on Stock Island looks like his home base. His ships are serviced there, but registered in the Samoa's." There was silence for another few minutes. "Curious. He has several older ships with United States registrations."

"That's gotta be it," Mac said. Thinking out loud. "Something is happening to these refugees after he gets them. I saw blood on the boat and drank some water that I was sure had some kind of drugs."

Mel took the phone and pulled up Google Earth. It wasn't real-time information, but towards the far end of the marina was a low rent district. "Here," she said, enlarging the area on the screen.

He heard a car pull up and looked over to the street and saw Trufante extracting his frame from the compact car. "We gotta go. Keep digging," he said, pressing the disconnect button.

"We don't need him now," Mel said, holding Mac back.

"Yeah, we do. At least to know where his is and what he's doing," Mac said. He went to the car, looking back to make sure Mel was following. "With Pamela out there he'd be a lose cannon.

"Hey, it's Kurt." There was a long pause on the line.

"I haven't had a chance to look at the drive yet," she said.

"I just wanted to apologize again for before. Martinez just got to me. I shouldn't have taken it out on you."

"Yeah, I figured."

"I'd like to try again, but there's a dead body in the way now."

"Way to seduce a girl. How'd you know I'd go for the dead body line?"

There was no way to top that one. "I decided to go back out to the mangroves and follow the tidal flow. I saw two men searching the area too."

"When do I get to play?" she asked.

"I just sat in on the autopsy—at least all I needed to. The man was definitely Cuban and had a head wound. The coroner agreed to run tests for the drugs too."

"Must be Sid. That guy that works days wouldn't give a fat rat's ass."

"It was. Can you shake free and pick me up?"

"Back to that again?"

"Come on. I'll show you my dead body."

"How can a girl refuse. See you in twenty," she said.

Kurt disconnected the call and smiled, wondering if this was the first time anyone used a dead body to get a date. He climbed the stairs to the main floor. Outside, he sat on one of the low walls around the entrance trying to figure out what his next step should be. Fortunately, it was Friday night, and Martinez would either be on a golf course or in a bar until Monday. Working weekends, something that some called the bad part of being low on the totem pole was exactly the opposite to Kurt. With his days off on Monday and Tuesday, he wouldn't have to report to Martinez until Wednesday. That left a lot of time to figure this out and ask permission later.

There was nothing the dead body could help with besides the proof that a crime had been committed. The cause of death was murder from a blow to the head, and he was sure the toxicology would come back positive. The chances of establishing the identity of the man were close to none, and the murder weapon was probably under several feet of murky water somewhere in the mangroves. That left the murder a dead end. The real question was what happened to the other people on the boat. Then he remembered the piece of cloth Janet had found. Something nagged at him about it, but before he could pin it down he saw headlights approach. He saw the light bar on the roof and expected it was Jane.

The large SUV pulled into the entry. He had always wondered why the government conspired against truck and SUV owners while buying the same cars and trucks for themselves. Janet got out and walked towards him. Not knowing if a hug was appropriate, he led her into the building and downstairs.

"Sid," she called out, entering the examination room.

Kurt watched through the glass window. He didn't want to suit back up and the smell still lingered in his nostrils. Janet had just grabbed a mask and goggles, knowing exactly where everything was. She went right to work with the examiner and Kurt felt a tinge of jealousy creep up on him. Pushing it aside, and wondering why he would have those feelings with two coworkers analyzing a dead body, he watched them work.

Sid was doing what he called the interior section, removing organs and handing them to Janet who placed them on a scale. She read the display and called the weight and dimensions to the recorder. Kurt was in a chair with his head flopping back when the door opened. A quick look at the clock showed him it was an hour later.

"That was cool. How about some dinner?" she asked.

Kurt wondered after watching these people, that if you worked around death long enough, you became immune to it. "Sure."

There was a lack of choices in picking a restaurant this late, and they settled on a diner nearby. Janet rattled off a play by play of the autopsy, most of which Kurt didn't understand. But he knew enough to sit patiently. His head was dead weight, supported by his hand and he sipped coffee hoping it served its purpose. There was something he wanted to get to and it wasn't bed.

"Well, that was fun," she said, winking at him. "Didn't know what you were in for with me, did you?"

Kurt let that go, not wanting to tell her that he was in for all of it. "I think, intriguing as the body is, that it's a dead end. I got a license plate off the truck those two men I followed took off in pulling the refugee boat."

23

Mateus Tabor sat back in his custom leather chair. It was supposed to be the latest in ergonomic luxury, but he still shifted his weight off his hips. He ran his hand over the burnished mahogany of the old ships hatch he used for a desk. The feel of the old wood distracted him for a minute, but he looked back at the computer monitor. On the display was a map showing his assets. Icons indicating which of his vessels were either at dock, or at sea littered the screen. He studied the ships for a minute, tracking their progress in his head, instinctively knowing where each should be. Making money in shipping was all about schedule and efficiency and after a quick overview he focussed on the Indian Ocean. A small cyclone had caused several freighters to divert from their planned routes causing delays. After clicking a checkbox in a window on the left of the display, the screen refreshed, and he saw the reason. The white swirl had enlarged since the last time he looked. He didn't need a calculator to figure his losses from the cyclone.

Besides fuel, insurance was his largest cost, and one he loathed. Each loss only increased his premium, and where once he had been reckless, putting his ships and crews in danger to stay on schedule, he was now more conservative. Money could be made other ways and shipping humans had proven to be a very lucrative business—and one he couldn't escape. It was in his genes. His great-grandfather had run slaves to the markets on the east coast of Africa back in the 1800s. Even before that, his family was based on the Ivory Coast in a country that had been renamed too many times to know its name. They had been rumored to have made many trips to the interior of the continent, bringing back prime specimens for market. As the trade evolved, it was necessary to venture further inland to find the right kind of slave and his grandfather had consolidated the family business, becoming brokers rather than gatherers.

After trying legitimate shipping, costs and regulations had spiraled out of control, forcing him to go back to his roots. At first, with his fleet of container ships, it was easy. But now with the advent of the internet, both the containers in the shipyards and the people themselves became harder to disappear. Adapting as his grandfather had done, he had used the change in immigration policy with Cuba to solve one problem. The refugees were invisible; generally never missed, or assumed lost at sea like so many before them to the difficult and dangerous waters of the Florida Straits.

The second problem was trickier. Getting the product onto his container ships where they could be transported to friendly ports where the authorities would look the other way for a small gift, had to be done at sea. Running small vessels into the Gulf Stream was risky and the numbers didn't work. He needed quantity and he had found the answer. Derelict ships had become a major problem in recent years, clogging both waterways and marinas. When the ships had aged or been neglected beyond repair, they were abandoned where they sat.

He had begun to buy some of the larger, more serviceable vessels and put just enough money into them so they could make the fifteen or twenty mile one-way trip to the inside edge of the Gulf Stream. After rendezvousing with one of his container ships, the product was offloaded and the derelict vessel sunk. Sipping his green blend drink, he reflected on his public service. Removing problem vessels from the waterways and marinas helped both the government and removed the ships cluttering the marinas. The beauty of this was that no one cared as long as they never came back. In one instance the sheriff had helped tow a boat out of Sister Creek in Marathon to open water, never realizing or caring what it contained.

He finished the drink, hoping the reputed effects would soon take hold and closed the window on his computer, opening another in its place. The grainy image showed his latest work in progress at a marina on Stock Island. The hundred-twenty foot ship sat on blocking barely elevating the keel from the asphalt. The resolution was not good enough to show the quantity of patches and repairs he had made, or the contents accumulating inside. Sitting back, he moved his hips again to relieve the nagging pain and watched the screen. Suddenly he sat forward, ignoring the pain, when he saw four figures approach the vessel, and recognized one as Billy Bones.

MAC SAW the ship and wondered what kind of idiot Billy Bones thought he was. But as he got closer, he evaluated the craft and started to piece together their plan. The old wooden hull showed its wear. He could tell by a quick glance at her lines, that at one time, probably seventy years ago, it had been a beautiful ship. Now, through age and neglect, the bottom looked like a patchwork quilt. His trained eye studied the first patch, noticing that although it looked rough, it was actually sound and well done. Each subsequent repair, though differed in method, had the same effect. The ship, though it looked bad was actually seaworthy. Not an ocean cruiser, as she had once been, but she wouldn't sink.

If Pamela was aboard, he thought he knew where this was going and they would need to rescue her before the ship was launched. From the look of things that was going to be soon. Mac had been around enough boatyards to know when they were getting ready to splash a vessel. The work area had been cleaned and cleared. Sitting a hundred feet behind it was a large blue lift, its slings ready to pick the boat off the blocking and set it in the water. It could be as soon as tomorrow.

"How do you get in?" he asked Billy.

"There's a hatch up on deck." He pointed to a ladder leaning against the starboard rail. "But I don't have a key."

Mac looked around the yard, finding what he wanted two boats over. He returned with a crow bar and went to the ladder. He stayed in the shadow cast by the hull, scanning the area. Headlights appeared on the service road, but turned into a complex of shipping containers converted to workshops. Waiting for another minute, he saw no threats and stepped into the light. Losing site of Billy would be a bad idea, and he motioned for him to go first. Mac looked up the tall ladder, spanning the fifty feet from the ground to the deck and waited until Billy was a few rungs above before following. Trufante was right on his heels.

For just a few seconds, they were all on the ladder at the same time. It wobbled slightly as Billy climbed aboard. He was already slightly unbalanced, when he heard Mel scream and then the world fell out from underneath him.

The next thing he knew he and Trufante were leaning against one of the braces below the hull with their hands bound behind their backs. He frantically looked around for Mel and tried to gain his feet, finding them bound as well. He was lucky the fall hadn't killed him and he scanned the shipyard for any sign of Mel when he heard the forklift start. A minute later, he saw the glow from the headlights and the large lift started moving toward them. It came to him in a flash— Mel was inside the hull, and he and Trufante were about to be crushed and left as an accident.

KURT LEANED over Janet as she entered the license plate number into her computer. He knew he was closer than colleagues should be, but it felt natural, and she hadn't moved. A name and address appeared on the screen and he took out his phone, opened the notepad app and entered the information. It meant nothing to him, but Janet sat back stunned. A drivers license picture appeared on the screen, and he saw why.

Before he could say anything, she had jumped up and pulled down the evidence bin. Removing the blood samples first, she set them aside, then took out the piece of torn fabric and fingered it through the plastic.

"It's him," Kurt said, "His suit was ripped the other night."

"Everything is pointing in that direction, but we need to rule out any coincidences." Moving to one of the stainless steel tables, she pulled out the piece of material with a tweezers and set it on the table. Swinging a light with a magnifying lens built in over it, she extracted several hairs from the cloth. "His DNA is on file. We just have to run this."

Kurt didn't need any confirmation. "The torn suit, the truck, and pulling the trailer with the boat? That's too much of a coincidence." Something clicked in his head and he went back to her computer. With Janet leaning over him now, he pulled up the picture he had taken of the front of the truck.

"That's Dwayne."

"It sure looks like him, but I'll run the tests to confirm. It's kind of a big deal accusing an officer of something like this."

Kurt knew she was right, but felt momentum gathering for the first time. "What about the hard drive. He's doesn't appear to be smart enough to be running this operation."

She went back to the evidence bin, retrieved the drive, and plugged it into her computer. They both stared at the screen as it scrolled through the file directory. Even with his modest computer skills, he was able to recognize most of the files as HTML, or web pages.

"There's got to be a link,"

She started clicking, opening one file at at time. It was a virtual internet, complete with clickable links and adds. "It's the Cuban internet. I read something about this. The island's Internet service is still restricted by the government. These are smuggled in allowing the user access to hundreds of sites without a connection.

"Hey, try this one," Kurt pointed at a file marked *visittheus.html*.

The page opened showing an aerial shot of the Keys stretching almost to Miami. There were several tabs above and he pointed to the one marked *travel*. A screen opened asking for a password and he felt the first rush of adrenaline.

"Easy Tiger," Janet said, leaning forward.

Kurt moved back, realizing in his excitement, he must have subconsciously moved too close. "Can you crack it?"

Her laugh sent him a few more inches backwards. "Encryption is over my pay grade. There's a guy here that does some hacker stuff on the side, but he's off until Wednesday and I'm guessing you don't want to wait."

Kurt didn't have to answer. "What are our options. I'm sure this is all related."

"Well it's not like it's on the Internet and we can track it down through servers and IP addresses to find the company that owns the domain. It looks like this entire drive is either copy and pastes of other sites, or created just for this."

"There's got to be a way."

"The FBI normally handles this kind of stuff. We can call them," she said.

"I don't think they'd get involved with as little proof as we have. They were reluctant to step in when I found that pot grow. The majority of their resources are all allocated to terrorism now."

Kurt moved back and started pacing. Running through every connection he had, he came up blank.

Janet turned in her chair. "There is someone I know, well know of. It's a couple that does freelance work for agencies. She used to be a CIA analyst, but when they culled the herd, she went solo."

"How do we get in touch with her?"

"Facebook is your friend. She lives with her boyfriend who runs a dive shop there and helps her out. I like to dive and follow their page." Janet said, picking up her phone from her desk.

Kurt moved back to her and watched over her shoulder as she opened the Facebook App and scanned through several screens before finding the pages she followed. She pressed and icon and a message screen appeared. It took several tries to compose the message, trying to humanize the request to get her attention. Finally she was satisfied and pressed the arrow to send the message. "All we can do is wait."

Before they could even think about what to do next, her phone buzzed. They read the message together and after several exchanges, they looked at each other.

"I'm good," Kurt said. "You'll have to drive though."

Janet shut off the monitor, stuffed the drive in her bag, and left her desk. Within minutes they were heading toward Key Largo.

24

WOOD'S
BETRAYAL

Mac didn't need to look behind them to know what was coming. The crunch of the wheels on the uneven pavement was enough. Instead he looked ahead. With forty tons of machinery coming at him, it was hard to concentrate, but he needed a plan.

He could barely hear his own thoughts over the roar of the engine and though he could only see the headlights approaching, he knew if the sun were out, the shadow of the lift would have been above them. It was impossible to not look back and watch the mechanism of his death moving toward them, and the quick glance was enough to see the forward wheels pass the stern. He had seen boats put in and out of dry dock many times, and knew what was coming. The four wheels were all visible now and the lift stopped. The next step would be to place the slings underneath the hull. He had to assume the two men who stepped down were the same that had captured them and there would be no help coming from the dockworkers. Their only way out was to bide their time until the straps were secure to allow their escape to go unnoticed. It would be better if their adversary thought he had succeeded.

He slid his hands over the pavement behind them, not finding anything large or abrasive enough to cut their ties. The bottom of the hull had been cleaned, leaving it free of barnacles as well. Their only hope was that the water would allow the rope to expand and they could squirm free. It was a long shot.

"When we hit the water, hold your breath," Mac yelled to Trufante over the roar of the lift. It had stopped now and he saw two men move underneath the hull, hauling the heavy straps that would lift the ship.

The few minutes that it took to secure the straps felt like seconds as the clock in Mac's head started its countdown to their death. The engine changed pitch and he felt the tug on his arms as the lift raised the ship off the blocks. Slowly the wheels started to move again and the lift carried the ship towards the ramp. Configured just for this purpose, the concrete walls on either side of the cut in the seawall were set at exactly the width of the lifts wheelbase, allowing the operator to drive the ship over the water. They were only feet from the ramp when he saw something on the ground and reached for it.

"I can't get it," Mac yelled to Trufante.

Like a contortionist, the lanky Cajun reached out for the screwdriver. Turning his body, he handed it to Mac who went to work on the bolt they were secured to. Inserting the shaft into its eye, he was able to use the additional leverage provided by the tool to turn the bolt, but just as he made the first turn, his body, which had been dragging across the pavement fell free and he found himself hanging by the rope.

The sound of the engine changed again, and he reached for the screwdriver. It was still in the bolt, held by the friction of the rope, and he grabbed for it with his bound hands. It was short enough for him to grip each end, but with the pressure of their combined bodyweight, it refused to turn. "Hold your breath," he yelled to Trufante, just as their feet hit the water. Slowly the lift lowered the ship, and he started the breathing sequence he used when free diving. Inhaling until his lungs were full, he held his breath for several seconds before forcing it out of his mouth. Repeating the sequence to enrich his lungs with oxygen, he tried to remain calm as the water crept up his body. When he was waist deep, the tension on the bindings loosened just enough for him to start turning the screwdriver again, and he was able to get several turns before he felt the water encompass him.

With his lungs full of air, he knew he had about two minutes before the convulsions started and things would only go south from there. Forcing himself to stay calm and concentrate, he worked the bolt. Their bodies were floating freely now that the hull was submerged. The straps were released and he could feel the movement of the ship sling their bodies, like flags in the wind. Mac's hands cramped as he continued to work the bolt and he knew he was down to seconds. Suddenly, just when he felt the bolt loosen, the ship moved, taking him by surprise. The forward motion spun their bodies and slammed them against the hull, but he realized they were spinning counterclockwise and if he could just hold on long enough the movement of the boat would free them. His hands cramped again, and in slow motion, he felt his grip fail and the screwdriver drop into the water. There was nothing he could do as it fell to the bottom.

The first convulsion hit and he doubled over, trying to hold his breath. With no idea what condition Trufante was in, he grabbed the bolt with his fingers and tried to turn it. Another convulsion hit and he knew he was out of time when he twisted it one more time and it fell free. His survival instincts took over and he worked his way along the hull, somehow knowing which way was up. Trufante was dead weight forcing him to pull against their negative buoyancy. He felt Trufante come to life behind him and with the added help, several seconds later, just as he had taken a mouthful of water, his head broke the surface. Gasping for air, he tried to stay afloat, but the water pulled him under again. Using his bound legs like a fin, he kicked toward the surface and took another deep breath. This time he was able to see the concrete seawall. Somehow, they were lucky enough to come up on the land side of the hull. If they had surfaced on the other side, they would have been fifty feet away. Their combined weight dragged them under again, but finally the water settled the argument with their buoyancy leaving their heads just below the surface.

Suddenly everything went blank, and he thought he was about to suffer a shallow water blackout when he felt a tug against his bindings. Trufante was ahead of him now, struggling toward the seawall and Mac realized that Trufante had burned another of his nine lives. Joining with him, he tried to synchronize his efforts with the Cajun's. Several seconds later, his knee struck something hard and he set his feet down, finding solid ground beneath them. He grabbed the still struggling Trufante, and they both stood.

There was no embrace or high after escaping death. They both gulped air and stared out to seas at the dark shadow of the ship that held Mel and Pamela.

Kurt tentatively knocked on the door, surprised when it opened after his first light tap. It was three in the morning and he had felt like a thief, skulking around the dark dock. Running next to the dive shop, it led around back to the stairs to the apartment upstairs. The lights bleeding through the Bahamas shutters told him the residents were up, but still he was tentative.

The door swung open and a medium height man, built like a fireplug with his hair in short braids stood in front of them.

"Hey man, I'm TJ. Alicia's back in the war room."

"Sorry to bother you so late," Janet said, stepping in front of Kurt. "I'm Janet Doeszynski from the FDLE crime lab. I called earlier." She held out her credentials, but TJ ignored them and waved them in.

He led them through the great room, past the kitchen to a pair of double doors. Kurt noticed the dinner dishes stacked on the counter. "We didn't mean to keep you up all night."

"No worries man. Somehow, I think this is tied into something we were working on already."

TJ opened the right hand door and the only thing Kurt could see was the glow from the multiple screens mounted on the wall directly in front of them. The door closed, and Kurt found himself standing on the bridge of *The Starship Enterprise*. A captains chair was set near the center of the room, surrounded by monitors. One of the displays had a map of the waters between Cuba and Miami. Icons were sprinkled across it, mostly along the coastline. Before he could ask what it represented, he was taken by surprise by a voice from the darkness.

"I'm Alicia. Do you have the drive?"

Janet moved toward the shadows and pulled the device from her bag. A hand reached out to grab it and seconds later, one of the screens changed to the directory they had seen before. Janet moved toward the woman and pointed out the encrypted files.

"What are you guys working on that dovetails with this?" Kurt asked TJ, while Alicia and Janet worked through the files.

"Dovetailed. Nice word, gotta remember that one," TJ said, moving toward the captains chair. He sat and started pecking at a keyboard. Another screen changed, this time, showing what looked like a dossier. "Mateus Tabor. Shipping magnate, turned slaver."

"How do you think this is related?" Janet asked.

"I'm not sure yet. We had a call from a friend asking for help, and discovered that charmer," Alicia said, pointing to the dossier on the far left screen.

Kurt studied the dark sunken eyes of the picture. He had the hollowed out features and the receding hairline of a man anywhere from forty to sixty, but something about his hard look made Kurt think it was the latter. He scanned the resume next to the picture, wondering how the couple could compile this much information so quickly. "How does a shipping magnate have anything to do with a dead refugee?"

"We'll just have to see," Alicia said, turning to TJ. "I'm swinging this file to you. Can you handle the encryption?"

TJ cracked his knuckles, took a second to look at the screen before typing several commands. The middle monitor blinked and changed with lines of code scrolling down faster than Kurt could read them. TJ sat back in his chair staring at the code.

"Not very complicated. Should only take a minute," he said. "Get anyone a drink?"

"You think this is going to work?" Kurt asked.

"He wrote that code to break into his gaming opponents accounts. It's better than anything I worked with at the CIA."

They sat in silence for a few minutes watching the screen. The door opened just as it stopped. "There you have it," TJ said, taking a can of soda and placing it in a built in cupholder in his chair. He sat forward, pulling the keyboard holder to him and entered the password in the space on the web page.

Nothing happened for several seconds and Kurt thought they had hit a dead end, when suddenly the screen changed and a plain text document appeared.

"Crap, it's in Spanish," TJ said. "I can run a translation program." He started typing again.

"Never mind. I got it," Kurt stared at the screen. "It's a list of directions starting with something about how to find your boat and then when to set off the EPIRB. What's that?"

"You're a Park Ranger?" Janet asked.

He shrugged. "I'm new here."

"I guess. It's an emergency position-indicating radio beacon," TJ said. "Most boats carry them now. They are either activated when the water level lifts them from a cradle, or manually, sending a distress beacon to the Coast Guard. These guys are using them to locate the refugee boats for pickup."

Kurt crossed his arms and continued to translate the instructions. "Exactly, and then they are drugging them and selling them as slaves."

25

T he two men moved away from the lighted ramp area into the shadows where they hauled themselves onto a small dock. Once they were out of the water, they collapsed. Mac rubbed his wrists, noticing the blisters that had formed like bracelets from the rope that had bound them. Trufante stood and starred out to sea. Mac followed his gaze, seeing the white masthead light disappear as the ship blended with the horizon. He looked back at Trufante and saw despair on his face, an emotion he had never seen before. For a long minute, he stood with him.

"We have to find a boat and go after them," Mac said, breaking the spell.

"Damn straight," Trufante said.

To their right were a string of finger piers with boats moored to them. "There," Mac said, running off the dock and past a steel building. On the other side he scanned the boats. Passing over the sailboats, he saw a fishing boat that looked to be about thirty feet. It wasn't the sleekness of the deep V hull, though he knew it was a fast design, or the comfort of the cabin that drew him to the Hydrasport. It was the four three-hundred horsepower engines mounted on the transom. It was easily the fastest boat available.

They ran to the dock and jumped aboard. Mac went right to the cabin. After setting the battery switch to *all*, he turned on the cabin lights and opened the service panel for the helm. The dim light revealed a mess of wires, and he knew it would take too long to find and override the ignition from here. He turned and was on his way onto the deck to find a simpler boat when he heard a loud crash.

Staying low, he looked over the gunwale, suddenly realizing he was alone. Seconds later, he saw the unmistakeable frame of the Cajun, backlit by the security lights, running toward the boat. The look of despair he had seen earlier was replaced by his thousand dollar grin. He jumped aboard and threw a stunned Mac a keychain. Mac grinned back and stuck the plastic key in the kill switch and the ignition key in the engine controller. The key turned and he started the engines one at a time. Before he could start the last engine, Trufante had already cast off the lines, and he had to work to control the boat. With all four engines running, he backed out of the slip and dropped the port throttle in reverse and nudged the starboard forward to spin the boat. It was more power than he was used to with each lever controlling two engines, and he wasted several seconds, after the boat had spun in close to a full circle, trying to straighten it out. Running out of patience, he judged there was just enough room to clear the dock, and slammed both engines to forward. Cutting the wheel, with only inches to spare, he pointed the bow to open water, and heard the whine of twelve-hundred horsepower behind him as the engines responded.

The boat was already on plane by the time they left the narrow channel. Mac set the autopilot to one-eighty, the safest bearing to deep water and studied the electronics. The maze of wires he had seen earlier were now his friend and he turned on the twin touch screen displays and waited. Seconds later, after accepting the waiver that nothing he did was the companies fault, he set the right hand unit to show a navigation chart and the left to radar. Estimating the larger ship had about a half-hour head start, but a maximum speed of somewhere around ten knots, he set the radar setting to ten miles. Several rings appeared and after its initial scan the unit showed a few dots around the five-mile ring. The boats shown were stationary and in the area of the reef, probably fishermen. Just past the ring was a dot, moving slowly.

Mac watched it for a few seconds, then set an intercept course in his head, and adjusted the auto-pilot to one-sixty-five degrees. Just before he looked away, he zoomed out to twenty miles and saw another much larger ship working southwest. This was not unusual. Typically, cargo ships and tankers traveling this direction, found the inside edge of the Gulf Stream to avoid fighting the six-knot current moving in the other direction. Conversely, ships traveling northeast ran inside the Stream. He watched the dot carefully, confirming that it was moving west, but it was further inland than he expected. Tracing the courses of the two ships in his head, they looked like they would collide somewhere around the hundred fathom line, but he knew better. This was a prearranged rendezvous. The timer in his head started ticking again knowing they had to reach the ship with Mel and Pamela before the two boats were in sight of each other. Once the container ship was on site, rescuing the women would be much more difficult.

He dropped the throttle slightly, showed Trufante their course, and pointed out the two ships on the screen. Boarding a moving vessel at sea was not as easy as the Pirates of the Caribbean made it look. They would need weapons and a plan. Assuming the men aboard the old ship were the same two men who had assaulted them and operated the lift on the boat, he knew they would be facing armed opposition. Leaving the helm to Trufante, he started in the cabin, pulling out anything that could be used as weapon. Several knives were in the galley drawers. He set them on the table, although they would probably be of limited use. A tool box contained nothing more harmful than a screwdriver and the requisite safety kit had a some flares in an unopened package that was several years out of date.

Looking at what he had, he doubted it was was enough to take down the larger ship, but just as he was about to give up, he saw the boats EPIRB sitting in its cradle. If he couldn't take them down, he could at least track them. Leaving the cabin, he checked on Trufante. A glance at the electronics showed all three vessels were now on a collision course. He adjusted their course slightly to intercept the older boat before the larger cargo ship reached them. Looking over the bow, he scanned the water for the navigation lights, but there were none. That didn't mean the ship wasn't there. Once out of the channel and away from shore, they were probably running dark.

They had just passed the reef and Mac knew they were out of time. Looking for anything that might help, he opened the hatches built into the deck. The fish boxes were empty and he found only dock lines and fenders in another. It was the last hold, when he had just about given up, that gave him his first hope. Reaching in, he pulled out the dive tank. A plan was already forming in his head. After laying it on the deck, he pulled out the buoyancy compensator and regulator, then quickly assembled the gear. His only fear now was that the tank was empty. He held his breath and turned the valve on. The hoses went rigid and the gauge showed just over three-thousand PSI—more than enough for what he had in mind.

He lay the tank and gear down on the deck and pulled out the mask and fins, quickly adjusting them to fit, then returned to the helm. The radar showed them within a half-mile of the ship, but the cargo ship was closing fast; only a few miles away.

"Give it all she has," he yelled to Trufante, bracing himself as the boat jumped forward. The GPS speed read forty-two knots and he looked up. On the horizon, growing larger every second was a dark shadow. As they approached it, the lines became defined and he could see the outline of the old ship. "Get around the front of her. Your going to have to keel haul me."

It was the last thing he wanted to do, but he knew the bottom was clean. Had the boat been in the water for any length of time and accumulated the inevitable barnacles, what he had planned might kill him. Trufante pressed standby and took control of the boat from the autopilot. Steering a course wide to the port side of the larger ship, he moved ahead of it, trying to look like a fishing boat running out to the Gulf Stream for the morning dolphin bite. Mac knew their biggest asset was surprise as the men likely thought they were still tied to the hull, dragging underneath the ship. Ironically, it was almost exactly what he intended to do. With only seconds before Trufante would be in position, he gathered the dock lines and sorted them out. Last he grabbed the flare pack, hoping the expiration date had no effect on their performance.

The longer line, he coiled around his arm, counting each loop as six feet. When he reached twenty-five loops he tied it off on the stern cleat. The shorter dock line he set by the dive gear. Looking up, he saw Trufante had them just about in position and ahead of the larger ship. Taking several large breaths to control his heart rate, he rinsed and spit in the mask before placing the strap around his neck, then slid into the BC and sorted out the hoses. With the fins on, he shuffled to the port gunwale and grabbed his supplies.

"Ready? I need you right in front of them. I'll disable the prop and drift behind them where you'll pick me up. Then we board."

Trufante nodded that he understood. Mac placed the mask on his face and the regulator in his mouth. After taking a quick breath to make sure it was functioning, he grabbed the end of the dock line and rolled overboard. The minute he hit the water he felt the current pull him back and he held the line tightly, knowing if he lost his grip he would either end up shark chum after hitting the propeller or drift behind the boat and into the open water beyond. At night, without a light, he would likely never be found. He wrapped the line around his wrist and tightened his grip, not liking either scenario. Even in the dark water, he could tell that the hull of the ship was above him and he tried to gauge where he was when he saw another eye bolt. He recalled there were four attached to the hull, just like the one he and Trufante had been secured to, used as tie down points in the shipyard. Under normal circumstances, they would have been removed and the holes patched, but once this ship offloaded its cargo, Mac knew it would be scuttled.

Grabbing onto the eye with his fingers, he let go of the lifeline, and threaded the end of the dock line through the bolt. Now, attached to the hull, he looked around, feeling the vibration of the propeller before he saw it. One foot at a time, he worked his way down the line and drifted back to the steel guard surrounding the spinning blades. He took several breaths, studying the mechanism and stuffing box. Forming a loop with the line, Mac tied himself to the guard and with both hands free, opened the package containing the flares. One at a time, he took them, pulled off the top and lit them. The light helped him work and he stuffed them into the wadding that prevented the shaft from leaking. When the last was in place, he unclipped the EPIRB from his BC, pushed the distress button, and clipped it to the propeller guard. Once that was in place, he released the line from his BC and floated back behind the boat. He watched the flares as he drifted, hoping they did as he intended.

Once he was past the stern, he inflated the BC and surfaced. Kicking his fins, he spun in a circle, finding the boat just where he had asked. Trufante must have seen him and the hull moved closer. Mac worked his way to the transom, climbed aboard and dropped his gear on deck. Standing next to Trufante at the helm they watched the larger ship. There was no great explosion, but it suddenly stopped. Dead in the water the ship drifted beam to the seas. Now they just had to get aboard.

26

Now that the bad guys had names, Kurt didn't know what to do with the information and wondered if the spreading tentacles of this operation were too vast for him to handle. He doubted the insider involvement stopped with Dwayne. In any case it was certainly out of the Park Service jurisdiction now.

Janet must have read his face. "We can pass the evidence to the Coast Guard or FBI."

Kurt nodded, still trying to get an angle on how he could remain involved. Although his tenacity often got him in trouble, he didn't want to hand someone a file and walk away. He thought about Dwayne again, knowing he was not going to drop it. "Whatever it takes to catch him," he said stoically. "

"We need to reach Mel and give her an update," Alicia said, picking up her phone. After a few minutes of what looked like several calls, she started to look anxious. "No answer on either her or Mac's phones. Can you track them?" she asked TJ.

He started working his keyboard and exchanged Tabor's face on the screen for another map of Florida. The mood seemed to lighten once the dark eyes were gone. "Nothing on Mac's, though that's not unusual. I got Mel here." A small blip appeared near Key West. "They're on a boat."

"Maybe she couldn't hear the phone over the engine noise. I'll text her too," Alicia said.

Kurt stared at the blip, looking at the same area on the screen with the EPIRB alarms on it. It was down by Key West, but the area was foreign to him. It looked like a string of islands running south and west from the bottom of the mainland. "She's in the area where a lot of signals were activated."

Just as he said it, another blip appeared and the group was silent. "Give me a minute," TJ said, knowing all eyes were on him. He pecked at the keyboard and wrote some numbers on a small pad near his drink holder. After another bout with the keyboard he wrote down something else, picked up the pad, and stared at it. "The signals are within a hundred yards."

Kurt digested the information. "Do you think they're in trouble?"

"Those two can handle themselves, but this is a pretty big coincidence," Alicia said. "Hopefully, the Coast Guard will be doing more than just making a phone call to see if the distress call is authentic now." She paused and lifted the phone.

The room was quiet again. "I'd take the dive boat and check it out just to make sure, but it would take almost four hours to get down there. By then, if they're in trouble, it'll be over," TJ said.

"Isn't it a two-hour drive? And then we'll have to find a boat." Kurt said. "I vote for the dive boat, especially if we can still follow the beacon."

"He may have a point," Alicia said. "I can track them from here and link the position to your phone." She said."It's worth some time and gas to see what's going on."

"Why can't you guys call the Coast Guard?" Janet asked.

"Now that's complicated," TJ said.

Kurt was glad they were willing to go this alone. He looked over at Janet. Even in the dimly lit room, he could see the creases on her forehead. His decision was already made. There was no reason to drag her down with him. "Why don't you go back to Miami and keep an eye on things there?" he asked looking back at her. "Maybe see what our buddy Dwayne is up to." Immediately her face lightened.

"I never did trust him. I'd like to see this through on that end," she said.

"If we're going we better get it on," TJ said.

"Right. Let me walk Janet out, and I'll be ready," Kurt said. They left Alicia alone in the war room. TJ gathered some things from the kitchen counter and dropped them in a dry bag, then went to the refrigerator and opened the door. After emptying half its contents on the counter, he started loading a cooler. Initially it had seemed curious, but as he followed Janet down the stairs, he realized they would likely be out for at least eight hours.

Kurt and Janet walked in silence around the building and she paused before getting into the car. "That Tabor guy sounds dangerous. Be careful out there," she said, leaning into him.

At first, Kurt thought she was going to fall, but had read the movement wrong and awkwardly grabbed her. But their bodies worked it out and their lips found each other. "I still owe you that dinner," he said, closing the car door. She started the car and the window lowered.

"You do, and I'm holding you to it."

Kurt watched the tail lights recede as she turned out of the parking lot. He stared for just a minute, then gathered himself and headed around the building. TJ was already aboard.

"Hey, lover boy. Hand me those gas cans," he said, pointing to a line of yellow plastic containers by the building.

Two at a time, Kurt brought them over. TJ poured the contents of several into the fuel tank and moved the rest to the transom where he secured them with a rope. Kurt looked at what he thought was a dangerous situation. "Don't believe in gas docks?"

"Bastards are over a dollar more a gallon. With what we burn, it really ads up, and doesn't take much longer. I usually make my dive masters do the grunt work."

After the last container of diesel fuel was loaded and secured, TJ started the engine and asked Kurt to remove the lines. He jumped aboard and TJ started to back out of the narrow canal. After the boat reached the main channel, he took it out of gear and allowed its forward momentum to straighten it before pushing the throttle forward. Kurt watched him as he worked, making mental notes. Running a boat was a skill he'd have to master before long if he didn't get fired.

"Be easier with twin screws," TJ said. "You can turn on a dime with one in forward and the other in reverse."

Kurt just nodded. They were in the main channel now and he could see open water ahead. After the last marker was in their wake, TJ pushed down the throttle and the boat responded. Just as it planed out, he turned toward the west and started working the electronics. "Read me the lat / lon from my phone."

Kurt grabbed the phone from the space in the dashboard and read off the two sets of numbers on the screen.

"Looks like their short of Key West; offshore of Sugarloaf Key. Makes sense if they're up to no good. Pirates and smugglers have been using those waters for centuries. Not nearly as many eyes watching as Key West either."

"That should cut some time off our trip then," Kurt said after studying the screen.

TJ reached forward and set the cursor on a point further east. "Currents going to help too. Check the Navionics app on my phone."

Kurt scrolled through TJ's phone, surprised that most of the apps were games. The rest were all weather or boat related. He found the Navionics icon and opened the program. After it located their position, he zoomed out and pressed the button to show currents. Arrows, some bigger than others populated the screen and he noticed the larger were further offshore moving against them. The course TJ had chosen had the current in their favor.

"Right. They show about six knots in the Gulf Stream," Kurt said.

"That's going to help our cause. It'll bring them to us. We'll stay in Hawks Channel so we don't have to fight it," he said and leaned against the chair.

Kurt moved to the other seat on the port side, and settled in for the ride. The engine sound made talking difficult, and TJ wasn't looking for conversation. With a couple of hours to kill, his mind had nowhere to go, but drift back to the kiss.

MAC THOUGHT his plan had worked, and had taken the wheel from Trufante when the old ship started to move. He cursed under his breath, knowing it had been a long shot. The only thing he had left was the EPIRB to track Mel and Pamela. By now the emergency dispatcher had probably reached the owner of the boat the device was registered too, confirmed that the boat was at the dock, and the signal was a false alarm. If the owner was local, he would assume the boat had been stolen and they could expect company. To make matters worse, the lights of the container ship were on the horizon. The window on rescuing the women was closing fast.

Without a phone the only way to communicate was the VHF. He turned on the unit, and after seeing DSC pass across the screen, shut it back down. The digital selective calling feature gave the user a unique ID. It was valuable for being able to use the unit to speak privately with other DSC equipped vessels, but that same number was tracked by the Coast Guard and if the boat was now listed as stolen, it would be among the first methods the authorities would use to locate them. After escaping from the interview room that was the last thing he wanted right now.

Ahead the lights of the container ship had turned into an outline as the two ships converged. He was about to back away when he saw a cloud of smoke coming from the ship ahead. The flares hadn't stopped the boat, but must have damaged something. It suddenly stopped and he knew this was the only chance he was going to get. Accelerating, he moved toward the ship which was now dead in the water and listing badly to port. He glanced at the depth finder; a hundred-eighty feet of water lay beneath the hull. The scene started playing out in slow motion. The container ship was closing fast and the old ship sinking slowly. It would be close, and he thought he had an answer when he saw a figure appear on the deck of the ship just ahead.

He was about to ignore it, when the man, outlined by the moon-light lifted a cylinder to his shoulder and pointed the end directly at them. Before Mac realized what it was, a flash came from the weapon and a fiery trail marked the path of the projectile as it shot toward them. There was no time to do anything except grab Trufante and push him overboard. Mac saw the tank and BC on the deck and just as the boat burst into a giant fireball, he grabbed the gear from the deck and followed Trufante into the water.

27

T he dark sky, lit by the burning boat, blocked Mac's vision. The glow from the flames helped him locate Trufante, and using the inflated BC for support, he kicked toward him. Well aware, from his past experience in these matters, he fought to reach the Cajun, knowing the boat could blow any second. Never a great swimmer, Trufante was struggling to stay above the surface and Mac could see his head submerge every second or third wave. When he reached him, he fitted the inflated BC around his torso, turned him on his back, and grabbed the tank valve. Urging him on, they kicked away from the burning boat.

Fortunately, the current was moving with the tide, and they were able to quickly distance themselves from the imminent explosion. Mac's biggest fear now was that the older ship, with the woman still aboard, was still close enough that a burning projectile would set the old dry wood ablaze. For now, there was nothing he could do but keep himself and Trufante alive. He doubted the initial EPIRB signal had done any good, but now that there was a ship on fire visible to the fishing boats on the reef line. The Coast Guard would do the math and send help.

As they drifted away from Mel and Pamela, Mac saw no way to

rescue the women. It was time to admit they needed help and the Coast Guard had the resources. Turning away from the blaze, he kicked again and noticed the bright flash from a strobe light attached to the BC. It shot out a bright signal every second or so and was their only chance of being spotted at night. The unit was larger than most, and he reached for it, realizing it was a PLB. Personal locator beacons had just become affordable to the diving community and if you were diving from your own boat in any kind of open water, a good idea. With the unit cupped in his hand, he slid the flexible antennae from its restraint revealing the distress button and activated the unit. Even if the first unit was ruled a false alarm, a second so close in time and location should trigger some kind of response. He wasn't looking forward to a reunion with the Coast Guard, but he had to put his own problems aside and save Mel and Pamela.

The boat was low on the horizon when it blew. The five or so minutes since they had bailed was just enough for the wind and current to push them far enough away to avoid the burning debris flying through the air as a result of the explosion. Finally, the fallout ended, and he turned to search the horizon for the other two boats, relieved when he saw both ships unaffected. He had hoped the confusion would buy them some time and the Coast Guard would reach the scene before the merchandise was shuttled to the container ship, but the two ships remained on their course and the rendezvous seemed inevitable.

Mac stopped kicking and floated on the surface until he was able to judge the current. Tides were something that many Keys residents had built into their DNA, and Mac didn't need a table or app to tell him the water was about to go slack. After so many years here, he knew the position of the moon and sun without thinking about them. With that in mind, he reversed course and kicked back towards the wreck. The tide wasn't a hindrance, but swimming directly into the wind driven waves was wearing him out, and he could hear Trufante coughing seawater every time one crashed over them. Sticking the regulator in Trufante's mouth, he continued on.

They were soon in the debris field and with a revived Trufante, the two men navigated the scattered pieces of flotsam, moving in the direction of the old ship. Both vessels had slowed to close to a stop and were in clear view now, and Mac guessed he had only a few minutes before they transferred the cargo. Kicking harder, he made up the distance to the old boat and reached out and grasped for its hull. His fingers found a small groove between two planks and he held on while he thought about their next move.

The seeds of an idea were just starting to sprout when he heard the sound of an engine coming towards them. It wasn't a boat, and he looked up seeing a searchlight scanning the water from a helicopter. The thump-thump moved closer and he subconsciously ducked out of its beam. For now, it was better to stay invisible. The helicopter would report the fire and soon enough he would have more company than he preferred. The sound of the rotors moved away as the pilot flew a circular pattern, probably searching for survivors. When the searchlight reached the old ship, it stopped and momentarily stayed on the deck, but seeing nothing swung toward another patch of debris. Mac saw the light moving back toward them and submerged when it passed. Some instinct told him he would be more effective without being discovered.

When the beam had passed, he surfaced and scanned the water, relieved to see the helicopter had caused the container ship to abort. It was now moving at a diagonal course toward the Gulf Stream, and would soon be riding the current north without the cargo in the old ship. Mac breathed a sigh of relief that was halted in his throat when he saw movement from the deck of the ship. A life raft was launched into the water and the silhouettes of the two men were visible in the moonlight as they dove off the deck and climbed aboard. A small motor fired and a trail of white came from the stern of the raft as the craft powered away.

It was a clean getaway. There was nothing tying the men to either boat and they would either be rescued by the Coast Guard with few questions asked, or reach land and be free. Mac guessed it would be the latter with the light from the helicopter scanning the water a hundred yards away. The sound of the outboard motor died just as the light moved back toward them and he ducked under again, this time hearing the worst sound one can hear at sea.

Sound was different underwater, and what he couldn't hear on the surface, he could underneath. Water was entering the hull of the old ship. The vessel was always intended to be sunk and provisions had likely been made to achieve this efficiently. With the valves open, it wouldn't take long before the ship was taken to the sea floor as initially planned, except this time Mel, Pamela, and who knew how many others were aboard.

The helicopter skittered about like a confused mosquito. Moving between the debris field and back to the ship, the pilot couldn't decide what to focus on and moved away swinging the search light back and forth through the debris field. The ship groaned and Mac knew it wouldn't be long before it reached the tipping point and lost buoyancy. That moment was both what he feared and what he needed. To gain entry to the interior he needed to access the deck. With no way to climb aboard, he had to wait for the deck to come to their level and that meant waiting for it to sink.

Checking the air gauge, he saw the tank was still near full showing twenty-five hundred PSI. He thought about taking the regulator from Trufante, but figured it was the only thing keeping him alive. The Cajun's face was wrinkled up and pale, like he was seasick. Mac and he had been out in pretty rough seas and he had never seen him sick before, but the minute he was in the water, he looked queazy.

"Not too long now," Mac reassured him. He heard a grunt back that sounded like he was okay and felt the ship groan and move again. This time it started to list and his grip failed. There was no telling how the ship was going down, and without being anchored to the hull, they would be sucked into the whirlpool and drown. Grabbing the octopus floating beside him, he placed the secondary regulator in his mouth and breathed. Cool air filled his lungs and he slowly submerged. Trufante was no diver and Mac watched him carefully as he swam to the propellor.

The steel guard he had fastened himself to earlier swung upwards as the ship listed further to port almost striking the two men. The movement did tell Mac how the ship was going to sink, and he reached for the dock line still fastened to the guard and attached it to the BC. The ship started to slide over on its side. Mac knew it was in its death throws and he grabbed the BC straps. Facing Trufante, he opened his eyes and saw the look of panic on his face, but there was nothing he could do except stay connected to him. Holding tightly, he adjusted the inflator to keep them neutral as the boat slipped below the surface.

His depth gauge showed thirty feet and Mac looked up, trying to judge if they were past the vortex caused by the sinking ship. Through squinted eyes the water appeared calm, but he knew that could be deceiving. There was no choice though, and he released the dock line and dumped the air from the BC. Staying as close to the hull as they could, and dragging Trufante behind him, he worked his way toward the deck, now below them.

By watching for escaping air bubbles he was able to find the hatch. The plywood door had been left open when the men had abandoned ship making it easy for Mac to enter. It had been dark in the open water, but the moon had provided some ambient light. Now below the surface inside the ship, it was pitch black. With Trufante behind him, Mac started to move forward, counting the seconds in his head. He estimated the ship had been down for five minutes, and could only hope that the hold the women were in was somewhat watertight and held some air. If not they would be dead before they could reach them.

Ascending into the depths of the hull in a sinking ship was a strange experience and vertigo hit when he felt stairs above his head. Forcing himself to breath deeply and feel the direction his bubbles travelled, he remembered the ship was upside down. With any luck, by the way it had sunk, there was still air trapped in the holds. Dragging Trufante behind him like a rag doll made it difficult to work. Pulling him by the air hose, they floated to what would have been the bottom of the stairs. With the deck above him, he worked his hands against the bulkheads feeling for any kind of opening. They were in a corridor now and Mac passed several openings. Wherever the women were, the hatch would certainly be closed. Finally when he thought they had to have reached the end of the ship, he felt a padlock.

With a hard pull he jerked the shackle, but it held fast. He would need something to break it open. Hoping to get some assurance this was the right compartment, he banged his fist against the door, and put his ear against the solid wood. From inside came the unmistakable sound of panic. He had found them, but now he needed a way in and time was running out. There might be a supply of air in the hold, but in a hundred-eighty feet of water, he and Trufante were in danger of both running out of air and decompression sickness. Reaching out to the BC, he found the hose and reached for gauges. Grabbing the computer, he pressed several buttons until a faint green light backlit the display. Squinting through the water at the unfamiliar display, it looked like the device was recording his second dive, and he realized his time on the surface had exceeded the ten minutes needed to reset the computer. What had seemed like hours been only a few minutes. But the no-decompression time became the least of his worries when he felt the air flow restrict and he knew he had only minutes before the tank was dry.

Desperate, he moved backwards, dragging Trufante to where he had previously felt an opening and pulled the Cajun into the hold. Pressing the inflator button, he kicked up and their heads slammed against what would be the deck, but in this case was the ceiling. They had surfaced in an air pocket and once he felt air surrounding him, he breathed deeply. He grabbed the regulator from Trufante's mouth. "We're in an air pocket. Open your eyes and breath."

28

WOOD'S
BETRAYAL

T he frequency and intensity of the sounds coming from the ship told Mac they didn't have much time. A well built steel ship might make it to the bottom in one piece, but falling through six atmospheres of pressure was slowly tearing the old wooden hull apart.

"We gotta go," Mac said.

Trufante only nodded.

Mac was becoming worried about the Cajun and needed to get him under control if they were to rescue Mel and Pamela. "Breathe like me." Mac started his routine, leaving Trufante in the air space with the tank. When he was ready, he ducked under the surface. The water magnified the distress calls from the sinking ship and he tried to keep his mind on the task. Panicking now would kill them all. He kicked down, towards the ceiling, which with the ship upside down was the deck. Reaching his hand in front of him, he swept it back and forth, as he worked his way around the hold. Everything in the space that wasn't permanently attached was scattered across the floor and when his hand hit metal he grasped for it, thinking it might be their only chance, only to find it attached to the ceiling, probably a light. Discouraged and with his lungs burning, he surfaced. Trufante gave a weak grin and he nodded back. Despite the ship breaking apart around him, he knew better than to rush. Shallow water blackout was a real danger for free divers. It didn't matter how deep you were if your brain decided there was no air.

He looked around them while he rested and realized from the upside down equipment surrounding them that they were in a mechanical room. That meant there should be tools below. After several deep breaths he submerged again. It was hard to identify the tools in the ink black water, and he settled on what he thought was a hammer just before his first convulsion. He knew several shorter dives would serve him better, but was wary of the time between attempts. The creaking and popping continued. On the surface, with the tool in hand, he breathed up for the last time and grabbed Trufante. Using the octopus would have been easier, but he knew the air was running out, and needed to save all he could to get them back to the surface. He stuffed the regulator in the Cajun's mouth and pulled him under the surface, out the hatch, and into the corridor. Moving his hands along the bulkhead, he felt nothing but solid wall. His lungs were burning when his feet hit something hard.

Stars were bursting in his head like fireworks and his lungs felt like they were on fire. Reaching for Trufante, Mac's arm bumped against a hose and he followed it to the octopus. After a few deep breaths he released it and revived by the air, he remembered where the locked hatch was. Moving to his left, his hand immediately felt the door jamb. With his free hand he found the hasp and lock and taking the claw of the hammer, pried the screws from the plywood door.

Mac paused before he opened the door. There was no way of knowing how big the air pocket in the room was and the change in pressure when the door opened could sweep the women out or crush them. taking another deep breath, he spit out the octopus, and grabbed Trufante's arm, pulling him with him into the room. Testing the door, he felt resistance and pushed harder. The stronger the resistance, the more equalized the two spaces were. Now, instead of worrying about the water flooding the compartment, he had to worry about it already being flooded, but he was sure he had heard a response when he banged against it earlier.

A loud crack echoed through the water and he knew he had to act now. Bracing himself against the adjacent wall, he used his shoulder to push against the door. It gave slightly and he could feel the water moving past him as it gravitated toward the lower pressure inside. Once he stepped into the hold, he tried to close the door, but found it impossible. When he let go, the current swept him off his feet and seconds later he found himself standing on a ledge. When he opened his eyes he saw half a dozen women floating around him. The water in the room was waist high and rising. He breathed deeply and rubbed the salt water from his eyes. Once he became acclimated he realized he was standing on the manifold of the old engine.

Thinking he was too late, he saw Mel in the corner, floating on her side in what looked like an unnatural position. For a second he thought she was dead until he saw the restraints holding her there. Still not sure of her condition he went to her realizing in another minute the water would be above her face. Pausing, he checked her breathing, relieved to feel her warm breath on his hand.

"Give her the regulator," Mac said. Before Trufante had stuck it in her mouth, he went to work on the restraints. The rising water had the ties at their limits. Another minute and it would be over her head. Even now, he had to push her down into the water, to retrieve enough slack to free her. The water continued to rise and he lost his footing. His hands fumbled with the knots and clinging to her, he tore at the rope, finally feeling a little slack. It was probably a simple fisherman's knot. One that he could have easily untied on land, but underwater everything changed and he struggled. He released her, took a deep breath, and submerged again. With both hands he worked the knot now. Fighting through the burning in his lungs, he clenched his jaw and found the resolve to endure another convulsion, determined to stay under or die with her.

Finally, Mac felt the rope give a little more and pulled the knot free. Grabbing Mel, he pushed for the surface, propping her up on his bent arm. He checked her breathing again and with Trufante now by his side, used the purge button on the regulator to feed her fresh air. Her eyes fluttered open and he thought he saw recognition, but they closed again. Twice more he hit the purge button, simulating mouth to mouth resuscitation until they opened for good. He rubbed his hand against her face to reassure her and went back to work.

"Hold her up. I'll get Pamela," Mac said to Trufante, and dove into the water. Pamela was only a few feet away and he reached her easily. Now that he knew what kind of knot secured her, he made short work of freeing her and dragged her to Trufante.

The water was quickly winning the battle against the air and there was only about a foot of space left; just enough for their heads to remain above water. Both women had their eyes open now and regulators in their mouths, but Trufante was struggling to hold them above the surface. Mac looked around at the other women in the room seeing they were all Cuban. They were all held underwater by their restraints and he felt their loss, swearing he would get vengeance on whoever was responsible.

Mel and Pamela had been lucky. Secured to the engine instead of the deck, the restraints had enough movement to allow the women to remain above water. There was nothing he could do for the other refugees. He said a silent prayer under his breath and looked at Trufante.

"You hold onto them and make sure the regulators stay in their mouths. I'll swim the tank ahead of you. Breath up like I showed you," Mac said inhaling deeply. After several breaths and just before the water level reached his mouth, he grabbed the tank and submerged. He felt resistance on the lines and the small assurance that he was connected to Mel pushed him harder. The weight of the near empty tank helped drag them to the bottom and he immediately started moving toward the hatch.

Just when they reached the corridor, he was thrown from his feet as the ship crashed into the bottom. It settled slightly and he hurried forward, knowing the hull could easily roll now and trap them inside. They continued forward in their awkward procession until Mac's foot hit the first step. Knowing there was no where to go but up, he reached for the inflator hose on the BC and pushed the button. Air flooded the bladder and they started to rise. A hurried ascent was never a good idea, but in this case there was no option. The women would probably be fine. They had been breathing the air trapped in the hull which had remained at the same pressure as the surface. The few minutes of tank air would probably not hurt them. For he and Trufante, it was another matter, but one that would have to wait. If there was any air left in the tank, they might be able to drop a few feet from the surface for a decompression stop while they waited for a rescue that he was not sure would come.

Whatever oxygen was in Mac's lungs was long gone when they reached the surface and he gulped a mouthful of seawater before his first breath causing his body to spasm. He coughed it up and inhaled the fresh air, looking around the surface for anything that might help them. Trufante was grasping the inflated BC, using it as a support and had Mel and Pamela beside him, but the combined weight of the three people and the tank was dragging it under. Mac swam to them and checked the air gauge. It was pinned at zero PSI, maybe a few more breaths at the most.

"Watch them. I have to ditch the tank," Mac said, reaching down and releasing the buckle. The tank dropped but the BC was coming with it. He had failed to release the inflator hose. Reaching down, he pressed the quick disconnect and the hose popped off. With the tank gone, the BC responded and popped above the surface. With all four of them grasping to it, they looked at each other too dazed to speak.

Mac came around first and evaluated each of them. Trufante looked better than he did down below, which was not saying much, but Mac knew it would take more than this to take him down. Mel and Pamela were slowly coming around. He urged them to tread water, more to retain body heat than to stay above the surface. Free of the tank, the inflated BC was easily supporting them. After making sure they were alright Mac moved his attention to their surroundings. He didn't know whether to be relieved or reassured that they were alone.

He'd been in similar situations before and escaped. Having to worry about the others made things more difficult, but he was sure they would make it. The worst case was they would be in the water for a while. The wind blowing gently at about ten knots from the southeast would eventually push them onto the reef, and if they weren't noticed there, they would make landfall somewhere around Islamorada. Something flashed in his face and he reached for the strobe light attached to the BC. He had forgotten about the PLB attached to the vest. The red light continued to flash every other second, broadcasting their position again.

KURT SAW TJ's phone dance around on the top of the console and reached for it. There was no way to hear the ring over the engine noise, so he had set it to vibrate. Kurt reached for it, saw a message from Alicia. He held the phone out so TJ could read it. After a second, he tapped the screen of the chart plotter indicating that Kurt should enter the coordinates she had just sent.

Between the bouncing motion of the boat and his unfamiliarity with the electronics, it took Kurt a few minutes to enter the coordinates of the PLB that Alicia had just sent over. "Looks like about eight miles. Gives us an arrival of about a half hour," he yelled over the engine noise.

TJ pushed the throttle all the way forward and the boat picked up another five knots. "Be less than that now."

Kurt watched them close on the icon. When they were within a half mile he started scanning the water. "Got any binoculars?"

TJ pointed to the cabin and Kurt came back with an old pair and put them to his eyes. After adjusting the focus, his stomach set off an alarm as nausea overtook him.

"Those'll get to you," TJ yelled. "We need to calculate drift. They won't be on the same spot now. Can you text Alicia for the latest coordinates?"

Kurt pecked out the text, having to correct it several times when the boat hit a wave. Finally he had it right and hit send. Staring alternately at the phone and the water he waited. TJ had crossed the reef line a few miles back and since then the horizon was void of any human activity. He turned back to the phone and saw the screen lit up with new numbers and he went to the GPS.

"Just let me see them," TJ yelled.

Kurt held the phone for him and he immediately cut the wheel. He starred out at the water until he saw what looked like a blinking light in the distance. "There!" he pointed. Somehow TJ got another few knots out of the engine and they sped toward the signal. With the wind and waves behind them, they covered the distance quickly.

"Drop the dive ladders. I see something ahead," TJ said.

Kurt was thrown off balance when TJ slowed and using the tank holders pulled his way to the stern. He reached the dive platform, released the bungee cord holding the ladders up and dropped them into the water. Custom made to bring a boat full of divers aboard quickly, they dragged behind the swim platform ready for duty. Turning his attention to the light Kurt saw what looked like four heads bobbing in the water. TJ skillfully moved downwind and past them before coming back and placing the stern a few feet from the group. He saw one man leave the group and reach for the ladder. He started on the first rung and fell back exhausted, but Kurt was out on the swim platform and dragged him aboard.

"Damn if it ain't Trufante," TJ called to the man now prone on the deck and turned to Kurt. "Get the boat hook and help the rest."

One at a time Kurt fished the bodies from the water, bringing them to the ladder and helping them aboard. A few minutes later, the four bodies were strewn across the deck.

29

M ac knew he had gone to the well one too many times and his breath came in gasps as he struggled to his feet. Fighting the pitching deck and his own lightheaded-ness, he moved to the helm. "We need to get out of here," he said, glancing at the compass. "Just head south. Going against the current will distance us from their search pattern."

The Coast Guard chopper had left the scene as soon as the cutter had arrived, and Mac guessed they had drifted outside of the search area while they were underwater. The only thing left on the surface after the old ship had sunk and the container ship had aborted the pickup was debris on the water. Even though they were out of sight, the PLB would send the cutter in their direction and they needed to move fast. He scanned the water, seeing nothing but a few boats on the reef, their windshields reflecting the first rays of the rising sun.

TJ changed course and the ride went from uncomfortable to near torture. Running into the seas, the waves pounded the bow sending spray across the back deck and forced Mac to grab onto the seat back. Once the course was set, he moved to the cabin to check on Mel and the others. A man he didn't recognize was working with her, and she seemed responsive so he turned his attention to Trufante and Pamela.

They were in each others arms and recovering. With everyone accounted for and no apparent need for medical professionals, he leaned back next to Mel.

"I'm Mac," he said to the man who appeared to be checking her vital signs.

"Kurt," he said. She seems to be alright. Maybe you could hold her so she doesn't bounce around too much," he said, and waited for Mac to slide next to Mel before he stumbled across the deck to check on Trufante and Pamela. Mac could tell right away that he wasn't used to boats the way he moved. An experienced seaman would have timed the waves.

"Thanks," Mac said, and looked down at Mel. A weak smile crossed her lips and he breathed out. "You okay?" he asked.

"Yeah," she said, trying to sit up. "Could use some water and maybe some food."

With the knowledge that they were alright, Mac's mood changed from worried to vengeful, but he tried to conceal it and went to the cabin. Inside a cooler he found bottles of water TJ used for his charter customers and grabbed a half-dozen. After passing them around, he went back to Mel. He helped her sit up and handed her the bottle of water. The strobe from the inflated BC that Kurt had used to support her head caught his eye and he was about to let some air out and give it to Mel to lean against when he saw the PLB. With the unit functioning, the course change had been for nothing; the device was still broadcasting their position and would lead the rescuers right to them. Grabbing the BC with both arms, he pressed the button on the inflator to release the air and squeezed. Once it was empty, he looked around and grabbed two five-pound dive weights from a milk crate. Inserting them into the pockets, he went on deck and tossed the vest overboard.

"You good?" he asked Mel when he returned.

"Yeah, more water?"

He grabbed another bottle for her before going to the helm "We have to change course. The PLB was still on. I weighted and tossed the vest, so it will stop broadcasting our position, but anyone watching would have seen our course."

"Where to boss?" TJ asked.

Mac thought for a second. This whole thing revolved around the marina on Stock Island and Billy Bones. Although Mel and Pamela were rescued, the bodies of the Cuban women drowned in the hold, stuck in his mind. He knew Mel would back him up. "Stock Island."

TJ zoomed out the chart plotter and set a course for the Boca Chica channel. With the boat now running almost due west, and the waves on their beam, the ride settled and Mac was able to move around easily. After confirming their destination with TJ, he grabbed a few more bottles of water and went back to Mel.

"What happened to the other women?" she asked.

Mac put his head down, "There was nothing we could do for them," he reached for her hand and felt her squeeze. "What are you thinking we should do about this?" He knew revenge was powerful medicine and it took a minute, but he saw her perk up as her brain now had a problem to work on. Mac watched her carefully, relieved that she was sipping the water now, rather than gulping it. He knew how this worked and waited patiently. She wouldn't speak until she had analyzed the problem from all sides and made a decision. It took less time than he expected.

"We have to shut them down," she said. Finishing the water, she tried to stand.

Mac pulled her back down. "We're headed for Stock Island. That's where this started, and I expect that's where it'll end. Rest, we've got a good hour or so until we get there."

She succumbed, but her posture changed when she sat and Mac knew she was fully engaged now. He looked over at Trufante and Pamela. They were in their own world, probably a good place for them. Kurt was at the helm talking to Cody. Mac needed his story before they proceeded. "I'm going to see what that guy's about. The uniforms a little unsettling," he whispered to Mel and got up.

Joining the two men at the helm, Mac looked at the instruments, knowing that TJ was as capable as he at navigation and running a boat, but he didn't want this to look like an interrogation to the newcomer. "Thanks for your help there. You've got good training," Mac said.

"No worries. I'm with the National Parks Service. I got the training through them."

Mac had to stop himself from counting the tax dollars that had taken in his head. "You guys involved in this?"

Kurt shook his head. "I'm a little off the reservation."

That set Mac instantly at ease. "We're going after the head of this operation."

He could see the man weighing his options. "I'm in, but officially there's not much I can do."

"That's how I like things—unofficial. Welcome aboard," Mac said, feeling Mel at his side.

"I need to talk to Alicia," she said.

"We're just crossing the reef and we'll be inside Hawks Channel in a few. You should get cell reception then," TJ said, handing her his phone.

Mel took it and went below. Mac followed and closed the door. Inside the cabin the engine noise was muted but still loud. "Only one bar," Mel said, looking at the phone.

Mac watched her closely. He needed to be certain about her condition before they went any further. A head injury or her time without food and water could cloud her judgement. Thinking about her captivity and what these guys were doing angered him. Trying not to show it, and knowing they needed food, he rummaged through the cabinets in the small galley. The best he found was an open jar of peanut butter which he pulled out and handed to Mel with a spoon.

"Can we do anything legally?" he asked after she had taken several bites.

"There's no proof. No paper trail to show these people actually exist. Undocumented immigrants that have been here awhile leave breadcrumbs: a drivers license, social security care, or government ID —all available with few questions. These women are Cuban. There's no record of them leaving their country and nothing showing they entered the US." Her brow furrowed. "What about the men and boys? There were only women and girls in the hold."

"I'm afraid they kill them. I saw blood on the boats we salvaged." Mac looked down.

She took another spoonful and reached for a bottle of water. After taking a sip she continued. "Legally the only thing left is the money trail, but I suspect, it's all offshore and well hidden by now."

Mac nodded and looked up as the door opened and Kurt entered. "TJ says you ought to have service any minute." He turned to leave when Mel stopped him. "What do you know about this?"

Kurt leaned against the bulkhead for support. The ride was easier now, but beam to the seas, the boat still swayed as it passed over the waves. "I found an abandoned boat inside the Park boundaries in Biscayne Bay. It turned into a murder and human smuggling ring. The name Mateus Tabor keeps coming up."

"Tabor," Mel said to herself, racking her brain for any memory of the name. She shook her head and looked at the phone. There were three bars now and she opened the browser and entered the name into Google. The more she knew before talking to Alicia, the more productive the call would be. She waited impatiently for the results to come back. After a few minutes, a picture of a dark-skinned, balding man with ebony eyes stared back at her. The first link was to a Wikipedia page and she pressed it. "Shipping magnate. That explains how he handles the logistics." Closing the browser, she pressed the phone app, found Alicia's number, and pressed connect.

Mac, Mel, and Kurt sat hunched over the table trying to hear Alicia's voice through the speaker. It was too hard over the engine noise forcing Mac to ask TJ to drop their speed while they talked. He turned over the wheel to Trufante and joined them below. Mel handled most of the conversation from their side, firing off questions at Alicia who, after having had a few hours to comb through the CIA and NSA databases, had answers to most. When they were done, they knew as much about Tabor as there was.

Alicia had been able to trace three passports to his half-dozen aliases, all from different countries. His company and most of his ships were registered in Samoa. Surprisingly, his tax returns were transparent, showing a good income from several companies. With few deductions, he paid his taxes and was not on anyones radar for an audit. Mac found this odd, and it worried him about the man. On the criminal ladder, this was one step shrewder than the average smuggler. They were meticulous about their assets and how they laundered their money, but had a problem with donating to the government. Many were constantly audited, the expense for which was probably more than paying the taxes in the first place. More high level criminals were incarcerated for tax fraud, than their actual crimes.

"There's got to be something we can use against him," Mac said.

Mel just nodded. She had her head down, working the keyboard of the phone. "We have to make this hit close to home and force him to run. We have his aliases and passports. Maybe he'll panic."

Mac had his doubts that anyone involved in this kind of scheme was going to panic, but forcing him into the open was a good idea. And there was only one way he knew to reach the man. "Billy Bones."

"You're going to trust that dirtbag?" Mel asked.

"Not trust. Maybe a little psychology. The last time we scared him, he ran right to Tabor. That was when Pamela was taken. This time we follow him and set a trap.

"What do you have in mind?" she asked.

Mac had no idea. He got up and paced the small cabin and poked his head out the door to get some air. Sitting on the deck with her legs crossed looking like she was meditating or in some kind of trance was Pamela. Turning back to the cabin he stuck his head in the door. "We make him see a ghost."

30

Mac had been around Pamela long enough to know that when she was committed to something there was no stopping her. She had snapped out of her near catatonic state after Mel spoke to her. The two women were far from friends, but after sharing the near death experience there was a bond between them. Both had felt for the Cuban women that had shared their hold on the slave ship and were resolved to avenge their deaths.

The toll of the last few days was evident on the drawn faces of the group when they pulled into the marina and took a slip. Mac figured they all needed some rest, and TJ's boat was unknown in Key West. As long as they stayed out of site they would be safe. There was no point in trying to find Billy Bones until the sun was on the backside of the Keys. They took turns in the hot cabin, getting what rest they could. Mel had taken the time to lay out a case on paper against Tabor that Mac hoped wouldn't be necessary. If he had his way, the man would never see a courtroom.

TJ and Luke, the least likely to be recognized, had just returned with provisions and had bought two burner phones which Mel and Trufante had in their pockets. With TJ and Alicia's number programmed in, they would all be able to stay in communication.

KURT WASN'T FEELING right about tagging along. He had his own backyard to worry about and after he and Janet had figured out that Dwayne was involved he was anxious to get back. After watching TJ, Mac, and rest of the group, he was confident if it came down to a showdown on the water, like it looked to be the case, they were considerably more competent than he was.

Mac and Mel were leaning against the transom. She was on the phone to someone, probably Alicia, and he waited patiently for her to finish the call before approaching.

"Hey, what do you guys think if I head back up to Miami and follow up on my end of things?" he asked.

"You don't have to ask permission around here," Mac said.

"I'm feeling like you guys have enough here to take them down. I've got a dirty LEO officer up there that I want to stop." Kurt was aware of the looks his uniform and gun belt were getting as well.

Mel glanced up from the phone. "That's actually a good idea. The minute Tabor sees that we're on to him, he's bound to call them and shut things down."

Kurt nodded. Now he needed transportation. "How about I take the bike?"

"That might be a problem," Mac said, "It's Trufante's."

Kurt thought for a second before heading to the cabin where the Cajun was with Pamela. It took a few minutes of negotiation, but as soon as he convinced Trufante that the government was going to write a check for its use, he handed Kurt the keys.

FINALLY, toward three o'clock, which might have seemed a little early elsewhere, but in Key West, where the motto was "it's five o'clock somewhere" ruled, they left the boat. Trufante and Pamela strolled down Duval Street, both holding the standard issue red Solo cup. TJ pulled over to the fuel dock to gas up. He would then take a position near Sunset Key.

Starting on the south side of the street, they walked up Duval. Using a sloppy front and follow surveillance scheme they worked the bars. It took practice to perfect the technique, but they were after Billy Bones who would likely be oblivious. It was also a given that Trufante and Pamela would figure out some way to drink and Mac preferred to control it and keep them in site instead of leaving them to their own devices. First, Mac and Mel would check a bar while Pamela and Trufante walked ahead to the next and waited outside. Once Mac and Mel appeared the other couple would enter the next bar. The process was then repeated, but on a street known for its bars, the going was slow. They were anxious, but knew they had all night and sooner or later they would find him. They had already checked out The Hog's Breath, Captain Tony's, and even the Smallest Bar in the World. There was no sign of him in the Bull and Whistle or Margaritaville. They decided to turn and check out Willy T's and The Irish Pub. Knowing the bartenders there, Trufante took those assignments and Mac noticed him sway slightly as he walked. Next up was Sloppy Joes, but he was not there either. Walking to the end of Duval they turned right on Front Street and found themselves at the A&B Marina. Charter fishing boats were lined up in front of them, and as they walked down the wooden boardwalk of the historic seaport, Mac instinctively checked their catch neatly laid out on the dock or piled in wheelbarrows.

After a hundred yards, the boardwalk made a hard right and they walked together to the Schooner Wharf Bar.

"He hangs here sometimes," Trufante said. "Me and Pajamabama got this."

Mac looked at the couple, realizing their cups were about empty. It would be wishful thinking, especially after watching them come out of the Irish Pub, to think they had only had the one drink he had bought earlier. Knowing half the bartenders on the strip, some had surely slid across a shot or two. But they were running out of real estate and he nodded his approval. He and Mel walked to the rope railing between the boardwalk and docked boats and watched Trufante and Pamela enter the bar.

"What if we don't find him?" Mel asked.

"He had a pocketful of money last night. He'll be around." Mac knew although he talked a big game, that Billy Bones was a tightwad at heart.

"But all the same, I'd feel better if we had a plan B," she said.

Before Mac could start to think about another option, two tourists went flying as someone burst through the door of the bar. The woman fell to her knees, dropping her drink and the man with the build of a linebacker, reached out and clotheslined the offender. Mac looked to the ground and saw the unmistakable Billy Bones laid out on the sidewalk. His first reaction was to walk over, set his foot on Billy's throat, and grind his Adam's Apple into the concrete, but he restrained himself, having to turn away in the process. Grabbing Mel's arm he pulled her down the boardwalk, reminding himself that Billy was only the bait.

Using a sign for a sunset cruise party boat for cover, they watched Billy get up and brush himself off. It was a half-hearted attempt, and the result only added to his semi-homeless appearance. The phone in Mac's pocket buzzed and he glanced at the message: *it worked*. Billy looked around, clearly unsettled, and pushed against the grain of the throng of people moving toward Malory Square for the nightly sunset celebration. Mac and Mel stayed toward the outside and followed from a distance. Billy cut the alley to William Street forcing Mac to push through the crowd to catch him. He dragged Mel by the hand finally reaching the alley that led to the municipal parking lot.

Just as they arrived, they saw Billy pounding on the hood of his old beater. They moved behind a minivan for a better view and saw the bright yellow boot on his front wheel; his parking tickets had finally caught up to him. This was good news for Mac. With one final kick of the wheel, Billy grabbed his flip flop clad foot and screamed in pain. Stomping across the parking lot, his open shirt flapping in the breeze, he walked to Caroline Street and signaled for a cab. Mac watched as his anger increased when the first two passed him by. The third slowed and took a long look. Billy reached into his pocket and pulled out a crumpled wad of cash which he waved at the driver before he finally stopped.

Mac and Mel ran to the street and hopped in the next cab. "Follow him," Mac said, sliding in beside Mel. The smell of weed was pervasive, and the dreadlocked driver nodded slowly, apparently in no rush. "We gotta go man," Mac said.

"There isn't no need for speed here, man," the driver said, slowly pulling away from the curb. "Where can I take y'all?"

"Wherever that guys is going," Mac said, pointing over the back seat at the cab now a hundred yards in front of them.

"This following thing is extra, man," the driver said. The cab sputtered as he accelerated.

Mac was about to reach forward and grab his dreadlocks when Mel pulled him back. "Same cab company. All he has to do is radio the other driver."

"Right," Mac sat back and started typing an update to TJ and Trufante. *I'm guessing Stock Island*, he ended the text and hit send. The two responses came back quickly indicating both were en route; TJ by boat and Trufante on his bike. Although Mel was right that with cell phones and radios they didn't need to be right behind Billy's cab, Mac needed the assurance of visual contact and he leaned forward straining to see the other cab ahead. The traffic was light until they crossed the Palm Avenue Causeway and turned left on North Roosevelt. As they passed the chain restaurants and stores, the traffic became heavier until Mac could no longer make out the cab ahead. He leaned back frustrated as they stopped for a red light, one that a motivated driver might have called yellow.

After crossing the Stock Island bridge, the driver pulled off the road. Just as Mac was about to jump over the seat, he reached for his phone. Seconds later, after speaking in heavily accented Rastafarian, he pulled back onto the road.

"Relax my friend, we've got your man. My friend, he says the man is a pig and he would drop him on the next corner, but I urged him to take him to his destination," he said turning to show Mac his two gold incisors. "You see, no reason to worry, man. I take care of you. He is going to Robbie's Marina."

Mac thanked him and got back on the phone. He texted TJ telling him to dock in an empty slip near the channel entrance to the marina,and then Trufante, to wait outside the gates. "Much appreciated," Mac said, biting back what he felt. "Is there a back way in?"

"Now you asking for my special stealth package. My friend says it is Billy Bones you are following; disgusting man that he is. If he is your enemy, then I am your friend. I know a way."

Mac looked out the window at the landscape he had passed just yesterday, then leaned forward and studied the road for anything that might help. The cab passed the sign for the marina entrance and went another hundred yards before slowing to a crawl when the road ended. The driver surprised him when he continued on, turning onto a small gravel path hidden by the brush. Bouncing along the unpaved road littered with debris, Mac saw that it accessed a vacant lot backing on the marina.

While the driver navigated the junkyard, Mac watched the dust cloud on the other side of the fence that he guessed was the other cab. After striking another large pothole that almost threw his and Mel's heads into the roof of the cab, the driver stopped.

"Through there my friends," the driver said, pointing to an opening in the fence.

Mac dug in his pocket and pulled out some bills which he handed to the man and thanked him. He exited the cab, and waited for Mel before taking off. Working from one junk pile to the next to stay out of sight, they reached the fence. Just as he was getting his bearings, the phone vibrated.

"A black Beamer. Big and bad, just pulled in," Trufante said.

Mac thanked him, hoping that Billy Bones had raised the alarm and flushed out Tabor. Looking to the left, he soon saw the car and knew right away from the custom gold trim and dark windows it was their man. He pulled up next to another boat in about the same condition as the one they had just escaped and stopped. The window opened just a crack, enough to speak, but not enough for Mac to get a look inside. When Billy Bones approached the car, Mac grabbed Mel's hand and with her behind him, they eased through a cut in the fence. He had thought about asking her to remain hidden, but knew from past experience, she would not be left behind. The best thing he could do was to keep her with him. With Billy leaning into the window, they ran for the cover of a large sailboat.

His phone vibrated again and he glanced at the screen. There was a text from TJ that he was in position. They had Tabor cornered now. The question was what to do.

31

Mateus Tabor kicked the sleeping man parked under a sun shade made from a section of an old sail. He rose and as soon as he saw the man standing over him, jumped to his feet, and stood at attention.

"Anyone been here?"

"Just Billy."

"Where is he?"

The man pointed to the hatch. Tabor left him without a word and walked across the deck to the plywood board leaning against the companionway. The first thing he noticed was the padlock was unshackled. The worry here was not someone getting out; the women below were bound and tied to eye bolts. The makeshift door was to keep people from boarding, mainly the OSHA inspectors and homeless people who frequented ship yards, the former looking for violations and the later for free accommodations.

He felt no guilt for the way he treated the Cubans. His ancestors had treated their slaves much worse on the trip across from Africa. Things were different now, and the women below had a different purpose. There was a fine line between holding them hostage and ruining the merchandise. Tabor leaned forward and pulled the door open. He sniffed the air and entered. It had been a long time since he had been a aboard any of his ships, let alone one of the junkers he used to transport the human cargo. At first he thought the smell of the unwashed bodies and waste would be repugnant, but he found it quite the opposite. There was something satisfying about the power he had over these people. Moving deeper into the ship, he called out for Billy, but there was no answer.

After several months of fine tuning, the operation was finally running smoothly. But now, it was threatened and he knew it was time, just like his ancestors had years ago, for a change. That was too bad, because the business had been profitable every step of the way. First the sale of the Internet hard drives, then the passwords, and if the clients were willing the charge for the boat and EPIRB. There was no reason any of that had to change. Drugging the worn out refugees with rohypnol in the bottled water had been a brilliant stroke. And then the recycling of the boats to start the cycle all over again.

Unfortunately, allowing the refugees their promised freedom was not an option. Even though he was dealing with a higher class of people; those that had the money to pay several thousand dollars for the service, they would still talk. Maybe more so than the hardened criminals that Castro had sent out in makeshift rafts during the Mariel Boatlift. Those refugees were hungry and tightlipped. The newer variety were not.

Just as he reached the locked hatch, the door opened and Billy Bones appeared. "What are you doing?"

"Checking things out. Figured you'd want to get out of here."

"I had thought about burning it," Tabor said calmly. He needed to know if he could trust Bones.

"These cats are smarter than that. They got forensics and shit. I know this chick from the morgue. Got some serious quirks, if you know what I mean."

Tabor didn't care what he meant, but knew he was right. The ship, along with its cargo needed to disappear. The timing had been good with one of his ships cruising northeast through the Gulf Stream right now. The operation usually worked in reverse using ships traveling to the Caribbean, South America, or Africa where the ports and officials were more receptive to his business. But to make his own escape, the northbound ship would work, though the cargo might need to get scuttled with the old ship. His gut had told him to disappear and he never questioned the fine tuned warning system. Throughout the last few centuries, his family had survived by trusting their instincts. He knew he would be back.

"Get the lift running. We're moving now," Tabor said.

He watched Billy climb the ladder to the deck and then took a long look at the closed door. The padlock was ajar, and he reached for it. Just before he was about to close the shackle, curiosity overcame him, and he opened the plywood door. Eyes turned toward him, and he felt the power he had over the women. These were not the dregs from Castro's jails either. There were no prison tattoos or bad die jobs. The women looking at him were highly marketable merchandise, and he changed his plan.

Smiling at his captives, he turned to leave the room, but not before taking one last look at a particularly striking women near the engine. He would return later for her. Closing the door, he secured the lock and went toward the light coming from the stairway leading to the deck. Just as he was about to start up the steps, the outline of a man blocked the exit.

"They're still working on the engine. It's not running yet," Billy Bones called down.

That was unfortunate news, but not a deal breaker. "Find a tow," he called back, turned and went back to the locked room.

Kurt sped north on Trufante's bike. Feeling more comfortable on the motorcycle than the boat, he gunned the engine and passed a truck pulling a boat. The rear tire swerved spitting gravel at the car behind. Before he fishtailed, he pulled the bike back onto the road and slowed to the speed of traffic. It wasn't the danger that made him slow, but the velocity the gravel shot back from his wheel that could easily shatter a windshield.

The Park service would get the bill eventually, and explaining his first visit to the Keys was not something he wanted to share with his boss. The news of an accident or cracked windshield would reach Martinez right away, letting him know where Kurt had been. Slightly more cautious now, he gunned the throttle again, using the pipes like a siren to clear his path and flew by another half dozen cars. Curses flew his way as he passed, but he ignored them and sped through the lower Keys. He soon had the traffic pattern figured out and relaxed through the islands knowing the bridges were four lanes and he could pass there. Finally, after the adrenaline faded, he began to heed Mac's warnings about the speed traps, especially prevalent at night. Wearing his uniform, a traffic stop would not result in a ticket, but the time and chance the FHP would call his office to check his credentials were not worth it.

After passing through several more Keys he blended with the bike. There was some adjustment from the off-road bike he had used on the fire roads of the National Forest out west and by the time he passed Sugarloaf Key, the Harley felt good beneath him.

A red light slowed him on Big Pine Key and he pulled out his phone and found the address the pickup was registered to, copied it, and pasted it into the maps app. The screen showed an hour and twenty minutes to Redland. The light turned green and he gunned the engine, impatiently waiting for the traffic ahead of him to start moving. Mac had warned him to be patient here, but that didn't make it any easier. Finally, he reached the bridge leading to Scout Key, and passed another dozen cars before the road narrowed again.

He repeated the process numerous times before reaching the twenty-mile two lane road connecting the Keys to the mainland. There were passing lanes every few miles which he chose to ignore. The road was straight and he used the wide shoulder as a passing lane. Entering Florida City, he slowed again and pulled over to gas up and check the map. The app showed him only fifteen minutes away.

After another mile, he turned left onto West Palm Drive, then made a quick right onto Krome Avenue. Passing planted fields on both sides, he turned left again and headed directly to the Everglades. Five minutes later, he slowed when his headlight hit the city limits sign.

The Redlands, as it was called by the residents was the center of the breadbasket of the south. Riding through the agricultural area, quiet now with flatbed trucks parked on the access roads, ready to be loaded by the pickers in the morning, Kurt thought for a minute that he was back in California, cruising I-5 through the Sacramento Valley. Reaching the town, he slowed again and pulled to the curb. Ignoring the looks from the mostly brown skinned pedestrians walking through town, he realized how he must appear in his uniform riding a Harley.

After memorizing the directions, he was back on the bike and through the small downtown. Turning left, he suffered his first casualty when a B52 sized mosquito slammed into his forehead. The closer he got to the Everglades, the thicker the bugs and he clenched his jaw and squinted his eyes to keep the bugs out. Finally he passed the last field, turned left again, and stared at the address sign hanging from a crooked gate.

He dismounted and walked down the driveway to see if the gate was locked. It was, and he went back to stash the bike out of site. He would have to go in on foot. Alarm buzzers went off in his head and he had a flashback to the pot grow. Entering a property like this, even one that didn't house a criminal enterprise, was dangerous. Suspecting what was going on here, he knew he had to let someone know where he was. He stepped to the side of the driveway, removed his phone, and texted Janet.

Without waiting for an answer, he shut off the phone and started down the dirt road. The red mud the area was named for muffled his footsteps and the property was quiet except for the mosquitos buzzing by his ears. He followed the road to a clearing where it forked, going to the left and right. Ahead he saw the glow from a light inside an old clapboard house.

Moving to the side of the driveway, he stayed in the shadows as he approached the house. It appeared vacant, and there were no cars in the driveway. Still cautious, he went wide around the front and started to approach the back when he heard the low growl of a dog. Reaching to his side, he withdrew his service pistol and with his finger outside the trigger guard, held it barrel down as he proceeded. The growl turned to a loud bark and he stopped, listening carefully in case the dog was approaching.

The red mud, kept constantly damp from the oolite limestone beneath it, allowed the aquifer to saturate the soil. The rich soil had been his friend on the approach, but was his enemy now. Kurt moved behind a large oak tree as the barking continued. He studied the house, but it appeared he was correct and no one was home. Slowly, he moved away from the cover and approached again, calling out softly to the dog. After a hundred feet, he saw the low chainlink fence and relaxed. He continued to whisper to the dog as it followed him along the fence.

At the back corner, he thought he saw water, and moving away from the house and yard, he walked to a wide canal. Tied to stakes in the ground were four boats, all identical to the one he had found in the mangroves.

A shot rang out and he looked back before jumping down to the closest boat. Another shot hit the dirt berm, and he lay down on the deck. It was quiet for a second, and he inched toward the low gunwale and looked up to find the barrel of a rifle pointed at his face.

32

WOOD'S
BETRAYAL

A shiver ran down Mac's spine when he heard the lift start up and approach the ship. Even though he was in no danger, and Mel was by his side instead of trapped aboard, both her captivity and the near drowning were still fresh in his mind. He watched Billy Bones and another man run the slings under the ship and a few minutes later the lift rolled slowly toward the water. It had been a while since they had seen any activity, and he wondered if Tabor was still aboard or if he had snuck off. The black BMW was still here, but that meant little. The boat yard was a maze of works in progress and stacked containers set up as workshops. He could have easily escaped, but Mac's gut told him the man was aboard.

Mac tried to work out a plan as the ship moved toward the water. He texted TJ to be ready, then grabbed Mel's hand and staying to the perimeter, worked their way toward the end of the pier. Looking back he noticed the lift had stopped. The two men were underneath the old ship looking at something.

"This is our chance. Let's get out to TJ's boat," Mac said, leading Mel to the end of the pier. With Tabor's men distracted they reached the boat. Each grabbing a dock line, they jumped aboard. With the engine already idling, TJ dropped the transmission into reverse and they moved away from the marina.

"What's up?" TJ asked Mac.

"They're splashing the big boat. Tabor's aboard. Head out a ways," Mac said. TJ had just started to back up when they heard the sound of a loud diesel engine echo off the seawall as it entered the channel. Mac heard the whine of the engine and knew they were in trouble. Stuck in the middle of the cut leading to the marina, they had no time to move as an old sportfisher barreled straight at them. The natural reaction would have been to push the throttles down and try to escape the inevitable collision, but TJ nudged the throttles backwards. With the help of the tide, he guided the boat back toward the slip. The bow of the incoming boat barely missed theirs, but the wake was another matter, and slammed the dive boat into the pilings.

"It's the *Shark Gunner*, and that's Wesley at the wheel," Mac said, staring at the boat.

"Bastard. That's way over idle speed!" Tj called after him, shaking his fist.

Mac stopped him before he could take any action. "This is tied together. Wesley and Billy Bones are buds."

After a quick check of the damage to his boat, TJ came back. "Mostly above the waterline. Not too bad. I'll deal with him later."

"Looks like you might get your chance," Mac said, looking back to the lift. Wesley was positioning the stern of the *Shark Gunner* at the bow of the Tabor's ship. The lift lowered the old ship into the water and they watched as Billy Bones ran to the bow of the ship and tossed a line to the old sportfisher. "He's going to tow them out."

TJ knew what to do and while the men were distracted hooking up the tow and removing the straps from the lift, he pulled out of the slip and into the channel. Once he cleared the last marker, he pushed the throttles forward and pointed the bow toward the reef where they would wait.

Mac scanned the horizon. He knew they were coming and paced the cockpit trying to think of a plan. There would be only one shot to get Tabor and save the women aboard. He knew Wesley, and though he didn't care for the man, he was an old conch, and Mac didn't want to see him hurt. He knew he was drawn into this from necessity, like so many captains before him. Faced with a choice of losing their boat and the livelihood it provided, most captains did what they had to.

Though Mac knew the shark hunter was down on his luck, and he was confident Wesley had no part in this other than providing a tow. He was just one of those guys that had a hard time adapting to new rules; not the kind of guy to be involved in the human trade.

They reached the sixty-foot contour line and TJ slowed to a stop. "This good?"

Mac leaned over and studied their location on the chart plotter. They were in the channel between the #32 light and the Western Sambo reef. "Wesley'll run straight out from the channel. He knows these waters and I'm guessing he'll be worried about his fuel bill and wanting to ditch the tow as soon as he can. Mac studied the chart and noticed the square area in one-hundred-forty foot of water. "That's the Vandenberg, isn't it?"

"I'm pretty sure," TJ said. "I have a dive chart below."

Mac took the wheel while TJ retrieved the chart. He spread it out on the seat and pinpointed their position. Just past their location lay the five-hundred foot long, ten story high wreck. Mac didn't care about the specifications, it was the surface buoys provided for the dive boats that attracted his attention.

"There's no way, old Wesley's going to pull them out to the Gulf Stream. I'm guessing, he'll drop them on one of the mooring balls, get his paycheck, and haul ass. Let's head there. There'd be nothing suspicious about a dive boat sitting out there setting up for a night dive."

Mel came toward them and placed TJ's phone on the chart. "I've been on with Alicia. She's tracked all Tabor's assets in the area."

The screen showed an overview of the Keys and adjacent waters from Cuba up through the Bahamas. They stared at the dots representing the AIS tracking beacons in the area. Mac knew the devices were required by the insurance carriers and any ship of size or value would have one. Even Tabor wouldn't risk a claim on a multi-million dollar ship by disabling it. The line of red and green icons clearly showed the path of the Gulf Stream. Mac was looking at one in particular. "That one's off course." Just as he said it the icon disappeared. "Can you confirm the ship's registry?" He asked Mel. She picked up the phone and started talking to Alicia, but Mac had seen enough. The course was apparent.

"Head out to the Vandenberg. That's where the meet is."

TJ pressed down on the throttles and turned toward the square area on the chart plotter. As the boat sped toward the wreck, Mac studied the horizon, both in front and behind them. He could only hope that Wesley was anxious enough to be rid of the tow and pushing his speed. For his plan to work, Tabor's boat had to reach the wreck before the cargo ship.

"There it is," Mel called out.

Her eyes had always been better than his, and Mac squinted. Finally, he saw the running lights of the *Shark Gunner* coming toward them.

"Which buoy would you use?" Mac asked TJ.

"I'd go for the outside right. He's going to need to be directly into the wind with that dead weight behind him. That'll force his decision." Mac had what amounted to a battlefield mapped out in his head. By taking the outside right buoy, they were forcing Wesley to the west, and placing him and the other boat downwind of their position.

"Go on and grab the hook. Should just be a second," TJ said.

The boat slowed and circled one of the blue and white buoys. Mac grabbed the long hook from under the port gunwale and went forward. Using the wind, TJ goosed the throttles and set the bow in position to place the ball just downwind on the port side. Mac leaned forward and snatched the loop of the thick yellow line. He hauled it in and using a dock line quickly bridled it, attaching the ends to both forward cleats. Once the boat swung, he moved back to the cockpit.

With the *Shark Gunner* slowly approaching, Mac went to the cabin and started laying out the dive gear. After assembling the BC and regulator, he pulled out fins and a mask. Looking at the pile of weights, he decided against using any—he would need to be as light as possible for what he had in mind. Lastly he pulled a speargun from its holders on the bulkhead. Checking the tip, he made sure it was sharp and secure. Then he counted the loops of line wrapped around the trigger and calculated it had about twenty feet of line attached to the spear.

Back at the helm, Mac scanned the water. He glanced to the north and saw Wesley and the *Gunner* steadily heading their way. He waited while they approached and when he saw him slow and line up with the mooring ball he started to get ready.

Mac grabbed a wetsuit. It wasn't the warmth he sought, but the buoyancy and protection from the hull of the ship. Where the other had been ready for its purpose, this ship was still being worked on. His brief survey at the boat yard had shown the bottom to be rough and unfinished. He fought his way into the neoprene and donned the BC and regulator. With the fins and mask in one hand, he reached for the speargun and carried the gear to the transom. Sitting on the dive platform, he put the fins on, spat in his mask and cleared it before sliding it in place, then swept his right arm around his back to retrieve the regulator. After taking a few deep breaths from the tank, he gave Mel a thumbs up and slid into the water.

KURT FROZE. Unable to see beyond the bright light shining in his eyes, he had no idea who was behind the rifle. It took a few seconds after the man spoke for him to realize who it was.

"Put your hands where I can see them, and stand up," the detective said.

It was Dwayne. Slowly Kurt stood, but the boat rocked with his movement throwing him off balance. Unable to gain his feet he tumbled over the gunwale and fell into the canal. Reaching for the boat, he ducked as several shots splashed around him. Remembering the man's stature, Kurt felt if he could get himself out of range, he would be safe. There was no way the detective was going swimming.

Kurt ducked under the surface and with a few breast strokes reached the bow where he released the single line holding the boat to the stake and waited.

"You've got nowhere to go," Dwayne called out. "There's a road that runs the length of the canal. I can follow you until you hit Florida Bay if I want. Either one of my bullets'll find its mark, or the gators'll get you.

Kurt allowed the boat to drift silently to the middle of the canal. He needed to think his way out of this. "I've got backup coming. They should be here any minute," he bluffed.

"Shoot, this is the Redlands. Back up don't come here."

He took the only shot he had. "Forensics has a piece of your suit that was found on the boat."

"Forensics? That girlfriend of yours has a history of losing evidence. Why do you think she's working the night shift."

"There's your blood on the boat."

"The boat you're using to try and escape? I cut myself trying to save you. Next ..."

Every way Kurt turned he was boxed in. He was about to reply when he heard the sound of tires on gravel. Using the distraction, he ducked under and kicked the boat across the canal. Two quick shots fired, both striking the boat where his head had just been.

Risking a glance, he slowly surfaced and looked toward the bank. The detective was moving away from the canal, in the direction of the driveway. Kurt took the opportunity to climb into the boat, but after seeing it was taking on water from the gunshots, he knew there was only one way out. Using his hands, he paddled across the canal, hoping he could disappear into the brush. He reached the bank and started climbing the berm. When he looked back his plan changed.

It wasn't until he reached the top of the bank, almost eight feet above the canal, that he could see across to the house. Headlights shone directly at him, and he moved to the side. With a better angle, he was able to see the car clearly now and his heart jumped. He almost called out to stop when he saw the dome light come on and the door open. The detective was moving alongside the house, staying to the shadows. Judging he only had seconds, he took a deep breath and dove head first into the canal. Swimming as hard as he could, he crossed the water and scrambled up the bank.

Pausing at the top, he saw the detective, still in the shadows, raise his rifle and aim at the figure emerging from the drivers side. Without thinking, Kurt ran across the yard and just as he heard the crack of the rifle, dove onto the detective and took him to the ground.

33

STEVEN BECKER

A MAC TRAVIS ADVENTURE

WOOD'S
BETRAYAL

Mac reached the buoy Wesley was lining up on and pulling a carabiner from a retractable cable on his BC, clipped himself to the the nylon line. With the vest inflated, he bobbed on the surface using the large mooring ball for cover. From the water, the waves blocked his view of the horizon and though he could hear the engine approach, by the time Mac saw the running lights from the *Shark Gunner*, the boat was almost upon him. With the red and green bow lights bearing down on him, he unclipped from the line, and descended several feet before the man moving toward the bow saw him.

Wesley was likely single-handing his boat and Mac tried to anticipate how he would moor the larger boat. If he were in Wesley's place, he would ensure the safety of his own boat first and then handle the tow. Though not what Mac would call an upstanding citizen, even in Key's circles, he respected the shark hunters abilities. It took skill to operate the old sportfisher without crew or even a deckhand.

Mac heard the RPMs of the engine drop and could envision what was happening only feet above his head. The dark hull of the fishing boat drifted past the mooring ball and then he saw the gaff snag the eye in the nylon line. The line lifted from the water and Mac knew

Wesley had tied off and it would be safe to surface. Ascending close
to the ball, Mac looked up at the bow and was reassured when he saw
the nylon eye looped directly over the forward cleat. If Wesley
planned on staying more than a few minutes, he would either have
rigged a bridle, or used a dock line to extend the scope of the
mooring line.

With one hand on the line and the other holding the speargun,
Mac waited in the shadow of the deep V hull while Wesley brought
another line forward. He dropped it around the other cleat for leverage, and tied a loop in the line. Without removing the mooring line
from the cleat, he used the now free bitter end of the tow line and
tied a sheet bend. Before the line became taught, he released the loop
from his cleat and his boat drifted freely. The old ship was now
secured to the buoy and he went back to the helm. Mac heard the
engine clunk and moved behind the mooring ball both to stay out of
sight and to use it for protection. As good of a captain as Wesley was,
it was past happy hour and there was no telling how many beers were
in him.

The sportfisher was moving forward now and Mac dropped to a
depth of ten feet just as the hull passed over his head. He heard the
RPMs increase and then fade into the distance. It was impossible to
tell the direction of sound underwater, but from the frequency of the
propeller, he knew Wesley was speeding away. Surfacing on the buoy,
he scanned the water. The old ship sat alone, now secured to the
mooring ball.

Looking back to sea, he saw a faint twinkle of a white, that he
guessed was the masthead light from the approaching container ship.
Sliding out of the BC, he clipped the vest to the line. Dumping his
fins and mask, and with the speargun slung over his shoulder he
swung feet first onto the mooring line and started to inch his way
toward the old hull.

Thankful for the wetsuit, he worked his feet forward. He
ascended until he was out of the water and just below the bow.
Looking up at the overhang, he followed the line and caught his
first break. The line disappeared onto the deck. But located just

below the rub rail on either side of the bow, were two recesses in the hull where the twin anchors typically hung. Without the anchors there was an open space big enough for a man to crawl through.

The problem now was that with the angle of the mooring line, they were almost ten feet away. Without pause, he brought the speargun to his shoulder, aimed at the port side opening, and fired.

Dry firing a spear gun was dangerous, and he was barely able to slide his head to the side to avoid the kickback. The sudden movement threw off his aim and the shaft slammed sideways into the hull, making a loud clunk, and dropped to the water.

Fatigue drained the muscles of his arms as Mac recrossed his cramping legs around the line for support while he retrieved the shaft. Releasing one hand, he loaded the spear back into the gun and with the butt jammed into his core, he pulled back the first band. The hard butt of the gun bit into his stomach, but he clenched his abdomen and pulled harder until finally, the small metal clip fell over the trigger release. Looking at the other two bands, he decided that one was going to have to be enough, and after taking a deep breath, aimed again. This time, he was ready for the kickback and the shaft flew through the opening. Relieved, Mac dropped the gun through his fingers and grabbed the line, pulling it slowly toward him.

The shaft caught several times but when he pulled back, it refused to take his weight. Finally, just as he saw the glint of metal through the hole it slid sideways across the opening providing him the support he needed. Hoping the line would hold his weight, he took another breath and released the mooring line. Knowing what was going to happen, didn't help the result, when he slammed into the hull. Fighting for a grip on the skinny line, he took several wraps around his hands. He was secure now, but the line was cutting through his skin and he fought to keep his grip.

With gritted teeth, Mac pulled himself hand over hand up the line until he was able to get a hand inside the anchor compartment. Hanging there for just a minute to allow his muscles to relax, he dropped the line, reached in with his other hand, and pulled himself into the ship.

It was pitch dark in the hold, and he banged his head several times, before dropping to his knees and moved to the opening. There were advantages to entering a ship meant to be scuttled and he caught another break when he found the hatch missing.

Slowly he crawled out of the anchor locker and gained his feet. He was in some kind of corridor now, and he walked toward the stern. Close to midships, a disturbing smell met him. It wasn't death, but the unmistakable smell of humanity, and he knew he was close. Armed only with a dive knife, he wasn't overly worried about running into either man aboard. It would take a rather large weapon to stop him and he doubted either Billy Bones or Mateus Tabor had either the weapon of the nerve to use it.

Moving down the dark corridor, he felt his way by brushing his hands along the bulkheads. Ahead a faint glow came from what looked like the crack from a door, and he went toward it. He immediately knew this was the source of the smell, and pulled at the plywood door. It resisted, but he quickly found the hasp and released the latch. The door swung open and he did his best not to stare. He thought he knew what to expect from his rescue of Mel and Pamela, but as their ship had sank, the water had washed away the waste and filth.

More than a dozen pairs of eyes stared back at him, lit by a dim lantern. He choked back the bile rising in his throat and went to the closest woman. She flinched as he reached behind her, but soon relaxed when the dive knife sliced through her bonds.

"Anyone speak English?"

A heavily accented voice came from the shadows. "Si."

"Okay. Get this woman to release you but stay here until I come back. I have another boat close by and as soon as I take care of the men above, I will be back for you.

He handed the freed woman the knife.

"One man just left," the woman said.

Mac nodded to her and walked out of the room. He closed the

door and replaced the latch just in case Bones or Tabor came behind him. Continuing toward the stern, he followed the dim light from the open hatch leading to the deck. Just before he reached the stairs, he saw a faint fluorescent glow.

Off to the side, in a small compartment without a door was a stack of EPIRBs. He had almost walked past when he decided to grab a handful of the units. He soon found the companionway ladder and started climbing. Mac reached the deck and paused to clear his head with a deep breath of the clean ocean air. He scanned the deck and not finding either Tabor or Billy Bones, looked past the bow at the container ship lurking just a half-mile away. The ship was dark, but with the moon behind it, he was overwhelmed by the size of it.

It was still moving, and knowing it would take a ship this large almost a quarter mile to stop, he wondered how they were going to make the transfer when he heard the sound of an outboard engine. The container ship's tender was moving toward the old ship and quickly settled against her port side. Mac ran to the broken railing and looked down, seeing what he had missed. Probably used to facilitate loading, a hatch was cut into the side of the old ship. He heard the grind of a chain and a gangway lowered.

Leaning over the side, he saw the silhouette's of the two men working the platform into position. He had only minutes before the women would be aboard. Winding up like a discus thrower, Mac had a moment of doubt that he might be signing his own arrest warrant, but continued the motion and tossed the EPIRBs to the sea knowing they would activate as soon as they hit the water. This was bigger than him, and with the container ship looming less than a quarter-mile away now, he knew he needed help.

He saw them splash and ran back to the companionway entrance. Two at a time, he went down the stairs to the lower deck. The minute his feet landed on the old wood, he crouched low and moved to the bulkhead. Light shown into the corridor now and he could clearly see the plywood door.

Reaching for the sheath on his leg, he found it empty and remembered he had given the knife to the woman. He looked around for another weapon when he saw Tabor speak to Billy Bones and cross the hallway to the plywood door. He opened it and Mac jumped. There was no telling what he would do when he saw the women were free. Barreling down the hallway he took Billy Bones by surprise. Lowering his shoulder, he drove him into the sea and without waiting, turned back to the compartment where the women were kept.

He froze when he saw Tabor standing in the doorway with the knife to a woman's throat.

"Back away," he said, twisting the woman in front of him.

Mac saw the desperation in her eyes, all he could do was watch as the women filed out of the hold like sheep to the gangway and were directed aboard the tender. He heard the engine click into gear. Just before the boat moved away, he crouched into a sprinters stance, ran towards the opening, and hurled himself toward the boat.

34

WOOD'S
BETRAYAL

urt had the detective pinned to the ground. He wound up to strike the man in the head but before he could land the punch, a blow to his groin threw him to the ground. The detective followed up his kick with another, but Kurt was already moving. Fighting the pain, stayed low and circled Dwayne.

He saw it in his eyes. The quick glance to the right and the second of indecision. Using the distraction, he went for the man, but stopped short when he heard the gunshot. The detective now had the upper hand and dove for Kurt. Taking him to the ground, Kurt felt the air leave his lungs and pain shoot through his torso. When he regained his wits, the detective had straddled his chest and was landing blow after blow to his head.

The rifle fired again. "Stop it," a woman's voice called out.

The detective paused for a second, and wound up for a last punch, but Kurt was able to block it with his forearm. He wound up again.

"I mean it," Janet yelled.

"If you had the stones to shoot me, you'd have done it already, Doey" Dwayne said without turning and released his punch. The pause was long enough for Kurt to deflect the blow. Just as the detective wound up again, Kurt saw something swing at his head and the man fell off him.

Scrambling to his feet, he looked at the trembling woman holding the gun and went to her. Without losing site of the detective, he took the rifle from her and pointed it at the man on the ground.

"He was right. I couldn't shoot him," Janet said.

"You did good. Probably saved my life," Kurt said, reassuring her. "Can you look around for something to tie him up with?"

Janet was back a few minutes later with a piece of rope, and went to the downed man. He looked unconscious but Kurt suspected the ruse before the detective moved. "Get back," he yelled at Janet and fired a shot in the dirt next to Dwayne who crawled backwards and collapsed on the gravel.

"She may not have, but I will shoot you," Kurt said, pointing the barrel at his head. He turned slightly to Janet and asked her to call back up.

"I did as soon as I pulled up and saw his car," she said.

Kurt saw two small dots of light in the distance. "Looks like you're done, detective."

HAD MAC WAITED ANOTHER SECOND, he would have missed entirely, but his hands found the rope running around the gunwale of the inflatable. The tender was moving now and he clung on as the water tried to tear him from the boat. Several of the women saw him, and with two on each arm, pulled him aboard. When he raised his head, he found himself staring at the barrel of a gun.

Several of the women moved to screen him and there was nothing Tabor could do without killing off his valuable cargo. Trying to read his eyes, he found himself staring into a dull black abyss; the pupils were indistinguishable from the corneas—Tabor's eyes were void of emotion. Mac sensed he was making a decision about the women. His hesitation worked to Mac's advantage, but the container ship was less than fifty yards away.

Just as he saw his finger tighten on the trigger, a large wave broadsided the boat knocking Tabor against the gunwale. Mac's body acted instinctively and rolled with the wave and in the time before his foe could recover, Mac wound through the women and went for the gun before Tabor had a chance to recover.

With his foot he crushed Tabor's wrist. Bones snapped and the gun lay free on the deck. Before he reached for it, he sensed something above him and when he looked up, saw several men standing on the rail of the container ship with weapons trained on him. Tabor must have seen it too, and with a pained smile on his face, started to rise, but Mac kept the pressure on him. The standoff continued for several seconds until one of the women, reached down and picked up the gun. The crew of the container ship, not knowing what to do, stared down at her as she lifted it toward Tabor's head and fired.

Mac went for the man at the helm. He had just slid the boat under the waiting davits and was looking up, when Mac pushed him aside. Two of the other women reached out and restrained him while Mac took the wheel and spun it away from the container ship trying to put as much distance as possible between them before the crew reacted.

This broke the spell on deck and bullets rained down on the small boat as it tried to make its escape. Using the sea to his advantage, Mac spun the wheel trying to pick a line that would keep them on the backside of the wave, using the wall of water as cover. From the height the men were firing this proved ineffective. The motion of the seas still aided him as the men's aim was thrown off. No one was hit yet, but several bullets pierced the inflatable. Between the screaming women and the air hissing from the puncture wounds the small boat was thrown into chaos, but Mac thought he had an idea. Instead of running from the ship and allowing a clear firing path, he used the bulk of the hull to his advantage and staying close to the ship, he sped toward the bow trying to reach the other side. With a ship as wide as a football field and its deck cluttered with containers, this would give him enough time to get out of gunshot range. He imagined the men above, running across the ship, weaving their way between rows of containers as he jerked the wheel to port to cross the bow. What he hadn't considered was the huge wake thrown out by the bow thruster.

Water flooded over the gunwales as he tried to turn away but it was too late. The small boat, already overweight with the women aboard, and sinking from the puncture wounds, turned beam to the seas. Water continued to pour into the boat and he looked for a way out. The ship was moving past now and several shots were fired at them, but the damage was done. They were sinking.

Mac was ready to abandon ship when he saw the transom of TJ's dive boat backing toward them. In the fracas, he had forgotten they were moored only a hundred yards away. Trufante was on the dive platform waiting for TJ to maneuver the boat close enough to drop the ladders. When the two boats were only feet apart, he held up a fist, and TJ dropped to neutral. Trufante dropped the twin ladders onto the gunwales of the sinking boat and started helping the women across.

TJ and Trufante took the driver aside, and restrained him with cable ties and the group stood watching as the boat, along with body of Mateus Tabor slid below the surface.

Mac felt Mel by his side and reached for her. She squeezed his arm and he thought she said something. He looked at her and saw her lips move, but no words were coming out. Before he could figure out what was happening, a flood light hit him in the face and he heard the thump-thump-thump of a helicopter above them. A loud hailer called out for them to prepare to be boarded.

Seconds later another light, from a Coast Guard cutter hit them and he could do nothing but watch and wonder how much trouble he was in as the inflatable cruised toward TJ's boat.

Mac sat on the deck as the Coast Guard boarded and searched the boat. When they were convinced that this was indeed a rescue, the officer in charge came toward Mac.

"I guess we'll forget about that EPIRB business back in Key West. It looks like you found a good use for them," he said.

Mac looked up at the man, too tired to respond. He nodded and watched as Mel took the man aside. Mac couldn't hear what was being said, but he knew Mel, and from the look on her face, he knew the officer was taking a beating.

When she was through, the officer called his men off, and they disembarked leaving the Cuban women aboard. Mel went to the helm and after giving TJ and Trufante instructions, the boat started moving toward Key West. Finally, when she was satisfied she sat next to Mac on the deck.

"Hey, you alright?" she asked.

"Hey back, yeah, I'm good. But how'd you get the Coasties to go home?"

"Just a little deal to keep the women here. Once they were aboard the Coast Guard ship, they would have been under the jurisdiction of the United States Government and with the current laws in place, would have been returned to Cuba."

"And you now represent them," he stated.

"Yup, I guess my new specialty is immigration law."

They both laughed and she sat beside him watching the women across the deck. He could see the relief on their faces and the light in their eyes knowing they had a future.

ABOUT THE AUTHOR

Always looking for a new location or adventure to write about, Steven Becker can usually be found on or near the water. He splits his time between Tampa and the Florida Keys - paddling, sailing, diving, fishing or exploring.

Find out more by visiting www.stevenbeckerauthor.com or contact me directly at booksbybecker@gmail.com.

facebook.com/stevenbecker.books

instagram.com/stevenbeckerauthor

Get my starter library First Bite for Free!
when you sign up for my newsletter

http://eepurl.com/-obDj

First Bite contains the first book in several of Steven Becker's series:

Get them now (http://eepurl.com/-obDj)

Mac Travis Adventures: The Wood's Series

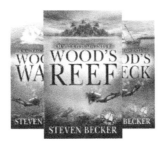

It's easy to become invisible in the Florida Keys. Mac Travis is laying low: Fishing, Diving and doing enough salvage work to pay his bills. Staying under the radar is another matter altogether. An action-packed thriller series featuring plenty of boating, SCUBA diving, fishing and flavored with a generous dose of Conch Republic counterculture.

Check Out The Series Here

★ ★ ★ ★ ★ *Becker is one of those, unfortunately too rare, writers who very obviously knows and can make you feel, even smell, the places he writes about. If you love the Keys, or if you just want to escape there for a few enjoyable hours, get any of the Mac Travis books - and a strong drink*

★ ★ ★ ★ ★ *This is a terrific series with outstanding details of Florida, especially the Keys. I can imagine myself riding alone with Mac through every turn. Whether it's out on a boat or on an island....I'm there*

Kurt Hunter Mysteries: The Backwater Series

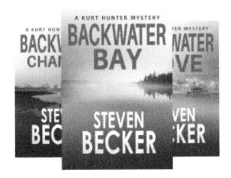

Biscayne Bay is a pristine wildness on top of the Florida Keys. It is also a stones throw from Miami and an area notorious for smuggling. If there's nefarious activity in the park, special agent Kurt Hunter is sure to stumble across it as he patrols the backwaters of Miami.

Check it out the series here

★★★★★ *This series is one of my favorites. Steven Becker is a genius when it comes to weaving a plot and local color with great characters. It's like dessert, I eat it first*

★★★★★ *Great latest and greatest in the series or as a stand alone. I don't want to give up the plot. The characters are more "fleshed out" and have become "real." A truly believable story in and about Florida and Floridians.*

Tides of Fortune

What do you do when you're labeled a pirate in the nineteenth century Caribbean

Follow the adventures of young Captain Van Doren as he and his crew try to avoid the hangman's noose. With their uniques mix of skills, Nick and company roam the waters of the Caribbean looking for a safe haven to spend their wealth. But, the call "Sail on the horizon" often changes the best laid plans.

Check out the series here

★★★★★ *This is a great book for those who like me enjoy "factional" books. This is a book that has characters that actually existed and took place in a real place(s). So even though it isn't a true story, it certainly could be. Steven Becker is a terrific writer and it certainly shows in this book of action of piracy, treasure hunting,ship racing etc*

The Storm Series

Meet contract agents John and Mako Storm. The father and son duo are as incompatible as water and oil, but necessity often forces them to work together. This thriller series has plenty of international locations, action, and adventure.

Check out the series here

★ ★ ★ ★ ★ *Steven Becker's best book written to date. Great plot and very believable characters. The action is non-stop and the book is hard to put down. Enough plot twists exist for an exciting read. I highly recommend this great action thriller.*

★ ★ ★ ★ ★ *A thriller of mega proportions! Plenty of action on the high seas and in the Caribbean islands. The characters ran from high tech to divers to agents in the field. If you are looking for an adrenalin rush by all means get Steven Beckers new E Book*

The Will Service Series

If you can build it, sail it, dive it, and fish it—what's left. Will Service: carpenter, sailor, and fishing guide can do all that. But trouble seems to find him and it takes all his skill and more to extricate himself from it.

Check out the series here

★★★★★ *I am a sucker for anything that reminds me of the great John D. MacDonald and Travis McGee. I really enjoyed this book. I hope the new Will Service adventure is out soon, and I hope Will is living on a boat. It sounds as if he will be. I am now an official Will Service fan. Now, Steven Becker needs to ignore everything else and get to work on the next Will Service novel*

★★★★★ *If you like Cussler you will like Becker! A great read and an action packed thrill ride through the Florida Keys!*

Made in United States
Orlando, FL
28 June 2024

48389148R20146